Remembrance

B Hamilton

sands press
Brockville, Ontario

Remembrance

Bess Hamilton

sands press

sands press

A Division of 10361976 Canada Inc.
300 Central Avenue West
Brockville, Ontario
K6V 5V2

Toll Free 1-800-563-0911 or 613-345-2687
http://www.sandspress.com

ISBN 978-1-988281-43-8
Copyright © 2018 Bess Hamilton
All Rights Reserved

Cover Design by Kristine Barker and Wendy Treverton
Edited by Katrina Geenevasen & Alyssa Owen
Formatting by Renee Hare
Publisher Kristine Barker

For information on bulk purchases of this book or any book published by Sands Press, please call 1-800-563-0911.

1st Printing March 2018

To book an author for your live event, please call: 1-800-563-0911

Sands Press is a literary publisher interested in new and established authors wishing to develop and market their product. For more information please visit our website at www.sandspress.com.

Dedication

In memory of Bill and Alice Lloyd.

Acknowledgements

Writing is a solitary act, but finishing a book sure isn't! Without these amazing people, this would not have been possible: Sarah Hamilton,Chad Martin, April Wozny, Laure Moody, Deborah Froese and the rest of the Critique Circle, all the wonderful people at my Stitch n Bitch who put up with me typing rather than knitting, Lindsey Henley, Denise Desrosiers and Samantha Beiko. Thank you to Janelle Desrosiers for a beautiful website and Terri Hofford for making me look like a pro. Thanks to my family for their support and love. All my love to Chris Taylor because he always believed I could do it and gave me the space to make it happen. And thank you to everyone I forgot to name but who encouraged me on this journey.

"The people you love become ghosts inside of you and like this you keep them alive."

Robert Montgomery

Part One

One

Maggie Lancaster suspected her time as a widow was almost over, but she couldn't be sure. She felt a change though. For so long, she had been like a rock in the river; life streamed past her while she stood in the same place. The Great War had frozen something in her that had just begun to thaw. For her, the years since had been one long, bleak winter.

Since supper time the day before, Maggie had overseen Mrs. Preston's labour in a too hot, stuffy bedroom. Mrs. Preston had been at school with Maggie, although, they had never been friends, only polite acquaintances. Mrs. Preston didn't question why young Dr. Mobley had left Maggie in charge. Everyone accepted Dr. Mobley's trust in Maggie as a nurse, built up over seven years of working together. Maggie could easily handle an uncomplicated, though drawn out birth.

None of Maggie's patients suspected she hated her work. She had long since learned to wear a mask of cheerful competence and knew her patients accepted it. Even old Dr. Mobley accepted her mask. Mrs. Preston and her mother had no idea that being closed up in a room with them on a humid night was a waking nightmare. Maggie smiled and murmured bland responses to every attempt by Mrs. Preston's mother to gossip.

Tonight, though, Maggie couldn't stop her happiness from breaking through. Her future had changed; it was no longer an endless stretch of days all the same.

While Mrs. Preston rested between contractions, Maggie stared out the window at the lightening sky. Night had shifted to dawn. Birds sang. She tried to pick out birds by their song. Her brother, Henry, had tried to teach her each bird's song, but she never had the ear for it.

Spring made Maggie wish she were anywhere but in the town she'd always lived in, the town she'd likely die in without ever really leaving. But she knew now she could choose to leave or stay.

A low moan from Mrs. Preston called Maggie back. Maggie wiped sweat from Mrs. Preston's face, smoothing back strands of hair that had caught in her mouth. Mrs. Preston gazed up at Maggie with tired eyes; exhaustion had taken away her words. Maggie squeezed Mrs. Preston's damp hand. "You're doing so well!" she said. "We'll have that baby out soon!" Maggie silently prayed she was right.

Maggie yearned for cool water to wash the sweat from her skin. She wanted to clear her nose of the smell of blood and stale sweat. She wanted to put her bare feet into new grass.

"So, Maggie, I hear you're keeping company with the youngest Cunningham boy," Mrs. Preston's mother said over her daughter's indistinct whimpers.

Maggie bit back the smile that came with any thought of Don. "He's hardly a boy, Mrs. Yorke."

Mrs. Yorke waved this off and picked up her knitting. Over the evening, she had completed a dress for the new baby and was very nearly finished a pair of booties. "You're all boys and girls to me. I can't believe no one's snatched him up before this. Has he asked you to marry him yet?"

Maggie couldn't control her blood. She sighed at the blush that rose up from her collar, and, in short order, reached her forehead. Before she could answer, someone knocked on the door. Maggie rushed to answer it before Mrs. Yorke could hoist herself to her feet.

"Is it Mark?" Mrs. Preston asked in a weak voice, struggling to sit up. Maggie turned to see Mrs. Yorke gently guiding her daughter back down to her soaked pillow.

Maggie opened the door, ready to shoo an anxious husband away.

"Are you going to tell me to go away, nurse?" Dr. John Mobley asked, laughter edging around his words.

"Doctor Mobley," Maggie said, emphasizing his title, "I didn't expect you back. She's close, no baby yet."

"Well, let's take a look," John said. He came into the room and set his bag down on a chair. He rolled up his sleeves and bent down to examine his patient. "You're right, it'll be soon. Mrs. Preston, Mrs. Yorke, if you'll excuse me, I'm going to wash up and speak with Mrs. Lancaster for a moment. Mrs. Yorke, could you get a basin of warm water? I think we'll be washing a baby soon."

John took Maggie by the arm and guided her down the hall to the washroom. "Thought you could use a break," he said. "Sorry to leave you alone. Wasn't too bad, was it?"

Maggie shook her head. "She's progressing nicely, if a little slow. And Mrs. Yorke filled me in on all the doings of everybody and her thoughts on the same. She approves of Don, so there's a weight off my mind." They both laughed.

"Well, people love romance. And you're giving it to them. Don't argue. You're a beautiful young widow," John paused. Maggie rolled her eyes. "You are! And Don's a handsome war hero. Of course people are interested. And, if you got married, I could hire a nurse who actually likes her job." Maggie shoved him with her shoulder and he winked at her.

"I'm glad you're here," she said. "How did it go with Bill Ward?"

John turned away. "Dead. Nothing I could do." His voice was flat. Maggie put her hand on his back. His shirt was soaked through. It was hot for spring.

"I'm sorry," she said. She felt him shrug beneath her palm.

"Let's deliver a baby," he said, turning back to her with a smile. The full light of sunrise filled the small room, covering everything in rose and gold. John's skin glowed, but dark shadows ringed his eyes. Maggie heard him wheeze slightly as she leaned closer to him. He looked gaunt. They were both too old to go without sleep and not wear it on their faces. She avoided her reflection in the mirror over the sink.

John had come back not because he didn't trust her to handle the birth on her own, but because he needed it. He loved delivering babies. Maggie liked to watch him do it, to see his joy.

Two

Less than an hour after John had returned, Mrs. Preston let out a great wail and pushed. The baby's head slipped into view. For a few moments, Mrs. Preston rested before pushing again. The baby's shoulders were followed quickly by the rest of its tiny, wrinkled body. John caught the baby with a grin, laughing at its first angry cries. Before passing the baby over to Maggie to clean, he whispered something into its little ear.

Once Mrs. Preston and her new son were cleaned and settled and Mr. Preston was allowed in, Maggie prepared to leave. She looked back to see Mr. Preston sitting beside his wife, stroking the baby's cheek while the baby fed at his mother's breast. *I could have that too, if I wanted*, Maggie thought and felt a blush rise up. She closed the door and stumbled down the stairs.

On the porch, she spread out her arms and took several deep breaths. Dew glistened on the grass. The day felt new, fresh. The breeze dried the sweat on her skin and clothes. She took off her white cap, not caring how frizzed her crown of braids had become. She stuffed her cap and stained apron haphazardly into her bicycle's basket.

"Maggie," John called from his car and gestured for her to come closer. "Need a ride?"

She reached through the open window to squeeze his shoulder. "I need air. I'll take my bike. Promise me you'll sleep when you get home. You look terrible."

"I'll try."

"I'm serious, John. You don't look well."

He waved his hand. "I'm just tired. Too many late nights and we're not kids anymore." John reached into his vest pocket and pulled out a small snapshot. "Look what Mum found the other day when she was cleaning out Dad's office." He handed it to Maggie.

"Henry," she said in a quiet voice. She ran her fingers over her brother's face. The photo had to be at least fifteen years old. She had never seen it before. Her brother held a paddle in one hand like a staff or a spear, his other arm slung around John's shoulders. They were both grinning. They looked so young. Their friend George stood on John's other side, glaring at the camera. They were all bearded, something Maggie had never seen before. George and John looked tan, while Henry, pale and light-eyed, almost seemed a ghost beside them.

"When was this?" she asked, handing the picture back to John. He looked at it again before tucking it back into his pocket. He tapped his pocket.

"After one of our camping trips. The only one George went on. He was miserable the whole time. It was funny Mum should have dug this up. I had a dream about him the other night. George, I mean."

"I haven't thought about him in a long time," Maggie said.

"I get a postcard from him every once in a while. Not sure where he is now."

"Do you still miss him?" she asked. Her voice was thick in her throat. She swallowed hard.

"Who? George? Sure. I mean, you were more his friend than I was. But I always liked him."

"No, I mean, do you miss Henry?" Maggie's voice wavered. John closed his eyes and rubbed his face.

"Every day."

"Me too," Maggie said. She leaned on the car door for a moment. Birds and frogs sang into the silence.

"If you see Lucy," John said, his voice much brighter, "tell her I'll stop by this afternoon. I think she's doing rounds with Dad today."

Maggie matched his shift in tone, forcing a smile into her words. "So you're going home? And here I thought I'd have to start charging you room and board." Maggie grinned.

"Oh, come on. I'm not at Apple View that much, am I?"

"Only every night. But I don't mind. I like the company. Now, go get some sleep!" She went back to her bicycle. "Oh," she said turning back to John. "That second call, after the one about Bill Ward, who was that?"

"It was strange. I only answered because I thought it would be the Wards again, but it was nothing. I could almost hear something, like voices maybe. It was so faint. Must have been crossed wires."

They said good-bye. John started his car. Maggie looked back once more before getting on her bicycle. John clutched the steering wheel. His forehead rested on it. Maggie rode away.

Three

The day promised to be hot. Late spring felt like late summer. The orchard at Maggie's farm had already bloomed and the fruit had begun to form. Maggie loved spring but it had ended too quickly this year. She pedaled along the gravel road, sweating, fueling herself with thoughts of a cup of tea, a cool bath and bed.

Tires crunched the gravel on the road behind her and she moved aside to make room. A truck slowed beside her. It had "Cunningham and Sons" painted on the side. "Want a ride?" the driver asked.

Maggie came to a stop. Relief swept through her. "Yes. Please. You're a godsend."

Don got out of the truck and put her bicycle in the bed. He lifted it as if it weighed nothing. His sleeves were rolled up, giving Maggie a view of the muscles in his tanned forearms. She blushed when she looked up to find him looking at her. He bit his lips and looked away.

They sat in awkward silence, glancing at each other sideways. *I'm like a schoolgirl*, she thought. She knew he was looking at her too. He didn't seem to mind her frizzy hair, the sharp tang of her sweat that filled the air of the cab. She fought to keep her hands in her lap, rather than letting them go to her braids.

She thought of what John had said about romance. She remembered passing Don his daughter Ruth while John covered Don's wife Mary with a sheet. Mary had died giving birth to Ruth. Maggie could still feel the weight of Don's body against hers as she held him up while he wept over his wife. She would never forget watching him struggle to soothe his newborn daughter while his wife lay shrouded on the bed.

Maggie had visited Ruth and Don every few weeks in the four years since that day. And for most of that time, she and Don had been polite with each other, but not close. She spent most of her visits playing with Ruth, listening to the little girl chatter about her dolls and cats.

The polite distance between them changed a year ago. Maggie couldn't say what had happened, only that she began blushing when he stood near her. He seemed to do the same. The air around him felt charged like a summer storm. He started taking her places without Ruth. They talked and talked and talked, but never about that day four years ago.

A week ago, they had kissed for the first time. Maggie hadn't kissed anyone in over ten years. She had forgotten what a first kiss felt like, the nervousness. How she could feel the excitement and tension through her whole body. The pent up attraction and loneliness of the past years had burst out of them. That first kiss broke a reserve in them and they had kissed and groped at each other as if they were half their age. They had parted, breathing heavily. Maggie had muttered good night and ran into her house.

She hadn't seen him since. She told herself it was because she had been busy with work, but she knew she'd been avoiding him. Was she in love? Was it loneliness? Lust? Did it matter? She didn't know. She'd asked Lucy, who had told her to relax and have fun for once.

"So, home or office?" Don asked.

She told him to take her home. Neither of them spoke as Don drove out of town and to her farm. Maggie had inherited Apple View from her parents. Even though it was out of the way and the house was too big for just her, she stayed. It helped to have Lucy around, but even still, she couldn't keep up with the demands of an old house or acres of meadows and orchards.

Apple View was in her bones, though. It was beyond love. Until recently, she had never thought of leaving it for good. Her brother had said once that their home was what he pictured when the minister spoke of heaven, or, at least the Garden of Eden before the apple.

Don stopped the truck in front of her house. He turned off the engine. He didn't speak or look at her.

"Don, about the other night—" Maggie began. She didn't know how to finish. She stared at her hands, clenching and unclenching in her lap.

"Yes. About that," Don said. Maggie looked at him. He stared up at the roof of the truck's cab. She wanted to touch his face, run her fingers along the line of his cheekbone, his jaw. But she kept her hands still in her lap. He bit his lip. Her heart beat faster. She watched his throat move as he swallowed. "Maggie, I love you," he said in a rush.

Maggie opened her mouth, but she had no words. So she pulled his face towards hers and kissed him. They were back to where they had been the week before. She pulled away. Her entire body throbbed. No, she had never felt like this when she was younger. Or, no, maybe she had once or twice, a long time ago. A memory of her husband, William, before they married, pushing her away, his harsh words, his face twisted into a sneer. She shoved the memory back.

"Do you want to come inside? Lucy isn't home," she said. *What am I doing?* she thought. He nodded. He got out of the truck and came around to her side to help her down. He took her bicycle out of the truck's bed and placed it carefully against the porch railings. She held the front door open for him and followed him inside. In the hall, he stopped and turned to face her. She let him pull her close. "Will you marry me?" he asked, murmuring against her ear.

"I don't know," she said. She had imagined saying yes. But now, her happiness felt so fragile. Any change could shatter it.

"You don't need to say yes or no today. Think about it. But I love you, Maggie."

She kissed him instead of replying. That seemed to be enough of an answer for him. She ran her hands along his back and arms, feeling the muscles just below the skin, feeling his warmth. "Come upstairs with me," she said.

He pulled away from her. She couldn't quite read the expression in his nearly black eyes. But she heard his breath catch. "Are you sure?" he asked.

She nodded. Maggie was surprised at her brazenness. She didn't know if she wanted to marry him, but she knew she wanted this. The telephone rang.

"Shouldn't you answer that?" Don asked. She took his hand and led him up the stairs and to her room. She ignored the phone.

"I haven't done this since Mary," he said and laughed. Maggie laughed too. Here they were in their thirties and as nervous as virgins on their wedding night.

"You're beautiful," he said. He kissed her. She stepped back and began taking the pins out of her braids. She avoided the mirror. She didn't want to know what she really looked like. Don helped her shake out her braids. He ran his fingers through her hair and she tried not to think of the silver running through the red-gold. "I always wondered what this looked like down," he said. She didn't say what she had imagined about him.

They tried to undress each other, but gave up when it became clear they were too out of practice. They laughed as they undressed and kissed and touched. Maggie hadn't been this happy in years. She wanted to stretch time out. Maggie had forgotten what it was like to see someone's body outside of a clinical way. The sound of her breath seemed to fill the room.

Don gestured at his artificial leg. "I suppose this should come off, too." In the war, he'd lost everything below his left knee. But since he rarely spoke of it, Maggie had forgotten. He sat on the bed and deftly unfastened the strap holding it to his thigh. "Now what?" he asked. Maggie kissed his neck and took his hand.

Four

When it was time for him to go, she helped him with his leg, knowing what it meant for him to let her see him without it. When she kissed down that leg to the scarred knee and back up, he had shivered and breathed out her name. He never told her how he'd lost it. He never told anyone or spoke of the war. She knew he had worked very hard to walk with only the slightest limp.

Before he left, Don took her hand and put a ring on her finger. It was much grander than the simple pearl band she remembered Mary wearing. Maggie's ring was a diamond flanked by rubies. "Red, like your hair," he said, smiling. She liked seeing him smile. He looked younger, more at ease. "Wear it while you think. Don't rush to answer. I can wait."

She nodded.

"I think about you all the time," he said.

"I think about you, too," she said. But she wondered if they meant the same thing. She had tried to imagine a shared life, the daily round of running a home, being a couple, but her imagination would slide to how his mouth felt on hers, how his hand felt on her, how her hands felt on him.

He kissed her, just a brief touch of the lips and then left.

Maggie leaned against the door frame. She was beyond exhausted and she still hadn't eaten. She went to the kitchen to make tea and toast.

"Tell me again why you haven't married that man?" Lucy asked. Maggie set the kettle down with a clatter.

"Jesus, Lucy!" she gasped. Well, she was awake now. "I thought you were doing rounds with Dr. Mobley."

"He's coming back for me in an hour. I wanted to pick up a few things, so I had him drop me off. Tea's not strong enough." Lucy pushed a glass of sherry towards Maggie.

"It's not even noon."

Lucy grinned, arching one perfect, pencilled eyebrow. "It's medicinal. You've had a shock." Lucy grabbed Maggie's hand and brought it closer to view her ring. She whistled. "That's beautiful. Congratulations!"

"I haven't said yes. Or no."

Lucy rolled her eyes. "If I had a man that made me yell like that, I'd marry him in a minute."

Maggie drank her sherry in one swallow and coughed. "Lucy," she said, "I have a room down the hall from yours. You're not married yet." Lucy smacked the table and laughed. She poured Maggie another glass.

"True. But John's never given me a ring either. Especially not one with a great big diamond like that. Anyway, I'm not the marrying kind. But I think you'd like it."

"I've been married. Remember? My husband? William? Tragically killed in the war?"

"Oh, right. Him. But Don's offering you a life. And you're so happy. It's like you've come back to life. You're like you were when we lived in Montreal. You were so fun."

Maggie started to protest that she was fun now, but she stopped. She wasn't. She hadn't been. Not for years.

"And," Lucy went on, "you hate nursing. I know you do."

Maggie sipped her sherry. She had to eat something or she'd be drunk soon. "You're right. I've been so unhappy and I didn't even notice. I was just—numb. But, I don't know if I love him enough. Or at all. I don't know what to do."

"And you thought fucking him would clear that up? Oh Maggie. That never works. If it did, I'd be the wisest woman in the world," Lucy said. She lit a cigarette.

"Don't be vulgar," Maggie said, but she laughed.

The telephone rang. Unsteady from sherry, hunger and exhaustion, Maggie wobbled to the telephone table in the hallway. She didn't want to pick it up. She wanted to sleep. It kept ringing, insistent. Lucy could go if it were urgent.

"Hello? This is Mrs. Lancaster," she said. Silence. She could hear the sounds of traffic in the background. Then a man said, "Maggie." He said nothing else. She said hello again, but got no reply. Anger pushed exhaustion to the side. "This isn't funny! Stop calling here." She slammed the receiver down.

The phone rang again. She answered it. She could hear indistinct voices, as if she were outside a room full of people talking. She couldn't make out any words.

"Maggie. Maggie. Hello? Maggie." The voice was muffled and crackled, as if it were a recording. The speaker was urgent, but couldn't seem to hear her.

"Who is this?" she asked. But she got no answer. The roar of many voices came back on the line. "Who is this?" she asked again. No answer. "Stop it!" she yelled into the phone. These calls had grown more frequent over the past few weeks.

Maggie smashed the receiver down, making its internal bell chime. The telephone rang. She picked up the receiver, but didn't speak.

"Maggie?" Lucy came into the hall. Maggie handed the receiver to Lucy. As she passed it over, she could hear a man's voice saying her name over and over. Lucy put the receiver to her ear. The smile on her face faded. She hung the receiver up and stepped back. The phone rang again. It kept ringing.

Maggie went to the sitting room and returned with a pair of scissors. She snipped the cord at the telephone's base.

"That solves that," said Lucy. "But what if John or Dr. Mobley needs us?"

Maggie put a hand to her forehead. She was so tired. "I'll go into town later and arrange for a new one. And I'll tell John so he knows he'll have to come out here if he needs one of us." Maggie set the scissors down beside the phone. She swayed and put a hand on the table to steady herself. She was falling asleep on her feet.

The telephone rang. Lucy gripped Maggie's arm. "Don't answer it," she whispered.

"It's probably electrical," Maggie said. She didn't believe it. She shook out of Lucy's grip and went down the hall, through the kitchen and out the back door. Lucy followed her.

"What are you doing?" Lucy asked. The phone still rang.

Maggie didn't answer. She strode across the yard to the old garden shed. She flung open the door. A thick layer of dust covered the work bench at the back. Despite the dim light coming through the open door and the dirty windows, she found a hammer in moments.

"What are you doing?" Lucy asked again. But Maggie didn't answer. The weight of the hammer felt powerful in her hands. Lucy followed her back to the house where the phone continued to ring.

Maggie gripped the hammer's smooth, wooden handle firmly. She swung it easily and connected with the phone, knocking it over. She continued to hit it until the phone was nothing but shattered parts. The ringing stopped. Before she smashed the receiver, Maggie could still hear the man repeating her name.

Lucy swept the pieces into a dustpan. Maggie could see the question on Lucy's face. Now what? Lucy bit her lip and glanced away from Maggie. "Something's trying to connect, Maggie," she said.

Maggie felt the anger rush out of her, taking any energy with it. "It was just a prank," she said.

Lucy shook her head, but she didn't press her point. She never did with this. They had an unspoken agreement to never discuss it. "I need a cigarette. You?"

"You know I don't smoke," Maggie said.

"You could start. It's very relaxing," Lucy said. They looked at the ruined telephone. Lucy nudged it with her foot. They looked at each other. Maggie still held the hammer. They started to laugh.

Five

The trench wall collapsed, burying him in an avalanche of mud and water. Dirt filled his eyes and nose and mouth and he couldn't breathe. The other men panicked, screamed. He dug away at the dirt. The hand he grasped was not that of one of his men, but a dead man's hand. The flesh slipped like a glove from the bones. He tried to scream and mud filled his mouth, choking him.

George Comstock woke gasping. He wasn't in the trench. He was sweating and shivering. Where was he? He opened his eyes and for a moment, didn't recognize his shabby apartment. For a moment, he had expected to be back at Apple View.

"I need to open the window," he thought. But the window was so far away from the bed. The smell, though, was overpowering. Sweat and alcohol, stale smoke and something else, maybe last night's meal, brewed together into a suffocating stench.

He sat up and threw off the soaked sheet. It had been a while since that particular nightmare. But four years in the trenches had given him a rich variety of horrors. Someone muttered, startling him. "Right," he said, looking over. He leaned across the sheet-covered body beside him for his cigarette case and matches. He coughed, maybe a little more loudly than necessary. The person didn't move. He lit a cigarette.

The problem was he couldn't sleep alone. If he did, the nightmares were worse. He'd wake up and be unable to move. That's if he slept at all. Usually, when he was alone, he couldn't relax enough to sleep. Every noise would jerk him awake. The other problem was he didn't always remember who he'd wake up to in his bed. He vaguely remembered Sally had been drinking with him, but the angles of the shrouded body told him that wasn't Sally.

Sally had broken the picture frame. Glass littered the floor still and the photograph, now with a smear of blood on it from a gash on his finger, was propped up against the bedside lamp.

George pulled the sheet back carefully. Oh right. Him. Alan? The one that smiled all the time. Asleep, with freckles scattered across his face, he looked young. But he wasn't that young. *And doesn't he look a bit like* — George's mind whispered before George pushed the thought aside. "I should open a window," George muttered.

A layer of grime on the pane obscured the city beyond. Was it cloudy? Hard to tell. Gingerly, George got out of bed and shuffled quietly to the window. It squealed in protest as he lifted the sash, but Alan didn't move. George leaned out and breathed in the city smells. He missed living in the country. Right now, farmers would be cutting hay and the air would be full of the green smell of freshly cut grass and clover.

Alan mumbled in his sleep. George turned to look at him. "I should stop," he muttered. He was tired. Tired of strangers, or near strangers, in his bed. Tired of being alone. Tired down to his bones. But George knew he'd get afraid and lonely and drunk and go knocking on someone's door. He was still young enough and handsome enough that he didn't need very much charm to tempt someone to be with him. And kissing and touching and licking and, well, not to put too fine a point on it, fucking, quieted his mind. He became nothing but sensation and he thought only of the other person.

He pulled on the shorts and pants he'd left lying on the floor. Coffee. He needed some coffee. While he filled the percolator and plugged it in, a memory of the night before floated up. Sally had rummaged through his things, asking questions. She wanted to know him, she had said. Until that point, she hadn't seemed to care. She'd picked up the picture and asked, "Who's this?" It had slipped from her grasp. She'd been drunk when she'd come to his door and had kept going.

He'd cut his finger picking up the glass.

Sally had picked the picture up from the floor. "Is that your brother? He's good lookin'. Uniforms always did it for me. He dead or something?" she'd slurred. George had slapped her hands away and snatched the picture from her like a child taking back a toy.

He must've cut his foot too. There were bloody footprints all over the floor. He had swept the glass into the corner with a newspaper. She had laughed while he tried to clean his blood from the photograph.

"Or is that your fella? I know what you get up to. I'm broad-minded. I won't tell." She had draped herself against him and he'd pushed her away. But he couldn't remember when Sally had left and Alan had come in.

He looked down. His right foot was bandaged. When he lifted it, he could see some blood had soaked through at the bottom. He unwrapped the bandage on his finger. It had been stitched. Had he done that?

He poured a cup of coffee. It was bitter, but hot and the smell at least covered the odour of the room. Eventually, though, fatigue won out over caution and he got back into bed, careful to keep as much space as he could from the sleeping man. Sleep pulled him back down into dreaming.

Something on the back of his neck woke George. He sat up quickly. A laugh. "Good morning!" Alan said. A kiss, it was a kiss.

"Morning," George muttered, turning his back to his guest. Why did they always stay? Why did they want to talk? Or touch?

"Bullet?" Alan asked, grazing a fingertip over the scar on George's back. George stiffened and leaned away. He stood up and went to the percolator. He felt shy. Usually he'd just tell someone if he wanted them gone. But now that Alan was awake, George felt embarrassed.

"Yeah. It went right through. From the front," he turned to face Alan and pointed to the matching scar on his chest. Was he blushing? He turned back to the coffee pot. "Coffee? It's still kind of warm. Don't have any sugar or cream. But it'll wake you up."

"Sounds delightful, but I'll pass. So, you were there too? The war, I mean."

"Yeah." George didn't know where to sit, what to do. He ended up in the one tattered armchair in the corner.

"How long were you in? Until you got shot?" Alan asked. He helped himself to a cigarette. He seemed relaxed. As if he woke up in a stranger's smelly apartment every day. And fine, yes, he was not hard to look at. But then George had always been susceptible to redheads. Although, Alan's hair wasn't really red. More auburn or chestnut. Maybe it wasn't terrible to wake up to a bright smile like that.

George smiled back. "Nah. That was just the first one. They patched me up and sent me back. I got to be there for the whole thing. But, if you want to sit around trading sad war stories, I know where you can go. It isn't here."

"I'm not looking for stories. Got enough of my own." Alan clamped the cigarette in his mouth and leaned over to rummage on the floor for his clothes. George turned his head as the other man dressed. What was happening? He wasn't usually this fastidious.

"Look, George, if you don't want me here, just say so. But, uh, just so you know, I'd been hoping since I moved in that you'd ask me over," Alan said. George glanced at him. He did look young, blushing like that. George remembered how far that blush could go and he felt his own face redden.

"Why?" George asked. "I'm a sad old drunk."

"Maybe. But you're also a really handsome one." Alan shrugged. "You looked interesting. And I thought, maybe, you were interested. Anyway, I heard you bawling out Sally last night, so I had to see what the hell was going on. Didn't expect to find you bleeding all over the place."

George stared up at the cracked ceiling. He'd forgotten how to talk to people. Just talk. Not flirt. He felt stupid, slow and very thirsty. "Look, I had fun last night, but..."

Alan nodded. "I understand. It's not the same. Mine's not dead or anything. But I know what it's like to lose someone."

George shook his head. His hands went to the metal disc he wore on a chain around his neck. "Yeah. What happened to him? He get married?" When he saw Alan's face change, when he saw how old Alan looked for a moment, he felt mean. But he couldn't stop. "Well, some of us are greedy. We're not too fussy if it's a boy or a girl." George got up and lit another cigarette. He ran a hand over his face. "I'm sorry. I'm...not used to talking to people."

Alan smiled, but not as sunny. George sighed. He did like that smile. Had since the first day Alan had moved in and grinned at George as he passed him on the stairs. "Well, uh, I guess I'll see you around," Alan said.

George nodded. "Okay." He didn't expect Alan to step towards him and kiss him. They broke apart and Alan left without saying anything. George dropped his cigarette in his coffee cup. He looked at the wrinkled shirt balled up on the floor, stained with blood. He pulled a cleaner one from a hook on the wall. He tucked the photo into his shirt pocket.

In his small bathroom, George avoided looking in the mirror as he splashed water on his face and brushed his teeth. A rub of his chin told him he needed a shave, but he didn't need to shave for this. A knit cap hid his unruly hair and a jacket covered his wrinkled shirt. Another cup of coffee? It was cold, but with a touch of whiskey in it, it would give him strength.

George stepped softly down the stairs. He didn't want to talk to anyone in the building. He was saving his words. He needed a pay phone.

He listened to the line on the other end ring and ring. No one answered. The street outside the booth buzzed with people, cars, streetcars, the noises of a city. What he would give to hear a clear bird song, to hear frogs again.

"Hello," a woman said on the line.

George's voice caught in his throat.

"Hello," she said again.

"Maggie—" he said, but faltered. What to say? Where to begin?

"This isn't funny! Stop calling here!" And the call disconnected.

He hung up the receiver. He turned to rest his forehead against the wall of the booth. Had he called before? He didn't think so, but that didn't mean anything.

Someone rattled the door of the booth. "Hurry up in there. I gotta make a call!" a man shouted.

"I want to go home," George said to himself. "I want to go home," he said again to feel the words in his mouth. And home meant Apple View. Not his sister's house in Vancouver or the tiny apartment above a storefront where he'd grown up. He wanted to walk among the fruit trees.

"Hey! I don't got all day!" the man yelled, beating the door with his fists.

George dragged a hand across his eyes. He opened the door and glared at the man until he stepped back. "Go fuck yourself," George said. But it didn't make him feel better.

Six

"Oh," Maggie whispered, "I need to get away from this place." Thinking over the past, considering what to do about Don, it pressed her down. What did the sea smell like? She wanted to know. Wanted to see mountains in the horizon. She wanted to see faces other than the ones she had looked at nearly every day of her life. She wanted to walk away.

Finally, the bath water was too cold. She dragged herself to standing and stepped out of the tub. Still wet, she walked naked to her room, dragging a towel behind her. She paused in front of her full-length mirror. Age was making her more angular, taking away any softness she had.

Seven

John felt old. Older than his father. No matter how much he slept these days, John was tired. Even more tired than he'd been during the long days and nights of the Spanish flu. He didn't tell anyone, though. He tried to hide it, tried to keep his step light, his eyes bright. John wanted to hold his fear and worry close, to nurse them in secret.

He called out greetings from the doorway, but no one answered save for the dog. Alone, an unexpected treat. Sometimes, he thought, he should move out of his parents' home. But, while he wanted to be alone sometimes, he didn't want to be lonely. After Maggie's mother had died, he had watched Maggie sink under her grief and loneliness. He didn't want that. And what would be the point of his own home if he was going to die?

For a long time, John didn't think about his heart, the damage from rheumatic fever. It had kept him out of the war. But he knew his heart was weak and becoming weaker. It was like a trade in a fairy tale. You'll be spared, but not for long.

His mother had left a plate for him in the kitchen. But he ignored it, setting it on the floor for the dog. Someone should enjoy it and he had no appetite. But he did have a piece of pie for a small spark of happiness. After he finished, he had to work hard to convince his body to stand and go upstairs to bed. Sleep kept ambushing him, pitching him forward only for him to jerk awake.

"Get yourself to bed, doctor," John said. His mother's cat squawked at him. "Sorry, Jimmy," he said, tapping it on the head lightly.

In his room, John pulled the heavy curtains across the window, blocking out the sun. He liked lying in bed during the day. He liked to hear the sounds of the street and the rustle of the poplar trees in the breeze. It felt decadent to be resting while everyone was awake and productive.

Sleep came quickly.

He was in a canoe on a northern lake that looked familiar, but not quite like any lake he'd ever seen. The water was still and clear, like glass. Pale morning light fought through a heavy mist rising from the lake's surface. Loons called to each other. Ravens croaked and laughed in the trees. His paddle lay across his lap.

Henry sat across from him, paddling the canoe. Henry had been young when John had last seen him. But in this dream, Henry had aged along with John. His red hair had faded to a dirty strawberry blond and deep lines bracketed his mouth.

"You're right. I'm dead," Henry said, answering the question John hadn't asked.

John said nothing. The canoe glided past dark green shadows. Islands, hidden in the mist. They were alone on the lake. He couldn't see any cabins or camps on the shore. Other than the sound of the paddle in the water and the birds, it was silent.

"Is this heaven?" John asked.

Henry smiled and shrugged. "Maybe."

"But I'm not dead, am I?" John asked. He put his index and middle fingers to the side of his throat. He could feel his pulse.

"Not yet," Henry said.

"What's that supposed to mean?"

"You'll be joining me soon." Henry frowned, deepening the lines on his face. "I thought you knew."

John looked down at the paddle on his lap. He stretched out his hands. His fingertips were blue. Henry set his paddle down. He leaned across and tapped John on the chest.

"Don't you feel it?" Henry asked. "Your time, winding down." He picked up the paddle and put it back in the water.

"I'm not ready." John covered his face with his hands to hide his fear.

"There's always a price," Henry said.

When John uncovered his eyes, Henry was gone. He was alone in the canoe, drifting on the lake. The loons cried out.

John woke up.

Eight

He stood up under the oak tree and looked about. Was this familiar? Did he know it? The green grass and the yellow, orange, white, blue and purple flowers were too colourful, strange to his eyes. This was a meadow. This was a hay field. Clover. That pink, sweet-smelling flower was clover. And he knew he could pull out a petal and suck on the bottom. It would taste like honey. Something landed on his hand, soft, almost weightless. It flexed its orange and black wings. A butterfly. The words were coming back. All these things had names. He knew them.

Cows lowed in the distance. Insects ticked in the ditch on either side of the road. Lazy summer afternoons walking on roads like this. Had he done that? He remembered mud. He remembered decay. This was neither.

Did he have a name? He tried to speak, to say his name. No sound came. What was it he was supposed to do? Walk. Go to her. When you're strong enough, you can bring her back. You promised you'd come home. You said you'd never leave. You keep your promises.

He looked down at his hands. Were these his hands? Shouldn't he know what his own hands looked like? His head ached and the sunlight felt too warm, too bright. He squinted up at the sky. His body felt heavy, stupid.

He was so hungry.

He stumbled towards the road. He knew where to go. It was coming back.

Nine

Before the war, Apple View had been a busy place. Maggie's mother had been in several groups aimed at improving the world in some fashion or another. Her father had split his time between his law office in town and his office at home. His clients and colleagues were often at the house. Henry had invited John and William over all of the time when they were children. Later, when they were teenagers, George had joined in with the older boys. Before that, George had come over to play with Maggie. She also had invited groups of girls from school over, in junior versions of her mother's clubs. There had always been people around and that hadn't even included the people who were needed to run the house and the farm.

Some days, Maggie imagined she could still hear the boys running through the house, her mother calling to them to take their hockey sticks outside. The house had thrummed with their young energy.

Most of her trouble was loneliness. She knew that. But it was hard to change after so many years. She lay on the couch in the sitting room. Lucy slept upstairs. Alone. John hadn't been by much the last couple of weeks. Maggie tugged Don's ring off her finger and held it up to let the light play off the stones. He was waiting on her. She knew that. But she couldn't decide.

He would want her to leave Apple View. He had a business. A home. Could she leave? If she did, it would be forever. Unless she convinced Don to move here. But would she want to? Would he want to?

She looked around at the parlour. Nothing had changed since her mother was alive. There were signs, here and there, of Lucy, but for the most part, Maggie had left the house alone. And it showed. The wallpaper had started to peel away in places. The curtains didn't look fresh and a strategic cushion hid a stain on one of the armchairs. Outside, she knew, was worse. The shutters and the trim had needed paint for years. The roses, left alone, were reverting to wild. John made sure the lawn was trimmed, but the rest of the farm had gone to seed. The orchard was beginning to resemble the woodlot. Did she love Apple View or did she just have nowhere else to go?

Maggie sighed and sat up. She idly flipped through the mail Lucy had left on a table. Curious, she picked up a postcard. John had mentioned that he sometimes got a postcard from George. Maggie had heard nothing from him since 1918. The card's front was a tinted photograph of a lavender field in France. She flipped it over. There was no stamp. Her address was scrawled on the back. Scribbled beside that was "Wait for me." No signature. The bodies were buried in France.

"I need to get away from here," she said out loud. When the boys had left, she'd been jealous because they were going to Europe. The memory made her laugh darkly. She had known nothing.

She'd been sitting still for years. She looked at the ring on her hand again and wiggled her fingers. She'd been in the sun and freckles were now scattered across her pale skin. William used to call them stars, tracing out constellations. Don wouldn't do that. He was too pragmatic. But he loved her. She would call him and tell him she'd made up her mind.

A knock on the door interrupted her. She was tempted to ignore it. John never knocked. And he was the only regular visitor. It could be an emergency. She sighed and looked at the phone on her way to the front door. Since she'd had it reinstalled, the calls had stopped. Another knock.

"I'll be right there," she called. Through the frosted glass of the large window, she could make out the dark shape of a man. He was too tall to be Dr. Mobley. Too tall to be John. Too thin to be Don.

She opened the door. A tall, gaunt man with fair hair stood there. He said something, but she couldn't hear what he said. Her name?

"William!"

Walls closed up around her. Each second she stared at him, another brick was added to her prison. He smiled at her, tentative, unsure. She felt her face move in an answering smile. He held out his hands and she took them. They were cold, almost waxen. Where had he been? His face was streaked with dirt.

"Come in," she heard herself say. Was she supposed to fall into his arms? Is that what he wanted? What was supposed to happen here? He followed her inside through to the kitchen. She sat him in a chair. He was too docile, too silent. Was it him? She felt outside herself, as if she were watching from a corner of the room. He sat very still. Only his eyes followed her as she moved around the room.

The telephone rang. She huffed out a breath. Everything came at once. She hesitated. The phone continued to ring. William sat so still, so quiet. "Stay here," she said. He didn't move or react. She felt him watch her as she ran down the hall.

"Hello?" she said, breathless. She heard only noise. Before she hung up, she heard a man say, "I'm too late." She stood in the hall, unsure what to do. She picked up the phone. The line was clear. She rang the operator and asked to be connected with Dr. Mobley.

John's mother answered. Maggie asked if she could speak to John as if this were a normal day, a normal conversation. She knew if she said anything to Mrs. Mobley, the news would spread through town and they'd be flooded with visitors.

"Are you free?" Maggie asked John.

"Yes. Why?"

"Good. I need you here right away."

"Are you all right? What's happened? Is it Lucy?" John spoke quickly. She hadn't thought he'd be worried. She hadn't thought.

"No. I'm fine." Was she though? "Lucy's sleeping." She hesitated. Could she tell him? "Don't tell anyone. William's here. John. William's here."

"What?"

"I know! Please come."

"Yeah. Yeah. On my way."

Maggie hung up the phone and paced in the hallway. She had to go back to him. She twisted the ring on her left hand. The ring. Don's ring. She pulled it off and hid it in the back of the drawer in the telephone table.

"Go back in there," she hissed to herself.

William sat exactly as she had left him, straight up in a chair with his hands resting on his lap. Mud covered his clothes and boots. A dried oak leaf stuck to his hair and burrs clung to his pant hems. When he saw her, he smiled, cracking the mud on his face.

She went to the sink and wet a cloth. "I'm going to clean you up," she said. He nodded. She pitied him. That was unfamiliar. He would never be this dirty. He would never submit so quietly to being scrubbed like a child.

"Where were you?" she asked.

He started to form the words, but gave up. He couldn't speak. He shrugged.

Maggie watched herself make tea and then slice bread and butter it. She put the tea and bread on the table and indicated he should help himself. He ate quickly, as if he'd been starving. Every now and then, he'd catch her eyes. He didn't seem to mind her watching him.

She had forgotten what he looked like, she realized. Or, rather, she had forgotten what the living man had looked like. He had green eyes. Had he always? How had she forgotten that?

John let himself in. "Maggie!" he called from the hallway.

"Kitchen!" she called back. Her mother would have been appalled at the way they casually yelled out to each other. Quick footsteps came down the hall. John was running. He paused at the door to catch his breath.

John set his bag on the table. "William," he said and held out his hand. For a moment, William didn't respond. But then he took John's hand and shook it. John put a hand on William's shoulder. "I—I don't know what to say," John said. "You're really here."

William nodded. His face remained calm, still. John rubbed his forehead and took a deep breath. "I don't know if you remember, but I'm a doctor. I'd like to take a look and make sure you're all right. Can I do that?" John asked. William nodded.

Maggie stood beside John. "I don't think he can speak," she whispered. John glanced at her to let her know he'd heard. William did not react.

"Let's get you upstairs and into the bath. And I'll give you a little exam. No needles. I promise," John said. He helped William to his feet and put an arm around William's shoulders to guide him to the stairs and up to the bath.

A bath. Of course, he was filthy. Maggie followed behind. She was useless. She hadn't thought. She hadn't noticed how tired and weak William was.

She ran the bath while John helped William out of his clothes. She could hear the murmur of John's deep voice, but she couldn't make out his words. When John and William came in, Maggie saw that John had put William in the robe he kept in Lucy's room. "His clothes are in my—I mean, in Lucy's room," John said.

"I'll put him in the spare room. If you could help him to bed after you're done in here," she said. "You've got pajamas here, yes?"

John nodded. He didn't say anything. Maggie was grateful. She didn't know what to say.

Once everything was ready, she left John to take care of William. Maggie ran down the stairs and out the back door and down to the river. She knew she had some time until John would need her. She ran across the foot bridge and through the long grass of the meadow. There was an old stone farmhouse across the river. It had been part of the property Maggie's father had bought years before. He had never gotten around to tearing the old house down. It had been a playhouse and then a place for courting.

Once in the little house, Maggie dropped to her knees on the dirty wooden floor, not caring if she bruised them. She screamed until her throat felt as if it would tear. Then she stood up to shake the dirt from her skirt. She ran back, hoping John hadn't noticed she was gone.

By the time John came downstairs, Maggie had composed herself with a cup of tea. She waited for him in the parlour and stared at her wedding portrait.

John sat across from her in an armchair. He tipped his head back to look up at the ceiling. "I didn't wake Lucy. Didn't think you'd want her just yet."

"Thank you," Maggie said. She put the portrait back on the mantle.

"This is very strange," John said. Maggie laughed. He laughed too. "He's asleep. Wherever he's been, he hasn't been eating enough. And he hasn't been getting regular sleep. But he's healthy enough. I had a bit of a time hearing his heart and lungs, but once I did, everything's strong there." John continued to look at the ceiling. "I am worried about his inability to speak."

John sighed. He turned his gaze to Maggie. "I don't think there's anything physically wrong with him that food and sleep won't fix. But the speaking...I think he's got battle fatigue."

Maggie sighed. "Now what?"

John shook his head. "I don't know. Have you called his mother?"

Maggie laughed. "Oh no. I forgot Mrs. Lancaster. She'll never forgive me for not calling right away. And Don. Oh my God, Don." She bit back a scream.

"I'll do it," John said. He leaned forward and stretched out to take Maggie's hands. "Once word gets out, you're going to be swarmed. People will want to see for themselves."

"You think it's him, don't you?" Maggie asked.

"I do. Don't you?" John asked.

"If this were a novel, I'd say this was unbelievable. But I think it's him. I do."

John put his arms around her. He was solid, real and she leaned into him, taking in the familiar smells of coffee, soap and the lavender sachets his mother put in closets and drawers. "It does seem impossible," he said.

Ten

George woke up in a dark, empty room. No light came through the curtains or under the door. It had to be night. Someone sat cross-legged at the end of his bed. Henry.

"Are you haunting me?" George asked.

"I'm not really here," Henry said. His pale skin glowed in the darkness. George sat up and reached out. Henry held up a hand. "You can't touch me. I'm not really here, remember?"

"If this is a dream, why aren't I waking up?" George asked.

Henry shrugged. "Why would a dream have rules?" He rubbed his chin. "Well, this is different. Usually, we don't talk in your dreams. It's nice though. Like when we were kids. Before. You'd be on my bed and I'd be on a rug on the floor, listening to you sleep. And wanting to touch you. Did you know that?"

George nodded. "Me too. What do you mean, usually?" Henry smirked and shook his head. George laughed. Fine. He didn't dream about them talking. "Is this really a dream? Or are you haunting me?"

"Don't you think I'd haunt you if I could?" Henry asked.

George reached out again. Henry didn't stop him this time. George expected his hand to go through, meet no resistance. He was surprised to rest his hand on Henry's solid, warm knee.

"You're here now," George said.

Henry huffed, annoyed. "I told you. This is a dream. It's different." His face was shadowed. He wore uniform pants, the wool felt scratchy. But his feet were bare and he wore only an undershirt. He was thin, very thin. Had he always been thin? No. George had known Henry's body better than his own. His hands remembered a lean, muscular body, not this skeletal one.

George tried to speak, but he could only make a choked sob. Henry's face contorted, his lips shook. "I know," he said. "Me too." He put a hand to his chest as if he was trying to catch his breath. "I'm so tired, George." He took his hand away and a red stain bloomed on his shirt. "So tired." He shifted to his hands and knees, crawled up to George and pushed him back to lying down.

"Can I lie down with you?" Henry asked. George nodded. He pulled Henry close.

George woke up in a sunny room. He covered his face with his hands. The coppery smell of blood was so strong he could taste it. When he turned to lie on his side, someone slung an arm across his body. "Bad dreams," Alan muttered, not quite waking up. "Go sleep. It's Sunday."

Eleven

John and Maggie waited until the next day to tell William's mother. What was one day compared to nearly ten years? Once Mrs. Lancaster knew, there'd be no keeping William's return a secret.

William's mother arrived within an hour of John's call. She came in alone, leaving whoever had driven her out in the car to wait. Her black silk dress rustled with every step. She still wore mourning for her son. She held out a hand to John. He took it. "I hope you're well," John said.

"I am. Where is he?" she asked, her sharp pale eyes darting side to side, as if they had William hidden in the sitting room.

"I'll go get him. He's resting. As you can imagine, he's quite tired," John said and disappeared with a half-smile to Maggie and Lucy. Maggie settled Mrs. Lancaster on the sofa with a cup of tea. None of the women spoke. They stared towards the archway, waiting.

John led William by the arm. William stood in the doorway, looking from Maggie to his mother and back. His face was blank. The pajamas he'd borrowed from John were too short for him. His wrists and ankles stuck out past the cuffs, making him look gawky and childlike.

Mrs. Lancaster made a sound somewhere between a sob and a scream and ran to her son. She gripped him in a tight embrace, the beads on her dress rattling. She pulled back and took William's face in her hands. She kissed him all over, cheeks, forehead, chin. "My boy! My baby!" she cried.

William said nothing. He didn't try to speak. His face remained still. He gave into his mother's hugs as if he were boneless. Maggie caught John's eye. "Do something," she mouthed. Did William know his mother? If he did, he didn't show it. He was like a doll in her arms.

John put a hand on Mrs. Lancaster's shoulder. "Mrs. Lancaster, please, have a seat. William's still quite tired, as you can see. So let's sit quietly for a moment and let him collect himself." His voice was gentle, but Mrs. Lancaster took a deep breath. Maggie knew that breath. Mrs. Lancaster was gathering strength to argue. Her face hardened. She turned towards John, raising a finger to point in his face. Lucy smoothly stood up and took Mrs. Lancaster's arm.

"Your tea is getting cold. There you go, just there. And John, bring William here, so he can sit with his mother. I'll get him a cup. And a plate of biscuits?" Lucy left the room.

"Margaret, he belongs in his home. Where it is familiar to him," Mrs. Lancaster said, her voice imperious. Maggie bit her lip to hold in a burst of laughter. Her memory gave her William looking at a statue of Queen Victoria and remarking how she resembled his mother about the chin. Mrs. Lancaster had sounded the same when, after William had left for training, she had ordered Maggie to move in with her because Maggie was a Lancaster. Maggie wanted William to go with his mother, to leave, to never return to Apple View. But her mother-in-law's commands sparked rebellion. She refused to hand William to his mother.

Wherever he had been, William had decided to return to Apple View and not his mother's home.

"Ask him," Maggie said. "William, if you want to go with your mother, I understand." He nodded.

Mrs. Lancaster took William's hands in hers. She wore black gloves. "William, will you come back with me?" William shook his head. "What are you saying?"

"He can't speak," Maggie said. "We don't know why."

Mrs. Lancaster kept her back to Maggie, but her shoulders stiffened. "William. Come with me. You belong at home with your mother."

William pulled his hands out of his mother's grip. He stood. His mouth formed "no". If he had a voice, he would have shouted. He tried again. No words came. He stamped his foot. He shook his head.

"But William!" Mrs. Lancaster cried.

John came in with a plate of biscuits. "Mrs. Lancaster, please take a seat. William, please sit there." John waved to an armchair some distance from Mrs. Lancaster. "Mrs. Lancaster, I understand you're happy to have William home and eager to have him with you. This is—this is a miracle. However, I think it's best we let William decide where he is most comfortable at this point."

"He belongs at home! Margaret isn't prepared to take care of him. How will she feed him? I know how she and that other one live. This isn't a suitable place for him," Mrs. Lancaster stared at John, her lips compressed until they disappeared.

"I am a nurse," Maggie said.

Mrs. Lancaster continued as if Maggie hadn't spoken. "He belongs at home," Mrs. Lancaster said. "There will be no more discussion. Margaret, pack his belongings. William, go get dressed, my dear."

The laugh Maggie had kept in broke free. "His belongings? He staggered in here yesterday wearing khakis and covered in dirt. He doesn't have belongings."

Before Mrs. Lancaster could reply, William stood. He pointed to his mother and shook his head. He pointed to Maggie and nodded. Then he left the room. Mrs. Lancaster stood to follow her son, but John blocked her way. "Please. He needs time." He guided her back to her seat. Taking Mrs. Lancaster's hand and speaking in his quietest, most sympathetic tone, John explained to her that he thought William had been quite ill for a long time, that his mind had been affected.

While he spoke, Maggie and Lucy cleared up the tea things. No one had been in the mood for tea. All the cups were full. The biscuits were gone. William had eaten them. Not even the crumbs remained. Maggie sighed. How would she feed someone whose appetite seemed limitless?

She had not forgotten Mrs. Lancaster's possessiveness of William. Fine, Mrs. Lancaster was lonely. Maggie knew loneliness. But Mrs. Lancaster had wanted William to stay with her always. The front door closed. John had seen Mrs. Lancaster off. But she would return.

"So she's lovely," Lucy said as they watched Mrs. Lancaster's car drive away.

"He is her son," Maggie said. "I can't imagine what it would've been like for my mother if Henry had come home."

"I'm sorry," Lucy said. Maggie sighed. She'd been speaking to herself, not chastising Lucy. She didn't want William here, but she didn't want to be ordered by Mrs. Lancaster.

Maggie went to the kitchen to wash the tea cups. William stood at the counter, holding the sugar tin. His head was tipped back and he poured sugar down his throat, swallowing quickly. "William!" she said. He started and dropped the tin. Sugar spilled out onto the floor.

"Are you hungry?" Maggie asked. He nodded. She opened cupboards.

What to feed him? What would satisfy his appetite? Mrs. Lancaster had been right. How could she care for him? Other than some cans of food and some dried goods like beans and flour, Maggie had almost no food. A bag of oats suggested porridge. Maggie made a huge pot of it while William watched her. He gazed at her as he had when they were in their teens. Maggie's back tightened.

He ate the entire pot methodically, barely pausing to breath between bites. Maggie sat at the table and marvelled at a man eating enough plain porridge to feed a family for a week. When he was done, he drew his hand across mouth. He smiled at her. Was he simple now? She didn't remember him smiling this much. Was that why he couldn't speak? He looked to her with a question on his face. What did he want? "You can go lie down in your room," she said. He nodded and left.

If he spoke, what would he say? Would it be anything she wanted to hear?

Twelve

George woke later in the morning. Alan was still there, sleeping. George slowly shifted out of bed. He threw on an old, faded robe. It had been red and was now a streaky pink. He tried to stifle his coughs, but the only solution was a cigarette. After a piss, a coffee with a bit (fine, half a cup) of Irish in it and a piece of toast, George sat at his desk and waited for Alan to wake. He watched Alan sleep. No, he didn't really look like him. George's dream was fresh in his mind and he could see the differences better.

Since the night of his fight with Sally, George had spent only a handful of nights alone. But he didn't know what to do. It had been two years since he'd broken off an engagement with a friend of his sister's, but he'd never slept with her. Before that he had lived with—someone. Only for a few months because he had wanted to be somewhere warm. Before that had been hospitals, trenches, camps. And before that, well.

Alan stretched and groaned. He opened his eyes. Amber eyes, not a thing like Henry's pale blue eyes. He was his own person. He smiled at George. "Good morning. Do I smell toast and coffee?"

Without saying anything, George got up and made more toast and poured two more cups of coffee. He set the plate and cup down on the bedside table. Alan sat up and grabbed the front of George's robe. He kissed him. "You spoil me," Alan said and smiled again.

George sat at his desk, far from Alan's reach. His breath caught in his chest. Oh. He was too old for this feeling. It was mixed up in his mind with that dream about Henry. The coffee was still hot and burned his mouth, but it brought him back to ground. He didn't know what to say.

"Do you want me to leave?" Alan asked.

George sighed. "Maybe? I don't know. I have work to do."

"It's Sunday. Wait. You have a job? I never see you leave at regular hours. What do you do?" Alan had a job. Something that required a suit and keeping this life far away.

"I write. Don't get too excited. I write boys' adventure stories. Sometimes I do scenarios for a friend in California. But mostly, silly books for kids with someone else's name on the front."

Alan laughed. "That sounds better than keeping accounts all day."

George shook his head. "I wanted to be a lawyer." He thought of Mr. Tate, Henry's father, his mentor, how disappointed he'd be if he could see George now.

"What happened?"

"The Great War." George lifted the cover off his typewriter. "Well, sort of. The lawyer I was supposed to go into business with died while I was away. When I got back, I—I don't know. I couldn't do it anymore." He had tried, but too much time had passed. When he'd gone back to the university, the students had all looked so open, so light and innocent. He had felt like a dark, tainted thing. He'd been out of place, out of time.

"Can I read one of your books?" Alan asked. George took one from the pile on the floor beside the desk and tossed it over.

"It's terrible." George turned to the typewriter. His publisher, who he had never met in person, had told him he had real talent. George suspected the man was blowing smoke up his ass. He probably had a stable of ghosts who figured they were the next literary lion. George had no illusions of greatness. It was easy work that let him keep his own hours. The publisher sent him titles and plots and he filled them in. Maybe he imagined himself, Henry, John and Maggie in the stories. Maybe he spun out his childhood memories. But better. They were always brave and kind and they always won.

It was easy to have Alan there. Usually, George couldn't work with anyone in the room. But this was like being alone, but not lonely. Occasionally, Alan laughed at something in his book, but other than that he didn't disturb George who had slipped into the world of his story.

A few hours passed without George noticing. "I'm hungry," Alan said, "and you don't have any food. Want to take a break?"

"You go ahead."

"You do eat, right? You don't exist on air, cigarettes and whiskey?"

"Yes, I eat. But I want to finish this first. Go eat if you're hungry. I'll see you later."

"I'll be back," Alan said. "Put some clothes on."

George waved him off. He wouldn't admit it, but he enjoyed writing these stories. He liked slipping into a world where nothing very bad happened and everything resolved by the end. There was just enough danger to be exciting, but no one died or was lost. No villain escaped punishment.

A sandwich and a bottle of ginger ale appeared beside his typewriter. Alan draped his arms around George's shoulders. "Eat," he said.

After they ate, George sifted through the pages he'd written. He'd lost momentum and his typing was beginning to become sloppy. He'd done enough for the day. But he stayed at his desk. Alan sprawled in the armchair, watching George. "You know," Alan said, "You look pretty happy, clacking away. Do you like it?"

George shrugged. "I like it enough. It pays."

"What was the lawyer like, the one you were going to go into business with?"

"Why do you want to know?"

"I don't know anything about you. But I want to," Alan said.

"He was like a father to me. I know it's a cliché. But it's true. Mr. Tate was a good lawyer. And a good man. He really cared about making the right decision. Not just legally, but in life. He paid for my education, even after— well, he kept his promises. He died while I was in France." George wanted a drink, but he didn't want to drink in front of Alan. Even though he'd been drunk their first night, he wanted to be better than that.

"Tate," Alan said, tapping his empty bottle against the arm of the chair. "Your ID disc. That says Tate. Wait. Your last name's Comstock, isn't it?"

"Yes."

"Was he killed? The lawyer's son."

"Not officially. Missing. Presumed dead. His trench was mined. There was nothing left." George got up and pulled a bottle of whiskey from the cupboard. "Drink?" he asked. Alan shook his head. George poured a glass and brought the glass and bottle back with him.

"You don't want to talk about this," Alan said.

"No. I don't. What about you? What's your sad story? No one lives in this shit hole if they have a happy story," George said. He downed his glass and set it down. He started drinking from the bottle. He could see Henry, sitting on the end of the bed, red blooming across his white shirt, his white skin.

"I don't have one," Alan said. "I don't," he said in response to George's snort. "People don't ask questions in shit holes. And the rent is cheap."

George admitted, despite the questions, he liked having company.

"You drink a lot," Alan said.

"What are you? One of those temperance people?" George asked. When Alan started to say something, George stood up and went to him, kissed him. "I don't want to talk," George said. He let his robe slip from his shoulders as he straddled Alan's lap.

"Yeah," Alan said, a bit breathless. He dropped the empty ginger ale bottle. It rolled and hit the baseboard with a clink. "Yeah."

Thirteen

Adaptation happened quickly, George knew. A hotel could feel something like home after a few days. Life in the trenches became normal and everything before it seemed a dream. After only a few weeks, he felt as if he had known Alan forever. It had been a long time since he'd stayed up nights talking about everything, learning everything about a new person, not just a body, but a mind, a past, a future. He felt young, or almost. Not quite. George saw how constricted he'd made his life. How he'd boiled it down to a dirty one-room apartment, loneliness, whiskey, cigarettes and sex with whoever was willing.

They didn't talk about the war, though. Alan saw it as something that had happened to them, but they didn't need to dwell on it. It was easy, being with him. Which was strange, too, because they still had to be discreet. George should have thought it had been easier with his fiancée and it had been, in some ways. But he had never been able to speak to Vicky so frankly and she hadn't been able to be open with him either. But he'd loved her. He knew that. But this was different. This was almost like, well, like before.

One morning, George woke up and couldn't remember what he'd dreamed. There'd been no nightmares. No memories. George rolled onto his side and looked at Alan sleeping, his eyes twitching below closed eyelids, lashes fluttering. Happy. That's what this feeling was. And how long had it been? He held his breath, not wanting to disturb Alan's sleep. He wanted to remember this.

Birds sang loudly over the city sounds. They were grackles and sparrows, but he didn't care. The sun shone, birds sang and he was possibly in love. A feeling like this was fragile, like a thin sheet of ice over a puddle. He didn't want to make the step that broke it.

Of course, it shattered.

While waiting for Alan to come home from work, George passed the time, opening his mail after ignoring the pile of bills and demands from his employer for several days. He saved a letter from his mother for last. George loved his mother, but her letters were dull, full of details of his sister's social activities and the clever sayings of his nieces and nephews. She always ended with a plea to come home. But his home wasn't Vancouver. His mother and sister lived there, but it wasn't home.

He skimmed her letter and almost missed the explosive information hiding in amongst the mundane details of card games and church lunches. "I don't expect you've heard, but Mrs. Leslie (you remember her, her daughter was in your Sunday school class) wrote me. She says Henry Tate has come home. He can't speak and no one knows where he's been. He arrived on his sister's doorstep like a stray dog."

With shaking hands, George set the letter down. His mind went in several directions, but came back to one point. He had to go home. He pushed up from his desk with enough force to knock the chair backwards to the ground. He forgot Alan. He had things to do. He had to get ready.

First, George went to the bank. He needed money. Then he went to a barber's for a proper shave and haircut. Finally, he bought some new clothes and a travelling suit. Usually, he dressed in the same work clothes the other men in the neighborhood wore. But he had been a bit of a dandy when he was young. He wanted the armor of nice clothes. Finally, he bought a train ticket.

On the way to his apartment, he stopped off to pay his last month of rent and give notice. He had no intention of coming back.

Packing didn't take as long as he had hoped. He had hours to pass before morning and he didn't want to drink too much. He wanted to be fresh. His hands still shook. He read his mother's letter again. "Wake up," he whispered. Nothing happened.

Alan came in. Alan. George needed a drink after all. He poured a glass, keeping his back to Alan.

"What's going on? Where are you going?" Alan asked. He put his arms around George's waist. George flinched. Alan let him go. "George, why are you dressed like a swell?" His voice wasn't as light as his words.

"I got a letter. From my mother. A friend, someone who's been gone a while, has come home." He shoved the glass aside and drank from the bottle. His lips were numb.

"A friend," Alan said. He wouldn't be put off. George knew that. He turned to face his, his what? Reflexively, his hand went to the identity disc.

Alan nodded. "I see. So a visit?"

George shook his head. "I don't think I'll be coming back here." He felt the happiness of the morning, of the news of Henry's return drain out. He'd seen Alan's expression before. The tight jaw, the frown, the eyes that wouldn't meet his. So many times before. But it hurt this time. "I'm sorry. I—" He took another drink from the bottle and set it down. He took Alan's face in his hands and pulled him in for a kiss.

Alan pulled away. "You what?"

"I have to go home."

"You made it sound like heaven when you talked about it. The orchard, right?"

"Yes."

"Must be nice. I don't have a home. I thought—well, it doesn't matter now. When do you leave?" Alan smiled, but it shook at the edges and there was no light in it. I did that, George thought.

"Tomorrow morning," George said.

"So he's back?" Alan reached out and pulled the chain out from under George's collar. "Henry Tate?"

George nodded.

Alan bit his lip. He smoothed his hands over George's sleeves. He pushed back George's hair where it had come out of the barber's arrangement. "You look nice. Really handsome now that you've scraped the derelict off. He'll be happy to see you, I bet. Even if you haven't heard from him, in what, eight, nine years?"

"Alan—fuck. I'm sorry. I wouldn't be leaving if it weren't for this. I'm sorry. I really like you. I do." George felt the lie, but he hoped Alan didn't hear it.

"I better go. Leave you to packing. Write me, if you want."

"Wait. Stay? One more night. Please."

Alan sighed. He put his forehead on George's shoulder. "Fine. One more night."

Fourteen

People in town shared theories about William in the first weeks when the news was still fresh, still exciting. Some thought he'd got into trouble and couldn't go home. No one said jail, but it was implied. Others said he's been a prisoner of war that had been held too long. Some speculated he'd been in hospital all that time. Remember that Jackson boy, they'd say. Just as crazy as could be. His mind was so affected; he'd never leave the asylum. Really, it would have been a mercy for his mother if he'd been killed instead. Not that you'd wish anyone to suffer, but it'd give his mother peace.

More cynical gossips wondered if some unhappiness at home had kept William away. Oh sure, he and Maggie had been sweet on each other since they were little tykes, but she seemed a hard one to live with. Too used to having her own way. Her father had spoiled her. And so serious! You hardly ever saw her smile. A woman ought to have a bit of fun about her. Like that friend of hers. What a great girl for laughing, that one.

Others remembered Henry and how his mother had taken the news he'd gone missing. Funny how things turned out, they said. All those years poor Mrs. Tate thought her boy was alive and here's her son-in-law, resurrected. It really made you wonder. Well, God worked in mysterious ways.

Fifteen

George hesitated at the gate. The house looked the same. It was as familiar as his mother's old apartment. Yet, as he looked at it, he saw small differences. Paint peeled on the window trim. The gardens were overgrown and filled with weeds. He saw Maggie crouched by the roses, trimming and pulling wildly. When she heard the gate, she turned.

He put on a smile, but she didn't smile back. "I suppose you want to see him," she said. Her anger had always been the freezing kind. They used to have dramatic disagreements and spells of not being friends. He'd always be the first to make peace.

George followed her. He wanted to shout questions at her, but knew Maggie wouldn't answer. He had meant to write or visit, but the years slipped away and the longer he went without coming home, the harder it became.

His heart beat faster the closer they got to the pond. What would he say? What could they say with Maggie there?

"William, look who's here to see you!" she called out. She turned to George. "He can't speak. We don't know why." She walked away before George could say anything. William raised a hand in greeting.

It was William who had returned. But William was dead. George saw William lying in the mud, half his head gone. George put his hand to his chest. His legs gave way and he landed hard on the grass. Under William's mute gaze, George sat by the pond and wept.

Sixteen

George found Maggie in the orchard, lying on a blanket, an open book beside her.

"Maggie, you haven't said two words to me since I got here." He remembered it had been best to ignore her temper, to keep on as if she hadn't been angry. "How many hours did we spend like this as kids?" he asked, as he lay beside her. He tipped his hat over his eyes. "I meant to write. And then I didn't. I meant to visit, but once my mother moved out west, there wasn't a reason to come out here."

"I wasn't reason enough? God damn it, George," she said laughing a little. "I could have found you. If I wanted to. I could've brought you back. Apple View is half yours. Dad left half to me, half to Henry. And Henry. He left his half to you." She cleared her throat. George wanted to lift his hat, to look at her, but he was afraid to. "I had him declared dead a couple years ago. Stay. At least for a few weeks. It's your home too."

George didn't have an answer. Apple View was home, after all. He should go back to the city. He should get on the next train and find out if he had a home there. If that's what Alan had meant. He thought of Alan's face when he'd told him about the letter. And now he owned part of Apple View. He laughed and could hear the hysterical edge to it. The way it was a step too close to tears.

Maggie said nothing. Once he stopped laughing, George said nothing either. They didn't speak for a long time. He could hear a grosbeak singing. His right hand came to rest on his chest.

"The rose-breasted grosbeaks are still here. Henry loved them. Like a robin's song, but more beautiful. You know, he tried to teach himself about the birds over there." George sighed.

"Why are you here? Why now? William finally came home a month ago. Now you. Should I expect Henry any day? What about my father? My mother? All my dead?" Maggie said. George caught the slight wobble in her voice, under the hard edge of anger. He wanted to take her hand, but the years were between them. He'd forgotten how much she'd lost.

"I thought it was Henry who had come home," he said.

"I wish he had," Maggie said.

"Me too," George said, the words out before he thought to hold them in. The grosbeak sang again. He concentrated on the lilting song of the black and white bird with a splash of red on its chest.

Part Two

One

Before the blossoms fell and the fruit began to form, the orchard felt magical to Maggie. The smell of the blossoms, especially the cherry blossoms, could be overwhelming, almost too sweet, tipping towards rotten. Since childhood, she had liked to lie on the grass and let the blossoms fall on her like snow while she listened to bees humming. This year, there was no magic. The early heat rushed the blossoms and now the fruit. But she was still in the orchard. The plants, insects and birds went about their business, oblivious to people and their troubles. It comforted her.

She heard a stick snap. Was William back from his mother's? She closed her eyes and feigned sleep. She had hoped his mother would convince him to stay the night as she sometimes did. The sound of someone stepping through the grass stopped beside her. She opened her eyes. Don sat beside her, lowering himself down carefully, keeping most of his weight on his good leg.

"Where's your husband?" he asked, looking over his shoulder.

"In town, visiting his mother. I don't think he'll be back until tomorrow. Why?" She sat up. Don's gaze flicked to her, but then he looked around as if searching for something.

"Maggie—" Don stopped. He picked up a fallen branch and ripped the leaves from it. She waited. It hurt to see him. He had lost weight. She wanted to run her fingers across his cheekbones and feel their sharpness. He hadn't shaved in several days, which was unlike him. Dark and gray stubble covered his chin and cheeks.

"I'm leaving," he said. He looked down at the branch in his hands. "I'm taking Ruth. We're going out west. My cousin has a farm out there. Cattle, wheat. He says there's lots of opportunity." Don threw the branch to the side and rubbed at his eyes. He looked over his shoulder again.

"But your business," Maggie said. He was going. She'd never see him again. What about her? But she had no right to ask.

"Sold it. I need a fresh start," he said. He looked at her, quickly, then looked away. "Before I go, Maggie, would you have married me? If he hadn't come back."

"Yes," she said. "Yes."

Don grabbed her hand. He crushed her fingers, but she didn't care. "Come with me. No one needs to know who you are. Leave him. Come with me. Don't waste your life on someone who stayed away for years." His voice was frantic, his eyes wide. "Leave with me, right now."

"Don. I can't. I'm married. I have to stay." She wanted to go. She wanted to leap up, take Don's hand and run and not stop until they were far away. But she knew William would follow. Eventually, he'd find her. He'd come for her. After all, he'd come back from the dead.

She stood up and held out her hands to Don to help him to his feet. He pulled her close to him and kissed her. She thought of their morning together before William came back. She was sure Don was thinking of it too because she could hear his breathing change. She could go with him and leave this all behind her. But William would follow. William may have taken a long time to find his way back to her, but now that he had, she knew he would follow.

"I'm so sorry," Maggie said. "You're a good man. And I do love you. I do. But I can't leave."

"I know," Don said. "But be careful, Maggie." He kissed her again. She could have kissed him every day, if things had been different. She wanted to laugh. No, cry.

He looked around. What was he looking for? "I love you. Goodbye, Maggie," he said. She sank back into the grass. She had loved him, after all.

Two

Maggie hadn't planned to leave Henry's room as he had left it. She hadn't meant to make a shrine. Her mother had wanted it to stay the same, lest he came home. She would remind Maggie that Henry would never let anyone in his room, even to tidy it. But once Mum was gone, Maggie saw no reason to preserve it. But she had never found the time or volition to clean it out. And now, she felt wrong in here. As if she were invading George's space. Yet, she wanted to see Henry's sketchbooks and she knew he had kept them in here. He had hidden them so his parents wouldn't show them to guests, so proud to share their son's talent.

George hadn't disturbed much in the room. His suitcase sat on a chair, clothes spilling out of it. She remembered Henry teasing George about being a slob. Maggie wondered how her meticulous brother could have shared an apartment with George while they were away at school. The sheets on the bed were rumpled and tangled. Maggie could make it, but she decided not to. It wasn't her place to.

She opened the closet. George had no clothes hanging in it. The closet still smelled like Henry. She buried in her face in his hockey sweaters. Her mother had put sachets of cedar chips in them to keep out the moths, but just under the smell of cedar, she could catch Henry's boy scent; sweat, outside and something indefinable that was just Henry. *I should empty this place of its ghosts*, she thought. But then the house would be empty.

On a shelf in the closet, she found stacks of sketchbooks. Every Christmas, Henry had asked for a hockey stick and a sketchbook. Maggie dragged over the desk chair so she could stand on it to reach the shelf. She carried some of the books to her room to look them over.

She flipped through pages of drawings of birds and trees and the river in different seasons. She set aside earlier books, when Henry's drawings were clumsy for him and fine for anyone else. She was not interested in anything before they were nearly grown.

In one book, she stuck a bookmark in at a portrait of her parents sitting together on the porch swing. Her mother was knitting and her father was reading. They were more alive in the sketch than in any photograph. Her mother, a beautiful woman, always looked stiff and awkward in photographs.

Finally, she found what she was looking for. Henry had pestered all of them to pose for him. There were several pages of her hands. He had spent weeks practicing drawing hands and she had obliged by holding different objects or making different gestures.

There were only a few drawings of William and none that clearly showed his hands or eyes. She pushed the book away. She didn't know what she had expected. William had never liked sitting for Henry. He said he couldn't sit still that long. He had been uncomfortable with Henry's artist's gaze, while the rest of them had got used to being seen as a collection of shapes rather than people.

Maggie picked up another book. Henry had written "1912" on the inside cover. He'd been in art school then. She flipped through the pages, past copies of classical statues and drawing exercises. There were nudes that would have shocked even their blue-stocking mother. Maggie had seen too many people's bodies to blush over a well-drawn nude man or woman. Her brother had been talented. Even with biased eyes, she could see that he had been gifted. What a waste. So much wasted and for not very much. How many talents were buried in French mud?

Towards the back of the book, Maggie came to sketches that were not school exercises. Here was a page that was just bits of a person's face, the line of a cheekbone, the angle of a jaw, an ear. A whole page of eyes in different moods. A beautiful mouth repeated on several pages. She kept turning pages. There was never a whole face or body, just scattered pieces, carefully rendered.

She felt on the edge of something, a riddle she could almost solve. The answer slipped away.

Three

Maggie had tea with William's mother once a week after she returned to Apple View when her father died. No one other than her father knew that she had planned to leave William. When Mr. Tate died, she had accepted she would be a Lancaster forever. It would be best if she tried to appease William's mother, to win her over even a little. Besides, Maggie felt sorry for the woman who loved nothing but her son. Still, Maggie hated these teas.

After William had left, his mother had assumed Maggie would move in with her. When Maggie decided to work as a VAD, William's mother had been even more furious than her son.

"You're a Lancaster now!" she had shouted at Maggie when Maggie and Mrs. Tate had visited to share Maggie's plans. "You do not do whatever you want with no consideration. You will follow my son's wishes!" Although Maggie's mother didn't agree with Maggie's plans, she bristled at the idea her daughter would be ruled by a man, swallowed whole by another family.

Still, when she came home for good, Maggie visited Mrs. Lancaster once a week to listen to stories about William. His mother would read his letters to her out loud and demand to see Maggie's. Maggie always pretended she had forgotten to bring them.

Mrs. Lancaster would talk at Maggie while Maggie sipped tea out of fine china cups, so thin they were transparent. Maggie would smile and nod and share only the most benign tidbits from William's letters. She would vaguely assent whenever Mrs. Lancaster mentioned future grandchildren and how they would take after their father. The parlour, thankfully, was stuffed with knickknacks of all kinds. Maggie would choose one just over Mrs. Lancaster's shoulder to make it seem she was making eye contact with her mother-in-law.

"Of course, when William comes back, you'll come live here," Mrs. Lancaster would say.

Maggie would smile and say something vague that could be mistaken as consent by someone willing to hear it.

Maggie got the telegram. After every large battle, everyone was nervous for weeks, expecting telegrams or letters with the worst news. But days of no note could be just as dangerous.

Maggie had been at home, alone. Her mother had gone off to do volunteer work. Maggie knew she should have gone to knit or sew or whatever it was, but she pretended to not feel well. Instead, she lay on the couch, thinking of not much of anything. The doorbell startled her out of her blank reverie.

The boy who helped at the post office stood there. He looked nervous. Maggie took the telegram from him and gave him a tip. He stood there. She tried to move him with a hard stare, but he stood there. She didn't care if it was rude. Instead of speaking, she shut the door in his face. Standing close to the door, she listened to his footsteps along the porch.

Her heart beat fast. Was it Henry?

Maggie opened the telegram. It was a form from the War Office. "Regret to inform you that..." Maggie crumpled it up. "William is dead. I must tell his mother," she said aloud. "William is dead," she said again. She felt nothing.

Years later, she would remember parts of that day, but not the bicycle ride to the Lancasters' home. Had she waved at people as she passed? Had she smiled? Had she grimly pedalled forward? In her memory, she had crumpled the telegram, shoved it in her pocket in her front hall and then opened the front door and was on the Lancasters' grand porch.

She hastily smoothed the telegram, trying to remove the wrinkles. Mrs. Lancaster would need to see it. Maggie lifted the heavy brass knocker. A servant answered and invited her in. "Is Mrs. Lancaster expecting you?" the woman asked.

"No. I got a telegram. About William," Maggie said. Oh, she was too quick to say it. The woman's apple doll face wrinkled more as she struggled to hold her tears in. Maggie put a hand on the woman's arms. She'd probably known William all his life. "I'm sorry. I need to speak to Mrs. Lancaster."

The servant pointed to the parlour. Her lips trembled. If she spoke, she'd cry. Maggie nodded and went to the parlour. When she looked back, she saw the old woman sitting on the bench of the hat tree in the entryway, covering her face with her crisp, white apron.

"Maggie! What a surprise!" Mrs. Lancaster said, setting down her knitting and looking at Maggie over the rims of her glasses. "But you really should have called. I'm afraid I can't have tea today as I'm due at a Red Cross meeting in an hour."

Maggie wanted to be soft, but she couldn't. How else to say it? "I got a telegram. About William," she thrust the thin paper towards Mrs. Lancaster. The older woman reached for it with trembling hands.

"Oh. I can't. I can't look," she said in a small voice. "What does it say, Maggie?"

Maggie read it and Mrs. Lancaster screamed. It was unlike any sound Maggie had ever heard a person make. Mrs. Lancaster kept screaming. Maggie stood before her, unsure what to do. Finally, she knelt beside William's mother and took her in her arms. Mrs. Lancaster stopped screaming and began to weep.

Maggie held her mother-in-law and knew she felt relief. He was gone. She was free.

Four

The long grass on the hill was slippery after a recent rain. Halfway down the hill, George's feet skidded, then shot out from under him. He landed hard on his tail bone and the pain of it radiated like fire. He flopped onto his back. If he didn't get up soon, he wouldn't be able to get up at all.

It'd been in winter when he'd slipped on this hill and changed his life. Could he leave Apple View and all its memories? He wanted to leave. He wanted to stay. He should leave. For once, he had someone waiting for him. Was home a place or where he had someone waiting for him? He sat up and lifted himself back to standing. Turning, he shuffled sideways down the rest of the hill.

It was a hot day. Perfect for a swim in the river. There was a deep spot further down, near the old boat launch that they'd used as a swimming hole when they were younger.

Easing himself into the water, George grimaced. Every movement was agony. He crouched in the water, letting it rise up above his shoulders. It smelled fishy and a little rotten. Slimy weeds wrapped around his legs. Mud squished between his toes. Minnows darted around him.

He sighed. Winter.

He had been fifteen years old, the winter he'd raced down the hill with Henry and slipped, sliding right to the bottom. They'd been racing down to the frozen river to skate. Everything sparkled under the full moon.

The snow was soft and light. It puffed around George when he fell. Unhurt, George laid there, mesmerized by the deep, velvet blue of the night sky, pierced by glittering stars.

"Are you hurt?" Henry called. George didn't answer, not wanting to break the stillness of the night.

Henry slid down the hill, almost as if he were skiing. George reached out to pull his friend to the ground. They lay in the deep snow laughing, hardly cold at all. And then it happened. Henry kissed him.

George had been kissing girls for several years by then. In fact, earlier that week, he had kissed Josie behind the church, after a youth prayer meeting. He enjoyed kissing girls. He liked that moment, just before their lips met, when he knew what was coming and anticipation slowed time, when the world became two people, the shared breath between them. But kissing Henry shifted something in him. It wasn't just fun or pleasure. It was something he hadn't known he wanted until it happened.

After, Henry scrambled to his feet and ran down to the river, leaving his skates behind. George picked them up and ran on shaking legs.

"You forgot your skates," he said, cringing at his commonplace words. Henry's skates dangled from his hand, the blades reflecting the moonlight. Henry wouldn't look at him.

"I'm sorry," Henry said. "I—" He waved his hands as if trying to wave his words away. George set Henry's skates on the bench. Not looking at Henry, George began to change out of his boots and into his skates.

"Are we skating or not?" George asked as he stood up. Henry nodded and laced up his skates. At the edge of his vision, George could see Henry glancing at him. He knew Henry was trying to read his reaction. How did George feel? He felt happy, confused, afraid. He knew they wouldn't be able to say anything to anyone. It was a mistake. He wanted to do it again.

They skated in silence, half-heartedly kicking a block of ice back and forth to each other. Finally, George grabbed Henry's arm, forcing Henry to face him. Henry turned his face away. His shoulders hunched. Did he think George would hit him?

"Remember when I told you how much I liked kissing Josie? I—I like you better," George said.

Henry relaxed and smiled. His face was flushed. "Really?" His smile faded. "Now what?"

George shrugged. "I don't know. We can't—I mean, boys—" What was he trying to say? What did he want?

"I won't do it again. I promise." Henry held out a mittened hand. "Still friends?" George shook his hand and agreed. They grinned at each other, not letting go.

They stood on the ice, holding hands and promised they'd always be friends and forget anything had happened. And Henry believed he'd keep his promise. And George knew they wouldn't. But he didn't care.

A fish nibbled at his toes and broke the spell of memory. He wasn't fifteen. He was old and sore. Despite the warm air and warm water, George shivered.

Five

Lucy found the solution to William's silence. She smacked her hand down on the table and said, "A Ouija board! Maggie, do you have one?"

Maggie caught up to Lucy's quick mind. "'I think we do. It might be in Henry's closet." They both ran to look. It was exactly where Maggie had remembered. Their mother had wanted them to throw it away, but Henry had rescued it before their mother could burn it. He hadn't been able to resist a chance to play with people's credulity.

It wasn't that their mother had had religious objections. Her superstition about the board had surprised her children. When Mr. Tate had brought it home as a harmless game, Mrs. Tate had muttered about opening doors that should remain closed. Still, Maggie and Henry had used it at a party just before Christmas. At the party, Henry had terrified some of the guests, both boys and girls, with dire predictions and uncannily accurate answers to questions. Each time, he had caught Maggie's eye and only she saw the slight smile.

"My mother was afraid of us inviting in something unspeakable with this," Maggie said as she handed the box to Lucy.

"Well, they shouldn't be toys. But it doesn't work like that. We should be safe." Lucy brushed the dust from the box.

"Did you ever use one, you know, professionally?" Maggie asked. They had played with one a few times in Montreal. Lucy hadn't been happy with Maggie's pranks on the other girls. It had been after one of those sessions that Lucy had told Maggie about her abilities.

Lucy shook her head. "I prefer writing."

Maybe it would be less onerous to talk with William this way, Maggie thought. Conversations tapered off when it became too hard to find a yes or no question to ask. William became frustrated when he couldn't communicate what he meant. More than once, he had walked away from her or John in the middle of a conversation. Could an old game give him back his voice? Would she want to know where he'd been and what he wanted now?

Six

Maggie shared Lucy's enthusiasm for the Ouija board. John and George were less excited. John worried William would not be able to read the letters and would get only more frustrated. George told Lucy he worried they'd learn things none of them wanted to know.

"I thought you were all old friends," Lucy said to George. "But you don't seem to like William very much."

George laughed. Lucy was learning his laughs. He had a big laugh of genuine amusement and oddly boyish giggles if he were really tickled by something. But those were rare. He also had a short laugh, like a bark, a cynical laugh. "I don't really like anyone. William isn't special."

"You can say it, you know. Whatever it is you don't want to say," Lucy said.

"There's nothing. I don't believe it's really him. I know I saw him die. I think we're all being taken in," George said.

"Maggie and John say it's him. Who else would it be?"

George shrugged. "I don't want to keep talking in circles about this."

*****

Lucy set the Ouija board in front of William. She picked up the planchette. "We won't need to use this. You can just point at the letters." William raised his eyebrows at her, his face amused. "I know it's a toy, but it's got an alphabet and some words. Do you want to talk to us?"

He nodded.

"Let's start. You point. I'll write," she said.

William had tried to write. But all that came were scratches. They tried reading his lips, but could rarely make out his words. Same with charades. No one had patience for guessing games, least of all William. He retreated to only nodding or shaking his head.

William stared at the board, frowning.

"William, please spell your Christian name," Lucy said. Her voice was low and calm.

William took a deep breath and began pointing to letters, gaining speed with each one. When he pointed at "M", he looked up at Lucy and grinned, like a small boy who had completed a difficult task for his teacher. Lucy smiled back.

"Good!"

Lucy flipped through the notes she and Maggie had written. There were so many questions. She didn't want to overwhelm him, but she wanted to know.

"Where were you before you came here?"

Do not know

"Were you injured?"

Do not know

"How did you get here?"

Walked

"Why did you come back?"

For Margaret

Sorry it took long

"Were you in hospital?"

Do not know

"What's the last thing you remember before you came here?"

William glanced at George. He smiled, but only with his mouth. George sat to the side of William, slumped in his chair, arms crossed.

"What's the last thing you remember?" Lucy asked again.

Trench raid

George shot

Shell burst

"You were with George?"

Yes

"And then a shell hit. Was it close to you?"

Ask George

They all turned to George. He uncrossed his arms and took his cigarette from his mouth. "I was shot. Here." He tapped his chest. "We were in a shell hole. And William was climbing out. A shell landed nearby and he fell backwards. I was lying in the mud and I swear I saw him fall back, missing half his head. And then I woke up in hospital in England."

George brought his cigarette back to his lips. He inhaled deeply, the end glowed brighter. "Are you really William? Prove it. Tell us something only one other person in the room would know."

William smiled. Lucy remembered George saying he thought it was a hoax. That this wasn't William. William looked sly. Maybe George was right. But how could this man fool Maggie and John?

Dangerous

Sure you want me to tell

Anger crackled between George and William like lightening. It wasn't they didn't like each other. Lucy realized they hated each other. Which made her wonder about George's doubts. This was an old grudge.

"Like cats in a sack these two. Always were," said John, cutting through the mood.

"What about something your wife would know?" George said.

William tapped his fingers on the board. He started to point to letters.

Margaret

Birthmark

Right hip

Maggie blushed from the collar of her blouse to the roots of her hair. Lucy laughed. "That is something only you would know," Lucy said.

Enough proof

George pushed back from the table and stood up. "This was fun. But I've got better things to do."

Drinking better

"Yeah. It is," George said. He slammed the back door behind him.

Lucy rubbed her forehead. She could feel a headache blooming.

"Brilliant idea, but don't push too hard," John said to her. He stood and kissed her forehead. "I've got to go. Promise me you'll take a break." Lucy nodded.

The group broke up. Maggie asked if anyone wanted tea. William tapped *yes* on the board. Lucy closed her eyes and listened to Maggie in the kitchen, the domestic sounds of a kettle being filled and set on the stove.

She felt a tap on her shoulder. She opened her eyes. William pointed at the board. She picked up her pencil and began to write as he spelled out words.

Voices bothering you

Lucy dropped the pencil. William smiled. He nodded towards the kitchen and raised a finger to his lips.

Seven

George knew Lucy from somewhere. She was so familiar. Her hairstyle had likely changed and she was older, but her laugh, her voice. He knew those. This was the trouble he made for himself. Sometimes, he would meet someone who he didn't quite recognize, only to realize, after the person looked angry or hurt, that he'd slept with them.

They were all sitting outside, enjoying a long early summer evening. Lucy clapped her hands, startling George out of his mental catalogue of past lovers. "I've got you!" she said. "You were at my hospital! You were the handsome one who wrote me that silly poem."

Relief forced George to laugh. He hadn't slept with any nurses. He hadn't wanted to cost them their jobs. And, honestly, it had been the last thing on his mind anytime he'd been in hospital. "You! The Canadian. I remember you now. You spoke to the man next to me and your accent sounded like home. I didn't recognize you out of your blue habit," he said.

"And you don't have your fancy mustache," Lucy said.

"A mustache?" John asked. "Oh, George. You dandy."

"I had nothing else to do. It looked terrible," George said, stroking his upper lip, remembering that mustache. It had been terrible.

"I wish I'd kept that silly poem," Lucy said.

"Should I be jealous?" John asked, laughing.

"Hardly," Lucy said. "It was a bit of doggerel meant to take the wind out of my sails."

"It's true," George said. "All the men were in love with her. I thought she needed a corrective. It was an awful, silly thing. You were right to throw it away."

He could see the younger Lucy hiding behind the older, more polished version. She'd been a pretty girl, but her features had refined. Henry would want to paint her, George thought. She had more confidence now.

At night, in the hospital, when he couldn't sleep, George would see Lucy sitting beside some poor doomed bastard, making sure he didn't go alone. She would hold a dying man's hand and talk to him in a low voice. He had heard from the other VADs that Lucy volunteered to work nights.

One night, Lucy had noticed George was awake and had come over to see if he needed anything. She had offered to bring him water. She had asked why he couldn't sleep. He had told her about the dreams that came whenever he closed his eyes. "The dead are all around me," he had said to her.

Lucy had nodded. "Yes. They are," she had said and squeezed his hand.

"Did you ever get to see your friend?" Lucy asked, bringing George back to the present, back to sitting on the lawn, having tea. "The last time I saw you, you were leaving to catch a train. You said you were going to meet a friend."

The last time he'd seen Henry. George sighed. "I did."

Eight

Later, after everyone had gone to bed, George crept downstairs. He knew every board to avoid, every step to miss so that no one would hear him. Maggie had changed nothing. He could still navigate through the house in the dark. He went out to the yard. He stood barefoot in the grass. Heavy dew soaked his feet, but he didn't care. The dead are all around me, he thought.

"Can't sleep?" Lucy asked. He gasped. He hadn't heard her come out.

"You surprised me," he said, laughing to cover his fright.

She handed him a lit cigarette and then lit another for herself. "You made me think of things I hadn't thought of in a long time," she said.

"Me too. Actually, no. I never stop thinking of them," he said.

"I remember once you told me you couldn't sleep because the dead were all around you. That kept repeating in my head, so I thought, well, I'll go and see if he's awake too."

They smoked in silence. George looked up at the sky. He had lived too long in the city. He had forgotten how many stars he could see at Apple View. "Look," he said, pointing up to the sky. "Falling stars."

"What happened to you after you left?" Lucy asked.

"Well, I went back," he said. "I kept getting promoted. Mostly by not getting killed. And just before Armistice, I got shot in the head. One of my men thought I was a German. After that, I didn't have to go back."

"Which hospital were you at for that?" Lucy asked.

"Here and there. You see, when I came round, I thought I was dead and in—well, not in heaven," he said.

Lucy said nothing. She put her arm around his waist and leaned her head on his shoulder. He blew smoke rings up at the night sky, up at the falling stars.

"So you see, when I came here and saw William, who I'm sure I saw die—I saw his head nearly blown off. When I saw him, I thought maybe I really had died after all. Maybe we're all dead and stuck here."

Lucy tightened her grip, but said nothing. She blew smoke rings too. For a while, they smoked and tried to blow their rings through each other's.

"They thought I'd gone mad when I came back," Lucy said. George nodded. "I like this. You understand. Maggie, John. They weren't there. They didn't see." Lucy sighed. "I always had a gift. That's what my grandmother told me. She was a Spiritualist for a long time. But even before that, she spoke with the dead. My parents were appalled at her beliefs. They never knew she told me. Who cares about a little girl and an old woman? We'd talk to the dead and bring their messages back to the living."

"What happened to you? When you were overseas?" George asked.

"What didn't? I could control it. And then, one day, a doctor handed me a severed leg and told me to take it to the incinerator. There were never enough orderlies. And something—shifted. After that, the dead spoke all the time. It got so I couldn't hear my own thoughts. I couldn't concentrate. It was just the dead. Eager to give me messages. Eager to reach out."

She crushed her cigarette out against the sole of her shoe and put the butt in the can she kept on the porch. When George turned back to her, she was standing with her hands over her face. He went to her and took her hands away.

"When you said the dead were all around you, I thought, here's someone who knows. But you don't hear them, do you?" she asked.

"Only in my dreams," George said.

Nine

George couldn't sleep at the convalescent hospital. It wasn't the other men. They were comforting. He'd grown used to the constant noise of other people living on top of each other. In the long hours of the night, he smoked and tried not to think of the shell hole.

After a few nights, George noticed that one VAD always had the night shift. She moved quietly between beds, fetching water or speaking gently to someone who had woken from a nightmare. Her eyes caught George's. She came over to him.

"Do you need anything?" she asked.

"You're Canadian?"

"You too! Where are you from?" She sat down on the little stool beside his bed. Her uniform veil framed her face like a Renaissance Madonna. Henry would want to paint her. He wished he could draw so he could show Henry.

"Nowhere you'd know. You?"

"Toronto. Do you need anything? I saw you watching me," she said.

"I was admiring the view. You're very graceful."

"Are you flirting with me?"

"If I were, I'd say you're beautiful. But you already know what you look like," George said.

She punched his arm lightly.

He lit another cigarette. He was smoking too much, but it was something to do. It broke the long nights up into ten minute increments. Life went smoke to smoke.

The VAD plucked the cigarette from his lips and took a drag. She blew out a smoke ring and handed the cigarette back to him. "We're not supposed to be familiar with the men. And we are not supposed to smoke." She winked.

George shivered. He tapped his chest.

"Does your sweetheart know you flirt with strange girls?" she asked.

George wasn't sure if she could see his face redden. His tan and the dim light might have obscured it. "My sweetheart knows I like to look at beautiful girls, but knows where my heart belongs," he said in the same teasing tone.

"The other girls are very taken with you. Your sweetie should be worried. They all think you're very handsome," she said.

"And you don't?"

She shrugged. "You're too Byronic. You probably have a mad wife in an attic back in Canada."

"Do you always work the night shift?" he asked.

"As much as I can. It's quiet. I like to prowl in the dark. Trouble sleeping?"

He nodded. "Every time I close my eyes."

"Sleep heals." She took the cigarette again. This time, she drew heavily on it. She tossed it into the ashtray and then stubbed it out. "Give me your hand and close your eyes."

Her hands were rougher than he had expected. She rubbed his palm with her thumb in circles. Her voice was low, no longer playful. "Close your eyes. You're not frightened. Breathe in. Breathe out. Breathe in. Breathe out. Where's your favourite place to sleep?"

"Outside on a sunny day. In the orchard."

"That's where you are right now. You can smell the fruit trees. The sun is warm on your face. You can hear birds singing. Keep breathing. You're safe."

He drifted into sleep without noticing if she let go of his hand.

Ten

Lucy didn't think about the past. Her memories of her service didn't disrupt her sleep, her life. She could recall the terrible things she'd seen and accept they had happened. If she could still remember the feel of a man's intestines under her hands (slippery, warm), it didn't keep her up at night. That had been worse for the man whose guts she'd held in place. She would sometimes see her hands at work and remember when her fingers had begun to go septic. But she'd been able to stop the infection and save her fingers. Another VAD had lost a hand.

Lucy knew some were not as fortunate as she was. For them, the memories were like the voices were for her. Intrusive, coming at any time and relentless. George remembered too much. Apple View was not a good place for him. John hoped the good memories here would push the bad memories out of George's head, but Lucy wasn't sure that all George's memories about Apple View were so good.

On nights they couldn't sleep, they'd taken to sharing cigarettes on the back porch and watching fireflies flicker in the hedges. Sometimes, they'd talk, swap tales of their pasts. Other times, they were silent, caught up in whatever had driven them out of bed.

When George grinned at her, she could see the shadow of the boy who'd made the schoolgirls swoon. John had told her that almost every girl in town had been in love with George. He'd gotten a lot in life with that grin, she knew. Flirting with him was like practicing with another professional. It meant nothing, but it kept their claws sharp.

"Anyone you want me to contact for you?" she asked one night. She would find whoever he needed to speak to.

His grin switched off like a light. "The dead are gone."

She shook her head. "They're not gone. They're—somewhere else. Beyond this world, but they can come to the edge of it to speak. I quit doing séances, but I'd do it for you."

"Thanks, but no. Did you quit when you got sick?" George asked.

"Sick?"

"Maggie said you'd been sick. That's why you came here."

Lucy laughed. "Oh, Maggie. It was more than that."

Eleven

Lucy stayed after Armistice. She wanted to go home, but she thought home wouldn't be there. Too much had changed. She had changed. And she had a duty to her work. When her mother sent a telegram to express her displeasure, Lucy sent one back saying five years of work couldn't be undone in months.

The convalescent hospital was quieter. No fresh patients came. The days settled into routine. As men recovered and left, the number of patients and staff dwindled.

The voices didn't leave. When Lucy was busy with work, she could tuck them to the back of her mind. When she was idle, when she was lying in bed, desperate to sleep, she couldn't ignore the dead with their pain and confusion.

In a fit of rebellion, tired of years of rules, Lucy arranged to meet a soldier at a local cafe. The nurses and VADs were still off limits to the men, but life worked around rules. After years of teetering on the edge of death, rules didn't matter much. They'd learned being obedient offered no protection, no salvation. They'd already lived through damnation.

Lucy and the soldier ate huddled in a dark corner. Lucy giggled, something she hadn't done in years. She felt strange in her dress, the first beautiful thing she'd worn since 1914. They went on to a nightclub. She didn't know the new dances, but she learned quickly. As different men took turns dancing with her, she found another way to ignore the dead.

As long as she laughed or danced or drank, she could be Lucy, the rich flirt. She could be Lucy as she'd been in 1913.

When she got a rare week of leave, Lucy found a better way than dancing to ignore the dead.

Her soldier had been sent on course to fill his time until he had a berth back to Canada. When he finished, he borrowed a car from someone and asked Lucy to join him on a tour. She knew she should say no. But she didn't.

They checked into a hotel under false names.

In their room, Lucy said. "I've read too many tragedies that begin with pretending to be newlyweds and end in disaster."

The soldier laughed. "Well, we're doing it backwards, so it should turn out. We've already had disaster."

"Well, I don't believe the wages of sin are death," she said.

"I don't believe in much anymore," he answered.

They were not in love with each other. Lucy knew that. But they were out of uniform and free from orders. They had spent years not thinking further into the future than the next day, the next battle. Lucy didn't know how to think about the future.

After the first time, Lucy realized she had not heard the dead. Not once. He fell asleep almost immediately. As she lay awake, beginning to doze, the voices began to whisper. But from the moment he had put his hands on her, she had not heard them.

When he woke up, she smiled at him. "What?" he asked. She kissed him. She had to be sure. She had been right. The voices didn't bother her.

Twelve

George woke up in a hospital. He felt his chest, but that was fine, no bandages there. He felt his head. It hurt. Sun came through the windows. Everything was white, brightly lit. It hurt his eyes. Of course, after you died, you would come to a hospital. You'd have to be fixed up for whatever came next.

He fell asleep or passed out. He didn't dream. When he woke up, he asked a nurse if anyone had sent his mother a telegram. The nurse said yes, of course, they had let his mother know. But would he like to write to her? She could find someone to help him. He wanted to shake his head, but that hurt. He fell asleep again.

One day, while he sat outside wrapped in blankets, a doctor sat beside him. George liked this doctor. The man was younger than some of the others and he had a kind face. George thought he looked a little like John. John had a bad heart, maybe he was here. The doctors and nurses were angels, of course. That made sense. John was good. He could be an angel.

George had asked one of the nurses to check if men he had known were here. The nurse had come back to say no. "Oh, well, maybe they died too long ago to still be here. They've probably moved on," George had said. The nurse hadn't said anything to that.

The doctor offered George a cigarette and took one for himself. It was nice he could still smoke here.

"I hear you think you died, George," the doctor said.

"I was shot in the head. Of course, I died."

"Where do you think you are?" the doctor asked.

George explained his theory to the doctor. Was this a test? He thought of the castle and the women. There were a lot of tests after you died.

The doctor nodded. He didn't say anything for a long time.

"George, you lived. The bullet went through here." The doctor gently tapped George's forehead. "Entered the skull, and as far as we can tell, followed the skull's curve and came out here." He tapped a spot on the back of George's head. "You have metal plates to repair the bone, but you're fine. I'm writing a paper about it, actually."

George shook his head. "No. I'm dead. I know it. The first time I got shot, I didn't die. But I did this time."

He wouldn't ask if Henry was here. Not yet. He had got the letter from Maggie telling him that Henry had been reported missing. He knew from one of Henry's men that he probably hadn't survived. George put his hand to his chest. Henry's disc was still there. Maybe that had caused problems when he'd been brought here. But no. The doctor had called him George.

The doctor sighed. "Do you think this is heaven?"

"If there were a heaven, how do you think God allowed the war to happen? No. There's no heaven. We're alive and then we move on to whatever this is. And we keep moving. There are stages. My body's gone. This is just a—projection."

The doctor sighed and patted George's shoulder. "All right, George."

Later, when his wounds had healed, they transferred him to another hospital. Everyone there was mad. George didn't think he belonged there. Perhaps it was another test. Eventually, though, the doctors there made him understand he had survived. That night, he went to his room. That was the only nice thing about this place. They each had their own room. After so long surrounded by others, George liked the solitude, although he couldn't sleep because he was afraid of what would happen if no one was watching for danger.

He went to his room, closed the door and cried. Because if he were alive, the others were dead and he'd never see them again.

Thirteen

Maggie was certain William had never cleaned in his life. His parents had always kept servants. He had likely never learned to. Yet, he spent hours cleaning Apple View. But other than that, he had no new habits.

Every time they had fought or he had been angry with her, he would follow with a campaign of wooing. Each time, Maggie would feel smothered by his attention and would long to go back to not speaking. All she had ever wanted from him was a simple apology. She'd start speaking to him again just to bring everything back to normal.

Now, there'd been no anger, no disagreement and the campaign had no end in sight.

Every day, Maggie found fresh flowers in her room and in the sitting room. Sometimes he gave her roses cut from the garden. Other times, he gave her bouquets of Queen Anne's lace, black-eyed Susans and chicory he'd picked in ditches or wood lilies and blue flags from the bush lot and river.

Maggie didn't feel as rested as she had hoped. She hadn't worked since William came back, the longest break she'd had since the Spanish flu. Maggie worried she was becoming ill, but she didn't tell John or Dr. Mobley. She thought of her father's heart giving out, her mother giving up during the flu and she wondered if she was dying.

Her mother had believed fresh air was a cure, so Maggie spent as much time outside as she could. She took cushions and blankets to the river's edge and spent hours reading or painting or doing nothing at all. Because Henry had been such a talented artist, Maggie had given up painting in her teens, but she had started again. Henry had told her once how he could think of nothing else beyond the painting when he worked. She needed that.

Lucy found Maggie by the river in her nest of cushions, her painting abandoned to the side. They didn't spend as much time together as they once had. At night, Maggie could hear George and Lucy talking on the porch.

Jealousy sent a sharp spear into her heart. But she didn't know who she was jealous of. They were both her friends. Still, she missed Lucy.

"How are you feeling?" Lucy asked, dropping down onto the cushions. Her normally smooth bob was frizzed in the heat.

"Hot. You?"

"That's not what I meant."

"Tired. But I've been in the sun all day, like a cat," Maggie said.

Lucy pulled her blouse away from her body. "To hell with this," she said and began unbuttoning her blouse, taking it off. She wore only her chemise. She pulled off her skirt and stockings. "Join me? It's so much better than stewing in sweat?"

This was their friendship. Lucy leading. Maggie following, forced to acknowledge Lucy was right. Maggie admitted it was cooler to sit in the shade in just her undergarments.

"Maggie, I think I should move out," Lucy said.

"No! Don't! You can't!" Maggie said. Her throat ached.

"You should have less people here. You should be resting, not worrying about keeping all of us fed and entertained. George and I are too much. I'll evict us both and find you a housekeeper in town."

"You're no trouble. You both help so much. And the house is so big." If they left, she'd be alone. In her moment of fear, Maggie forgot about William.

Lucy took Maggie's hand. They were lying beside each other on the blanket as they had on so many nights in Montreal. "All right, I won't leave yet. But think about it."

Fourteen

Maggie was eleven years old and William thirteen when he told her he was going to marry her.

After Sunday school, the children milled about outside, waiting for their parents to stop talking to each other. Spring had finally come. The children tried to play quietly because it was Sunday, but the warm sun made it difficult to not want to run and shout.

Maggie and George picked violets out of the grass, competing to see who could pick the most, whose mother was going to get the biggest bouquet. Henry, John and William sat on the stone wall that surrounded the church yard, swinging their legs, whispering over something. William broke away from them and joined Maggie and George. Stooping down, William kissed Maggie's cheek.

"I'm going to marry you," he said.

Maggie wiped her cheek and made a disgusted face, sticking out her tongue. "Ugh. Don't kiss me. I don't want to marry anyone. Especially not you."

William scowled at her. But he moved to give her another kiss. George stepped between them. He was the smallest boy in his class and two years younger than William, but he still pushed William hard enough to make the bigger boy stumble back.

"Leave her alone," George said. He raised his small fists. His dark eyebrows knit together.

William laughed and stepped towards George. Maggie held her breath, letting out in a rush when William punched George, knocking George to the ground. William leaned down and whispered something to George. "She is not!" George cried out. He yanked William down by his ankles. The two of them wrestled in the grass.

Attracted by the fight, the other children had gathered in a ring around them. "Oh, Maggie. Two beaux fighting for you!" one of the girls said. Maggie tossed her violets to the ground and crushed them under her foot. She pushed her way out of the circle of children. Henry pushed his way in. Maggie looked back to see Henry and John pulling George and William apart.

The next day at school, the girls fussed over a cut on William's face, fretting he would be scarred. He recounted the fight, not mentioning that George had nearly won, despite being smaller and younger. George glowered from the back of the classroom. His left eye was swollen shut and his face was one greenish bruise. Maggie sat with him at lunch, but he wouldn't speak to her. When the bell rang, George said, "I'm not your beau."

"I know," she said. "You don't need to fight for me." She didn't tell him that she had cried before bed. She hated two boys were fighting over her. Henry had told her it wasn't her fault, but she felt guilty.

"I can't come play after school today," George said. His hand went to his injured eye and he flinched. "Or any day this week. Because I was fighting at church."

Trouble rippled out from her, Maggie thought. Maybe she should have let William kiss her and not done anything. The other children filed into school. Maggie hugged George and ran in, leaving him standing alone in the schoolyard.

After school, Maggie walked behind her brother and kicked rocks down the road. She was angry Henry wasn't paying attention to her. But she didn't want him to. Her feelings were jumbled and she was angry about everything. She wanted to scream.

William came panting up beside her. "I'm sorry. I didn't—I—you're—anyway, sorry," he said and pushed a paper bag into her hand. He kissed her cheek again, but she didn't mind this time. She blushed. She hoped he didn't see that. He ran off again.

"Maggie! Walk faster!" Henry shouted. He stood several feet ahead of her. She ran to catch up. "What's that?"

"William gave it to me. He's sorry." She opened the bag. It was full of candy. She held it out to Henry. He plucked out a caramel.

Through the sticky candy, he said, "He should apologize to George, not you. I can tell him to leave you alone if you want."

Maggie shook her head. She held out the bag again. She couldn't tell Henry that she'd enjoyed the attention from the other girls. Or that the girls had envied her because William was rich and the best looking boy in school.

Henry looked at her, but she couldn't tell what he was thinking. He was only two years older, but sometimes he seemed far more grown up. He'd grown tall over the winter. He was taller than their father now and their mother said he was losing his baby fat.

"Let's go home," he said.

From that time on, William brought Maggie little gifts, was at her side at school picnics and tried to be with her as much as he could. The other girls wanted to know which boy she would choose: George or William? No matter how much Maggie tried to explain, they preferred the excitement of a romantic triangle.

Fifteen

After consulting with friends from medical school, John had decided part of William's treatment would include reminding him of the past. William's memories were spotty. He could remember who they were and his parents, but he couldn't remember specific incidents. John asked George to stay a little longer at Apple View when George began to talk about leaving. "You remember things I don't," John had said. George thought of a small apartment with a dirty view of a dirty city. He wanted to go. He wanted to stay.

"I'm sure I do," George had answered. It was petty, but he wanted to remind William of the times he'd been cruel. George wanted to remind William of the war. He wanted to know why he'd been so sure William had died.

They went through old photo albums and told stories about the people in the pictures. Maggie found a box full of ephemera from their school days that her mother had saved. Sometimes William would respond. Mostly he wouldn't. Only John seemed to enjoy it. Well, maybe Lucy liked it too, hearing about Maggie and John when they were younger.

George played along. He hated it. He would have been happy to never see William again.

After dinner, they played cards. It was too wet to go outside and William seemed to enjoy cards, particularly if he won. Maggie and George refused to let him win, even though John had thought it would be good for William's confidence. Still, William won most of the hands. John shared a steady stream of memories with Maggie filling in details where she could. They avoided any unhappy memories.

"Do you remember the time William broke your nose, John?" George asked. Immediately, he was ashamed. John reflexively touched his crooked nose and glanced up at George.

"Of course. But it's not worth talking about. It was a misunderstanding," John said with a tight smile. He rubbed a hand over his head.

"Was it?" asked George. He couldn't stop now that he'd started. Maggie shook her head at him. He moved his leg away from her kick under the table and she caught his chair leg. He tried not to laugh as she swallowed back a curse.

"So," George said, smiling at Lucy and then John. He pretended he didn't see the flush spreading from John's cheeks, turning his bald head red. "We were playing, what was it? Rugby? I think rugby. I hated that game. Never played it after I left school. Anyway, John was on one team and William the other. I was on John's team. We won. Which was unusual for our team. William thought the referee had made some bad calls favouring our team. At the end of the game, you know, when you all shake hands, he said something to John. What was it? Oh. He called you a cheater."

John's flush had gone. He was pale now. "Look. Let's not tell this story. It's not worth remembering," John said.

George continued. "So John pushed William. Just a small push, just enough to make William step back. William started to walk away, but then he came back. And he punched John. Just like that. Right in the nose. John didn't have time to put a hand up. I heard his nose break. For a long time, it was the most disgusting thing I'd ever seen. War took care of that." George paused and took a drink from his mug. The others were having coffee. He was sure they knew his mug was mostly whiskey.

"There was blood everywhere," he continued. "John was yelling, the teachers were yelling and William, what were you doing? Oh, right. You were laughing. Because you'd made John cry. Which you can't help when you get hit in the nose. One of the teachers pulled you off the pitch. I gave John my sweater to catch the blood. And I sat with him while we waited for his father. John had the worst black eyes for a week or more. And William, what happened to you? Your father threw some money at the school. You were never punished."

John looked down at his cards. George could see him as he'd been. In that moment, John seemed very young. He was the nicest one of them, the easiest to hurt. God, George was an ass.

"It was a long time ago," John said so quietly George could hardly hear him. "And William apologized. Right? Still mates. Tempers get hot during matches."

William didn't react. He watched them, his eyes moving from John to George to Maggie and back.

"But that's what he always did, isn't it? 'I'm so sorry. If you hadn't made me so angry, I wouldn't have done it. I'll never do it again. I swear. It's just this rotten temper. We're all still friends, right?'" George stood up with his mug in hand. He was as bad as William. He was led by his temper too. George tapped John's shoulder. "Fuck. I'm sorry, John."

George left them to finish their card game. He paused at the door and looked back. No one looked at him. Lucy had her arm around John's shoulders and he leaned into her. Maggie was sorting the cards by suit. William looked up at George. He smiled and wagged his finger.

Sixteen

The night was beginning to have all the hallmarks of one that he'd regret, but he kept going, pushing through it. When Maude asked him to go with her, George had accepted and had intended to put on a nice suit and behave himself. But when he saw a girl look at him with a curled lip, when he saw a group whisper and stare at him, he changed course. Fine; if they thought he was beneath them, he would show them what that meant.

George had caught Maggie's eyes as he had pulled Maude towards a dark, secluded part of the garden. Even under the warm glow of the Japanese lanterns, Maggie's face was pale, ghostly. In her glare, he saw Henry. He tightened his grasp on Maude's arm and yanked her almost off her feet. Maggie shook her head and walked away.

In the dark corner, where they could hear, but not see the rest of the party, Maude let George kiss her and they both let their hands go wherever. Because the secret that George had learned about the people who looked down on him was as long as no one saw, as long as there were limits and technicalities, they would let him take whatever pleasure he could find. So, Maude would allow his hands to roam over her so long as she stayed dressed and she would touch him through his clothes too.

He could feel Maggie's white hot glare, though. The judgement and disappointment burned through him, making his chest ache. He knew there were rumours about what he had done to be cast aside by the Tates and sometimes they made him laugh because they were so far from the truth. No one, not even his mother or his sister, could see that his heart had been broken, was breaking every day.

So he slipped his hand under the girl's dress and at first she laughed and said his name in a breathless way, but then she came back to herself and pushed him away. Then she slapped him. Hard. And left him standing there, rumpled, his cheek already swelling. He watched her walk away while hurriedly adjusting her dress and hair. George laughed. He laughed so hard he began to cough and then, he was surprised to find himself sobbing. He sat down on the dew soaked grass and cried until he felt sick with it, until he could hardly breathe.

When he rejoined the party, he paused to take a glass of champagne and when the server turned to open a fresh bottle, he scooped up a bottle of whiskey and hid it in his jacket. He wandered through the crowd of beautiful young people, picking up half empty glasses and draining them. He spoke to a few people, but hardly any knew what he was saying.

He left the party, but didn't know where to go. He sat on the low stone wall that bordered the Suttons' property and looked up at the clear night sky. He thought that he saw shooting stars streaking across the sky. But then again, he was really drunk. He remembered the bottle of whiskey in his jacket. He could be drunker. But then he couldn't go home. The last time he had stumbled in, pickled, close to vomiting, his mother was already up, getting ready for work and she had hit him with a broom. He didn't blame her for it. Just as he didn't blame Maude for slapping him.

George sat on the wall and watched for falling stars and took sips out of the bottle, feeling the warm numbness spread through his blood. He started, nearly dropping the bottle, when he saw something white out of the corner of his eye. He remembered when they were kids they used to say this street was haunted.

"George?" Maggie asked. He laughed at his own foolishness.

"Hey, Maggie. Have a good time at the party?" He smiled at her, knowing she'd smile back even if she was angry with him.

She smiled and shrugged and he saw Henry again. "I hate those things, but Mum thought I should go. I'd ask if you had a good time, but I can see what kind of time you had," she said. She gestured at his face. He touched his cheek and yes, that hurt.

"Drink?" He wiggled the bottle at her. She laughed and held up a bottle of champagne.

"We think alike," she said. "I've never been really drunk, but—I want to be. Does it help?"

"Help with what?"

"Everything."

He shook his head. "I don't know if we can get that drunk. Did you bring something to open this with?"

She laughed and he laughed with her. God, she lit up when she laughed, just like—and he pushed it away. But she was usually so serious, too serious, so very few people had any idea how her face changed when she smiled. It was like the sun coming out from behind a cloud; it changed everything. "Ah. I forgot. Oh well. So much for that idea."

He took out a pocketknife. It was Henry who had got both him and John in the habit of always having a knife. It could be almost any tool if you knew what you were doing. He pried out the cork and they both jumped at the pop as the pressure let go. Maggie clapped her hands as he brought the bottle to his mouth to catch the foam. "You look like a rabid dog!" she exclaimed and he barked.

The sky was light by the time they left their perch on the wall. Maggie tried to walk in a straight line, but wobbled. George knew that walk, had done that walk. It was never convincing.

"Lemme take you home," he said, taking her arm.

"You're not — you're not supposed to be there. Mum — what did you do?" Maggie struggled to enunciate.

George sighed. "Doesn't matter. None of your business."

"Was it bad?"

He laughed. No, it was wonderful, he wanted to yell out. This part was bad. "Can't tell you."

"That's what Henry said. I hate secrets." She stumbled and George brought her back up to her feet. "I miss you." And she hit him in the arm. Women were always hitting him. "You were my friend first and I miss you!"

He hugged her close and kissed her forehead. They were nearly the same height. "I'm sorry," he whispered.

"Me too," she whispered. They didn't talk the rest of the way back to Apple View. At the gate, Maggie stopped and turned to George. "I can't go in. Mum will have a fit and I'll never hear the end of it. I gotta sober up."

George nodded. He took her hand. "Come with me." He led her through the yard and over the footbridge and through the woodlot and past the old burial ground to the stone house. He hadn't been there since, but it was a place to hide. It had always been a place to hide.

They sat beside each other, on the dirty floor, neither caring about their clothes. Both were already covered in grass stains and dust from the road. They didn't speak, but dozed next to each other. George put his palms to the floor, trying to still the spinning world. He idly wondered what it would take to burn this place to the ground.

He dozed and let his mind wander through memories of other nights he'd spent in the old farmhouse. He jerked awake when he felt hands on his face and a mouth on his. For moment, he thought perhaps he was still dreaming and he kissed back. But then he woke up and pushed Maggie back. "No!" he shouted at her. It was too strange to have now kissed both brother and sister.

"Why not?" she asked and pulled him towards her. He fought out of her grasp and she slumped a little against the wall.

"It's a bad idea," he said.

"You kiss lots of girls. I saw you at the party," she said, her voice slurring. "You do lots of things."

"It's different. And you're engaged. To William. I don't play around with other people's girls," he said, lying to her. Of course he did. And other people's boys too. Anyone who would have him and make him forget the constant ache inside.

"I'm not property," she said, shaking her head. "I've never kissed anyone else before. It was nice. Different."

George stood and lifted her up to standing. "I think it's time you went to bed. I'll help you back to the house."

"You're so nice to me," Maggie slurred and smiled at him. She looked so much like her brother. It was wrong. He was wrong.

He helped her walk back up to the house, but instead of taking her through the back kitchen door or through the front, he took her to the side of the house. "I thought you were taking me home. There's no door here," she said and giggled.

"Is your brother home?" he asked.

She looked at him, her eyes sweeping over his face. Their eyes, he thought, those are different. Hers were darker, almost gray, not nearly white like Henry's. "You don't know? But you're so much in each other's pockets. What happened? What did you do?"

"Is he home?"

"No. He's been at the lake all summer. Got a job as a guide. Takes rich Americans around in a canoe. Dad's going up next week to see him. Something about buying some land or something. I don't know. You're not going to tell me what happened. No one tells me anything."

George sighed. He wanted to tell her. But it wasn't his story to tell. He couldn't say anything that would take her love away from her brother. He couldn't do that to Henry no matter how much he hurt and how much he hoped Henry was suffering too.

From behind the ivy crawling up the bricks, George pulled out a rope ladder. It went up to Henry's window. Maggie stared at it, open-mouthed. "He's been keeping secrets!" she exclaimed. "Is it safe?"

George nodded. "I'll be down here, holding it steady. There's a handle on the outside of the window. Use it to pull the sash up. I used to do this all the time. Up you go."

He watched her climb, her concentration making her more steady-footed than he had expected. She looked over her shoulder, down at him, and grinned. Why couldn't they have stayed eleven years old forever? And then she disappeared through the window.

Seventeen

On a warm, sunny day after a few days of rain, Maggie decided to wash her hair. Usually Lucy helped her, but Lucy had been so busy since Maggie had quit nursing. With a house full of men, for some reason, Maggie had been shy about washing her hair on a day when they were all there. Lucy would always tease her while helping to wet and lather her hair. "Just bob it already," Lucy would say. But Maggie couldn't cut her hair. She loved it. It wasn't exactly vanity, although she did think it was beautiful. It was more that it was part of her. She only trimmed the ends when they became ragged, so it had grown past her waist. Even before bobs came in style, her hair had been unfashionably long.

Maggie went out to the backyard wearing one of her mother's old house dresses. It was a loose, ugly thing in a hideous print that her brother had always said looked like rotting roses, all smudgy browns and grayish pinks.

She awkwardly scooped water out of the rain barrel with a chipped china ewer. As she poured water through her hair, she very nearly hit her head several times. The pitcher was heavy even before she filled it with water. When she looked up through a curtain of dripping hair like reddish seaweed, she saw George leaning against the porch railing. "What?" she asked, hoping to drive him to turn around. He grinned at her.

"I was thinking of Henry's pre-Raphaelite phase when he made you pose as every damsel and princess ever. He'd paint you as a sea witch if he could see you now."

"Thanks. You could stand there or you could help," she said.

But before George could reply, William came out and jostled George, just a little, as he walked past. George glared at him. William began to say something as if he had forgotten he couldn't speak. He frowned when no words came. Maggie thought of their Sunday School fight.

"It must be terrible to not be able to use that sharp tongue of yours,"

George said.

William shook his head and went back inside. He came out with a chair and a towel. He winked at George. When he set the chair down by the rain barrel, he indicated that Maggie should sit in the chair. With a gentle touch, he guided her head back. Her hair nearly brushed the ground. She closed her eyes against the bright sun.

William poured water through her hair, combing the water through with his fingers. To Maggie, the world was all sensation and the orange glow of the sun through her closed eyelids. William's fingers felt good against her head and she leaned into his touch like a cat. He was kinder than she remembered.

William worked shampoo through her hair. Maggie thought she could hear him humming, but she couldn't make out a song. She wasn't sure if George were still there, watching, but she thought so. She felt drowsy, relaxed. It was almost like when her mother would wash her hair.

She opened her eyes when William gently took her shoulders to get her to sit up straight. He held up the comb and began combing out her tangled hair, beginning at the ends and working his way up to her scalp. She looked over to the porch. George was still there, watching, frowning. When Maggie caught his eye, he dropped his cigarette into the coffee can of butts and went back into the house.

William pressed a kiss to the top of her head. Maybe she could be happy with him, if he were like this now.

Eighteen

The sound of bones crunching under his foot roiled his stomach. He lifted his foot to reveal a headless, disemboweled mouse, now squashed, blood seeping out. George fought the urge to gag as he hopped off the porch to wipe his boot in the grass.

Don't think about bones under your feet. Don't think about rotted flesh slipping under your hands.

Just underneath the porch, he saw more tiny corpses in pieces. Bits of birds and mice were strewn about. There was even a snake. As he debated what to do about the mess, Maggie came outside with William following close behind.

"Maggie, do you have a cat?" George asked.

"No. There may be cats in the barn, but I don't have any on purpose. Why?"

"Something's been leaving you offerings," he said and showed her the bodies.

Maggie grimaced. "This is why I don't like cats. Little murderers." Behind Maggie, William smiled and licked his lips.

Birds sang and the morning air still smelled fresh and new. But George couldn't keep hold of the feeling he had when he woke up that it would be a good day. He went to the barn for a shovel and a pail. He'd bury the bodies under the roses so at least something beautiful would make a meal of them.

Nineteen

George wasn't sure if he should stay. He didn't want to be involved in whatever was happening. And Alan. He wanted to see Alan again. He'd written about the mistake and Alan had accepted it. George hadn't expected it and he was sure the longer he stayed here, the less likely Alan would be to welcome him back. But it was good to be back at Apple View, back in Henry's room. He could see the danger of staying.

When he was a child, he'd liked to stay at Apple View and pretend Mr. and Mrs. Tate were his parents. His mother was often tired and too worried about surviving to lavish much attention on her children. She loved them, he knew that, but coddling was a luxury. The Tates hadn't spoiled their children, but Maggie and Henry had lacked for nothing. And their friends had been treated the same.

George had never known his father. He knew Mr. Tate knew something, but he had never asked. He hadn't wanted to know. His mother had owed Mr. Tate for something and since Mr. Tate had been a lawyer, it had likely been some misdeed his father had done.

When George had showed an aptitude for learning and a curiosity about Mr. Tate's work, Mr. Tate had hired George to act as a kind of clerk. George had assumed that he would have to leave school to work, but Mr. Tate had made sure that he and his sister had been able to stay at school and even go on to university. George's mother had been a bit in awe of the Tates and had let them talk her into taking money for her children's education. Usually, she had refused charity, but she couldn't deprive her children of a chance at a better life. When he thought of his mother able to spend her days as she pleased in his sister's fine house, George sent a prayer of thanks to the Tates.

*****

Although he had slept in Henry's room many times over the years, George couldn't easily sleep there now. He felt as if the bed were swallowing him. He had forgotten about the feather beds at Apple View. So each night, he had a little night cap, a little taste to help him sleep.

After drinking himself to sleep, he woke and couldn't move. Not safe, not safe, his mind blared, but he couldn't make his limbs obey the order to run. Even his voice stuck. He had no words, only moans. The room was dark. He could hear the big clock in the sitting room ticking.

Under the door, light leaked from the hallway. A shadow passed. It passed again. It stopped in front of his door. He fought against whatever held him still. The doorknob turned and the door opened. At first, he saw nothing. Just the empty hallway. The door closed. And William stood in the room. He smiled. His teeth gleamed in the dark.

George tried to scream, but only succeeded in making a strange howl. William crept to his bedside. If he touches me, George thought, I shall go mad. William lifted the covers. A cold breeze raised goosebumps on George's skin. William slid into bed beside George and put a clammy hand over George's mouth.

"My old friend," William whispered. "Don't you think it's time you left? You're not wanted here."

George closed his eyes. The smell. The sick, sweet smell like the cherry trees in spring suffocated him. But William couldn't talk.

"I have lots to say, when the time comes," William whispered, his breath tickling George's ear. "You didn't see what you think saw. Battle fatigue. Makes you see things. And who would believe you? A drunk, a deviant. You belong locked up. I should have taken care of you that night. A favour to an old friend."

George thought of the night in the shell hole, when they were sure they were going to die. He thought of what they'd said to each other, although they had been long past pretending to be friends. And then he'd been shot and William's head had been taken off by a shell. He'd seen it. He had.

George wiggled his fingers. He could move a little. He struggled against William's grip.

"Do you like this?" the terrible voice hissed in his ear. "Is that what you want?"

And then William was gone and George was alone, gagging. He rolled out of bed, onto his hands and knees and threw up on the rug beside the bed. "What the hell?" he asked aloud, his voice hoarse. He pushed the rug away and collapsed onto his side. He fell asleep on the floor. In the morning, when he woke with a headache and a sour taste in his mouth, he told himself it had been a nightmare.

Twenty

At night, the barriers thinned. The voices were louder. Or they would be. Lucy could control them more than she had been able to after the war. But that control seemed to be slipping away.

Tonight, she was alone. Some nights, she relished having her bed to herself. Other nights, like tonight, she missed hearing John's slow breathing beside her. Lucy could make herself sleep by following his breathing. And the dead rarely spoke to her if he was there.

Even on a warm night, she needed the weight of blankets to hold her down, to let her body know it was time to sleep. She would wake up soaked in sweat, but she had tried sleeping with lighter sheets and would only toss restlessly.

There were no clear voices, only a constant, unintelligible murmur in her head that matched the sound of the wind rustling the leaves of the cottonwood trees outside her window. She wanted a cigarette, but she didn't want to get out of bed to get one.

Something scratched at her door. Like a cat, but there wasn't a cat in the house. Maybe one had sneaked in. George had mentioned finding dead mice on the back porch most mornings.

Lucy turned over to look at the door. The room was dark, but she could make out dim shapes. The hall light wasn't on. Everyone in the house was asleep. Another scratch at the door and she saw the glass knob turn. The door opened a crack. William slid through.

Her heart caught in her throat and her pulse quickened. She wanted to pretend to be asleep so he would leave, but she couldn't close her eyes with him in the room. The murmur in her head grew to a roar. It was the sound of a crowded station or the street during a parade. It was all sound and only a few words and phrases coming clear.

William sat on the end of the bed. Despite the dark, she could see him clearly. His pale skin was luminous. His teeth flashed as he smiled. He put a finger to his lips and made a hissing sound.

"You know," he said. His lips didn't move. His voice was in her head.

"Know what?" she asked aloud. He pouted at her, mocking her.

"Shhhh." His finger to his lips again. He tapped his head. "In here."

"Know what?" she asked in her mind. He nodded.

"Good girl. You know what I am."

There was a flash like lightning, but the night sky was clear. But in that moment, she saw him. Most of his head was gone, the edges of the skull ragged. Blood covered his torso. His jaw showed through torn skin and muscle on the left side of his ruined face. And then it was gone and he was as blandly handsome and whole as before.

A scream rose up in her throat, but she held it in, clamping her hands over her mouth. Bile rose up behind the scream.

"What do you want? I can help you," she said.

He shook his head. He slid closer to her, lying beside her. He took her chin in hand and turned her face towards him. The smell made her gag. "I don't need your help."

"I'll tell Maggie."

He laughed and she thought of that ruined jaw flapping. "She won't believe you. You're mad. And if you tell, I will take everything away from you. What would that do for John and his tired heart? Not much. I'll have him unless you keep quiet."

Lucy leaned away from him. He grinned. His teeth were long in his face, his lips pulled too far back somehow. She turned her face away, but he pulled her back by her chin. He kissed her, suffocated her. Lucy tried to fight against him and only when she began to see spots did he let her go. She took deep, greedy breaths. He licked his lips. "Oh," he said. "I see why John keeps his whore around."

The roar in Lucy's mind grew louder. It sounded like the battlefield. All shouts and explosions. She pushed William, knocking him from the bed. He got his feet under himself like a cat. "God damn you!" she yelled. "What do you want?"

"My wife. And when I'm strong enough I'll have her. And you and John and everyone else she cares about. I'll have them all." He slid back through the doorway.

Lucy fumbled for the lamp beside her bed. She knew her jaw would be bruised.

Someone knocked on the door and she stuffed her sheet in her mouth to stifle a scream. "Lucy? It's me, George. Are you all right?"

"Please—" she said, but she didn't know what she wanted. George came in and eased the door shut. He sat on the edge of her bed. He reached out to touch her jaw, but she flinched from his hand.

"I heard a noise. Did you fall? Your face—"

She leaned forward and threw her arms around him. He pulled her close and put his hand on the back of her head, smoothing her hair as she cried. He smelled good, comforting. His shirt was soft and smelled of tobacco. The tears cleared her mind. In George's tight embrace, feeling him breathe, she felt safe.

George tipped her back on her pillows, releasing her once she was laid back. He used the hem of his shirt to wipe her face. She tried to smile, but her face wouldn't move beyond a grimace. "What happened?" he asked. "Was it William?"

She nodded. He muttered something she couldn't quite hear, but she was sure it was a curse.

"Stay. Please. I don't want to be alone," she said. She could smile at his hesitation, his doubt. "I'm not asking for anything except for you to be a warm body beside me. I don't think I can sleep alone tonight."

"I don't want to cause trouble," he said.

"I know it's hard for you. For a woman to not throw herself at you," Lucy said.

George smiled. "There's my girl. All right. But if John challenges me to duel with pistols at dawn over your honour, I'm making you my proxy."

"He knows I don't have any honour." She lifted the sheets. The brief spell of humour died. "Please. I can't be alone."

"All right." He kicked off his house slippers and pulled off his belt. He unbuttoned his shirt and draped it over a chair. Still wearing an undershirt and pants, he got into bed beside her. Lucy put her hand to his chest. She could feel his heartbeat. All of the boys she had done this to and the heartbeats she had felt fade away. All the ones she sat with as they slipped over the barrier.

George put his hand over hers. "Go to sleep," he said.

The wind picked up and rattled the cottonwood leaves. But the voices were quiet and Lucy could hear George's regular breathing. It wasn't quite the same as John's, but it was close enough. The fear was fading and she was tired.

"George?" she whispered, but he was already asleep.

A voice in her head said, "Wait for me."

Twenty-One

Lucy realized it was both easy and hard to slip back into her old life. Her room hadn't changed. Her beautiful dresses, several years out of style, still hung in her closet. She had grown used to her uniform and the riot of colourful silks made her think of butterflies and orchids. A stack of old school books stood by her bed.

When she saw herself in her vanity mirror, she couldn't pretend the last five years hadn't happened. The morning light through her window was harsh, but she made herself look. Lines cut across her forehead and fanned out from her eyes. Too many sleepless nights had tattooed dark circles under her eyes. She'd lost weight, and with it, her soft prettiness.

Lucy undid her braids and let her hair fall around her shoulders. In London, she'd seen women with short hair. A change would be good.

Her mother was glad to see Lucy take an interest in her appearance. They made a day of it. Lucy put up very little protest to dedicating a day to frivolousness. She hoped it was enough of a distraction, that it would keep the dead from speaking.

It did not.

Drinking helped. Or at least it made it easier to pretend she was still herself. She always carried a flask and used mints to hide the smell. If her parents noticed, they said nothing. They wanted to believe the last five years hadn't happened.

Her grandmother would not be fooled.

On a particularly bad day, Lucy refused to come out of her room. She took her meals on trays brought up to her. Her mother didn't want to push and her father was away on business. But her grandmother let herself into Lucy's room.

"How long?" her grandmother asked, standing over Lucy. Lucy pulled the sheets over her face. Her grandmother yanked them down.

"About three years," Lucy said. "But it's getting harder to ignore. They won't stop. They talk all the time."

"What do they say?"

"I don't know. There are too many."

Her grandmother sat beside her and smoothed her hair back from face. "Well, let's talk to them."

Mr. and Mrs. Stoppard preferred to overlook old Mrs. Stoppard's Spiritualist beliefs. Her son only asked that his mother attend regular services at the Anglican church. For others, Spiritualism had been a fashion, but old Mrs. Stoppard believed.

Lucy allowed her grandmother to attempt to tease apart the voices with a séance. When she agreed, Lucy thought her grandmother would do only one or two sessions and they'd be joined only by her grandmother's friends.

But word got out. A stream of women began to call on Lucy's grandmother. They wanted to speak to their dead. They wanted Lucy to find out if their missing were actually gone.

Her grandmother's castle-like home no longer seemed romantic to Lucy. The heavy drapes blocked out the sun, creating a permanent dusk. They held séances in the dim, wood-panelled parlour.

A grieving mother or widow would bring a friend. They'd be dressed in black. The grieving woman would offer a token of the dead, a photo or some small possession such as a watch. Lucy hated the photos. She hated seeing their young faces, frozen forever.

The women, and sometimes a man or two, would sit at the table. Candles were the only light. Everyone would hold hands and concentrate on the spirit they were calling. Lucy's grandmother would call to the dead, but Lucy was the conduit. She wrote what the spirits dictated.

Lucy answered questions from the family or passed on messages from the grave. The messages were usually banal. Death didn't grant anyone abilities they didn't have in life. She wished the grieving wouldn't ask for details about the moment of death. As a dead man whispered to her, she would see his memories. She held back the worst, but the grieving were driven to know.

"I wish they'd just pray," Lucy said.

"The dead want you to speak," her grandmother said.

"Do they? I don't know. They're not going away. It never stops," Lucy said.

"You bring comfort," her grandmother said.

Lucy poked at the pages of automatic writing in the fireplace. They always spoke to her. Even after she wrote down their messages, they kept speaking. They were alone, afraid, confused. They never stopped.

Twenty-Two

The heavy brocade curtains were pulled tight against any outside light. Candles flickered around the room, casting weird shadows. Everyone was dressed in black except for Lucy. She refused to wear dark colors. Instead, she wore a pale lilac dress. She felt like a moth, pale against the sombre room.

She felt sorry for the people who came. They wanted comfort, but she didn't have any to give. She worried they'd think she was a charlatan. Sometimes, she wondered if she was. Maybe she was crazy, hearing voices and there was nothing on the other side. But they believed. They wanted to believe.

Lucy refused to take money for her services, but she had seen a woman press an envelope into her grandmother's hand more than once.

Her grandmother's staff were discreetly absent for séance days. Lucy always wondered what they thought of it. Did any of them believe? Surely a few did. The others probably thought Mrs. Stoppard was a harmless eccentric. Did any of them think her grandmother was mentally disturbed? Or a crook?

Lucy hung up her coat and went to the powder room to adjust her hair and dress. She was always nervous before a session. She remembered how calm she felt when she was nursing. She had never hesitated to do what was needed. Her hands shook as she smoothed her short hair behind her ears. Should she put on a bit of lipstick, to give color to her face? She lit a cigarette.

In the parlour, her grandmother fussed over the arrangement of chairs. All the furniture was heavy and old-fashioned. Everything was shrouded in heavy, dark cloth, often with fringe and beads. Dead relatives stared out mournfully from old daguerreotypes and crayon portraits.

The doorbell rang and Lucy's grandmother bustled to the door, her silk dress making a swishing noise as she walked. Lucy heard her warmly greeting the new clients. Lucy sat at the table and breathed deeply. The steady roar continued in her head, but she was almost used to it now. It was like the sound of traffic in the streets.

Her grandmother brought in the clients, a woman about Lucy's age and a middle-aged woman. Both wore black dresses. The young woman was dressed very fashionably while the older woman looked like portraits of the Princess of Wales, all pigeon breast and tiny waist. They were both pale and hollow under their eyes. They introduced themselves and sat down at the table.

"What is it you wish to ask the spirits?" Lucy's grandmother asked.

"I want to know if my Teddy is happy. If he suffered. If he's with Jesus now," the older woman said. "My minister says this is a terrible sin, us being here. But I need to know."

Lucy felt the younger woman stare at her. She met the woman's gaze and saw a non-believer.

"I'm so sorry for your loss," Lucy said in a voice not much above a whisper and the younger woman sneered at her.

Mrs. Stoppard told them to hold hands and to concentrate their thoughts on Teddy. His mother had brought not only a photograph, but a ragged little stuffed dog. The much loved toy pierced Lucy. More than the photograph, it spoke to her of Teddy.

Lucy closed her eyes and listened to the voices. She pictured herself in a great room that was full of the dead. It was crowded, but no one was distinct. It was like being in the foyer of a busy concert hall with people pushing past to get into the show. "Teddy?"

The others faded away as one man grew distinct. She recognized Teddy from his picture. He was very young. His skin was as smooth as an infant's. "I have this for you," she said and handed him the dog.

"Patches!" he cried and snatched the dog from her hand. He cuddled it against his cheek. That side of his face was ruined. A large wound gaped in his temple. He'd been shot. He'd probably died instantly. At least he had not suffered long.

They were now in a green field full of wildflowers. The light was warm and golden. She knew this was Teddy's vision. Everyone's was different, she had learned.

"Teddy, your mother is here. And your sister. They want to know if you suffered. Would you speak through me to them? To comfort them."

Teddy tucked Patches into the breast of his uniform. He looked at Lucy. "Do I know you?"

"No. My name is Lucy. I worked as a VAD during the war. Now, I help families talk to their dead."

"Then you know the answer to your question. Did I suffer?" He stepped closer to her. She wanted to step back, but she didn't. "Did I suffer? What do you think?"

"That you were shot and probably died very quickly," she answered. He was so close to her that if they were in the real world, she'd feel his breath on her.

He pointed to his temple. "You mean this? I couldn't take it anymore. The constant noise and mud and never alone and always cold and wet. So one day, I put my gun to my head. And that was that. Do you think my mother needs to hear that? Do you think that will comfort her?"

They stood almost nose to nose for a long, tense, silent moment. Lucy threw her arms around him. He sobbed into her shoulder.

"Is there any message you want me to take back to them? Families don't need to know the truth so much as they need to know that you're safe. They want to tell you one last time that they love you and they want to hear it from you too. Can you do that? For your mother?"

He nodded.

Lucy opened her eyes and could feel Teddy looking out of them and at the people in the room. He had control of her body and her voice.

"Mummy! Mummy, don't worry. I'm sorry. But I do love you." Lucy's hand took the woman's hand and squeezed it. "Thank you for bringing Patches to me. He'll comfort me until we can be together."

"Oh, Teddy!" The woman was crying. "I miss you so much. Please tell me. Are you suffering? Are you in heaven now?"

"I didn't suffer, Mummy. I'm in a better place now."

"Oh, thank God," the woman muttered. She wept into an embroidered handkerchief.

Lucy's hand now took up the hands of the young woman. She tried to escape from Lucy's grasp, but she couldn't. "Laura, please believe that it's me, Teddy. Remember the time we didn't go to school, but spent the whole day playing by the pond? I think of that a lot. It was the best day. Take care of Mummy for me. I'm so sorry."

And then he was gone.

Lucy's grandmother left to fetch a tea tray. Clients often needed some time to refresh themselves and prepare to face the outside world again. Their loss seemed fresher after a session.

The two women clung to each other, sobbing. Lucy felt awkward sitting beside such open grief, but it would be rude to walk away. She bore witness to their suffering. Silently, she wished Teddy well on the other side. The voices still roared. Her mind was still a busy hall.

"We didn't tell you the name of the dog," the sister said to Lucy. "You couldn't know that unless you really did speak to Teddy. It's a great relief to know he didn't suffer." Lucy nodded and tried to smile.

After they had gone, Lucy told her grandmother what Teddy what told her. "I'm not doing another séance," she said.

"But, Lucy, what about the voices?" her grandmother asked.

"It's not helping. And this, this is awful. We're reliving all this pain and suffering. We're making these people feel their loss again. And then they pay you! I've seen you take money. I won't do it again," she said.

Lucy's grandmother sighed. She went to a cabinet and took out a crystal decanter and two small glasses. "Sherry," she said. Mrs. Stoppard briskly drank her glass and poured another. "Lucy, I have taken money. I've put it into an account in your name. Oh my darling, I only want to help you."

Lucy patted her grandmother's arm. "I know."

Twenty-Three

Lucy needed distraction. She needed dancing. She needed a man's body next to hers, over hers. She needed passion and pleasure. Her mother's decorous parties were not enough, so she went out to find what she needed.

She hid her distractions from her parents. But rumors started. Her brother tried to shield her. He'd been in France. He knew. Their father had tried to get Garnet a safe position with the War Office, but he'd refused. He didn't ask Lucy what she saw because he'd already seen it. He only asked that she try to be cautious.

But Lucy couldn't be cautious. She didn't care about rules. It seemed to take more to quiet the voices. People started to notice she was drunk most of the time. Her parents said nothing.

They were forced to speak to her after she was found sleeping in the stable, curled up with one of her brother's friends, neither of them clothed. But her parents only asked that she curb her behavior. It wasn't so much they wanted her to stop; they wanted her to not attract notice. Their wealth gave her some protection, but not against too much of that.

When Lucy collapsed at an afternoon tea, clutching her head and screaming at the dead to be quiet, her parents had to do something. It could not be ignored. Lucy had fought to keep her secret, but after nights without sleep, she became overwhelmed.

The clatter of teacups set her on edge. The chatter of the women faded to the background as the messages from the other world grew louder. Lucy saw their memories in a confusion of blood, smoke and dirt. There was too much noise. Artillery, shells, horses screaming, men shouting. She was sitting in a pretty room wearing a silk dress, she was in a hospital carrying a limb down a hall, she was in the mud, clutching a rifle. Her teacup shattered against the tiles of the sun room floor. She fell to her knees, not feeling her skin split against the hard floor. Pain blared across her head like a spike.

Someone screamed for quiet, over and over. It was her. She was screaming and couldn't pull it back into her throat. Someone picked her up. Her brother. He whispered in her ear and carried away to her room while her mother's friends stood, silent, shocked.

Lucy woke to voices muttering around her. Garnet and her parents argued about what to do with her. Garnet wanted to take her away. He wanted them to go somewhere quiet, with fresh air, to convalesce. Her mother cried. Her father wanted her in a hospital somewhere. "It's brain fever," he repeated, as if just by restating his opinion more forcefully, he would convince his son.

"I don't want to go to a hospital," Lucy whispered. She licked her lips. They were cracked and sore. Her knees throbbed.

Garnet came to her side and gave her a glass of water. "Shhh. I know. I'll take you out west. Remember you wanted to go to Banff? When you're better, we'll go. Me and you."

But her parents brought a doctor who recommended that her father send Lucy to an asylum for her own good, her own safety.

The night before she left, Lucy sat in her room, listening to music and smoking. Her brother came in without knocking, walking in stocking feet. The doctor had asked Garnet to avoid speaking with his sister since he disagreed so strongly with the plan for her. Or that was what the doctor had told Lucy.

"Lucy, let me take you away," Garnet said.

"No. They're right. I need help. I'm sick."

"You're not. It's not—it's not in your head. I believe you. That you hear them."

Lucy laughed. No one in her family had talked to her about what she had claimed to hear except her grandmother.

Garnet sat on the floor across from her. He picked up her flask and took a drink. "I do."

"Really?"

"I saw things. Things I can't explain. Once, we were stationed in a village. We'd loaded explosives into the basement and were waiting for orders. Suddenly, I felt a cold hand on mine. It was my friend, Smitty. Remember, I wrote you about him? He was dead. Had been for months. But he was there, in that basement. He grabbed my hand and told me to go outside. Then he ran up the stairs. I followed him. Shortly after that, one of the men accidentally shot one of the barrels. He was cleaning his gun or something.

Anyway. Boom. The whole place went up. Everyone died. But me. Lots of men had stories like that."

"Where would you take me? I can't travel. I can barely leave the house. I—I don't know what to do. I need to rest. I'm so tired." Lucy lay down on the rug. She twirled the colorful strands of wool between her fingers.

"But I believe you. You're not sick. You have a gift," Garnet said. He took her cigarette out of her hand and smoked it for a little bit. He gave it back to her.

"Maybe. But it's a curse."

"Promise me, though, if you're unhappy there, tell me. I'll get you out. No matter what Mum and Dad want."

"I promise."

They sat up the rest of the night, listening to records, smoking and telling each other stories about the war. In letters, they had avoided talking of the terrible things they had seen or done. But that night, they told each other everything.

Twenty-Four

Maggie wondered where William had been and if he even knew. He said he didn't know, but was that true? All those missing years, she'd been in her parents' home surrounded by the past and he had been somewhere. Not with his mother though. His mother swore she had not heard from him since shortly before he died.

Maggie suspected he had been with his father. Mr. Lancaster had run off years ago with a mistress. It had been the scandal of the town until the war had swallowed it up. He probably wasn't with the same woman. His eye had always wandered after pretty women. He had never come back to town. Everyone allowed Mrs. Lancaster to maintain the fiction that he was looking after another branch of the family business.

But then, William's father had sounded genuinely surprised about William's resurrection when Maggie spoke with him on the phone. It was easier to lie over wires, when no one could read your face along with your voice, but he had seemed sincere. Still, he hadn't returned to see his son. The one time Maggie had suggested William call or write his father, William had walked away from her and she didn't see him for the rest of the day.

The telephone calls had stopped briefly after William came back, but after George came, they started again. Maggie got more calls every day. No one ever spoke clearly on the other end. She only ever heard snatches of songs and poems, her name and an odd word. Once, she came to the phone and William held the receiver to his ear.

William smiled. He looked cunning, his face in shadow in the dark hallway, weird shafts of light from outside making his expression sinister. He hung up the phone and laughed soundlessly.

"Who was that?" Maggie asked. He stepped towards and the shadows on his face shifted. His smile softened. He shrugged. "No one?" she asked. William nodded.

Twenty-Five

Maggie ran her hand through the water and looked up. As the sun set, the sky gave way to soft purples and pinks. Bright orange clouds moved slowly across her view. Frogs began to sing. It was a beautiful night to be in a boat on the river.

"Margaret," William said, breaking her reverie.

"Yes?" She brought her attention back to him. He held something in his hand. His free hand came to rest on the back of her neck. The row boat swayed. He began to kiss her. First, her mouth, then her neck. Her breath quickened.

"If we married—" he said as he moved his hand to her waist and kissed below her collarbones.

She sighed. To marry just for this would be foolish. But there was no alternative. Not for her.

"If we were engaged—" she countered, sighing as he moved his hand up from her waist, along her ribs, stopping just before it got dangerous.

Abruptly, he sat back. The boat shifted wildly. Maggie gripped the sides. William's face was pale, his lips thin. She had made him angry. She did that without meaning to.

"What are you suggesting?" he asked.

Maggie closed her eyes. Talking to him, being with him, was like being in a field full of hidden traps. She never knew where was safe. He seemed to lead her one way and then change direction.

"If we were engaged, if we were promised to each other, it wouldn't be bad, would it?" she asked.

He didn't speak. William rowed the boat back towards Apple View. He tied it beside the foot bridge. He helped Maggie out of the boat and then walked towards the stone house. She stood at the bridge and watched him disappear into the woods that separated the stone house from the river. She could go back to Apple View.

She followed him.

He sat on a worn stone in the old cemetery. Lilacs grew wild between the plots. Maggie felt sad here. The marble lambs, worn by years and weather broke her heart.

"William?"

His eyes were red rimmed. "It's just, Maggie. My father wants me to travel with him for the next year. And I—I don't want to leave you. This," he held out a ring, "would make it easier. Will you wait for me? Will you marry me?"

She sat beside him. He slid the ring onto her finger. The diamonds couldn't sparkle in the low light. "Yes." And even as she said it, she wanted to take it back.

He kissed her. And their kisses became urgent. They were a confusion of hands and mouths and bodies. Maggie pushed herself away.

"I love you," William said. She couldn't speak, so she kissed him again.

When they came back to Apple View, Henry sat on the back porch. "Mum will have a fit you're out after dark, Maggie. And you'd better fix your hair. William, you're covered in grass. Here." Henry stood and brushed grass and dandelion fluff from William's shirt. He helped Maggie arrange her hair and shake out her skirt.

"Congratulate us, Henry. We're engaged," William said.

Henry bit his lip. "Oh. Well, congratulations. You'd better go square it with the old man. He's in his study." Henry shoved William towards the door.

Henry held out his arms to Maggie. She threw her arms around him as he held her close to him.

"Are you sure?" he whispered.

"Don't tell George. I want to," she said, not answering him.

"Yes, well." Henry stepped back. He shifted a chair. Then he picked up and set down the book he'd been reading.

"Are you quarreling again?" she asked.

"Go tell Mum your good news. I want to see her face when you show her that sparkler," he said.

Twenty-Six

"I think we should wait," Maggie said. "We should wait until you get back. They say it'll be over by Christmas." She stiffened, waiting for William's answer. It felt like waiting for a blow, like when she was younger and roughhousing with George.

"I don't want to wait," William said. "I want to be sure you'll be here for me when I come home."

She forced a smile and hoped it reached her eyes. "I'll wait for you. We're engaged, aren't we?" And she could see herself taking that ring and throwing it into the river. Its weight on her finger was a constant reminder of her cowardice.

"Don't you want to be my wife?" he asked and her face must have betrayed her even though she tried to keep it still, to keep her smile, wide, sunny. A cloud passed over William's eyes. They turned cold. He grabbed Maggie's shoulders.

"Maggie. Margaret. You wouldn't go back on your promise, would you?"

Maggie shook her head. She tried to shrug off his hand. His thumb dug into the space below the bone. Pain radiated out from it.

"Because if you did, I know something that would ruin your brother if people found out. You wouldn't want to hurt your brother would you?" He pressed harder into her shoulder. Tears filled her eyes and she blinked hard. She didn't want him to see her cry.

"You're hurting me," she said. She tried to pull his hand away from his shoulder, but he gripped her wrists with his other hand.

"You're hurting me," he said. "I love you. I've always loved you."

She closed her eyes against his gaze. Henry. She'd only seen her brother for a few days at Christmas. He'd been gone for a year and no one would say why he'd gone. Something had happened. William knew. She couldn't hurt Henry more. At Christmas, he'd sat as far from everyone as he could, not speaking.

"I'll marry you. As soon as you want," Maggie heard herself say. William released her hands and pulled her to him. His kisses were hard, desperate.

"I'm so glad. Oh, Margaret. You've made me so happy."

Twenty-Seven

After her father died, Maggie kept busy helping her mother with all the tasks generated by death. She often spoke for her mother at these appointments. Mrs. Tate had frozen in her grief.

At the end of long, sad days, Maggie would retreat to her father's office and light one of his pipes, pulling on it just enough to keep it going, so she could wrap herself in the familiar smell. And then she'd organize his papers, determining what to give to the lawyer who was taking on his clients. It should have been George's job to do this, but he was in France. And wasn't this what women were doing? Taking up the work men left behind?

Of course, she searched for the key to Henry's secret. In her father's desk, she found receipts for suits long since given away, notes he'd made to himself about a broad range of subjects and articles clipped from newspapers and magazines for no reason she could discern. Her father's diary yielded no clues either. He hadn't recorded the daily details of his life. Instead, he wrote about his orchards, recorded poems and unconnected phrases.

Reading through his things, Maggie realized she didn't really know her father. How could any child truly know their parents? She knew his preferences, like what sort of tobacco he had liked and that he preferred rhubarb to strawberry pie, but she didn't know what had kept him awake at night or why he had fallen in love with her mother. She felt she understood why he had never really left Apple View because she felt the same. But perhaps his reasons had been different.

Mr. Tate had wanted to be buried in the orchard, but her mother had balked at that and so he had been placed in the cemetery at the edge of town in a corner close to the woodlot that separated the dead from the living. Maggie and John had visited a few days later to plant a cutting from one of Mr. Tate's apple trees.

"I sent a telegram to Henry," John said as he wiped sweat from his face.

Maggie worried about him digging in the heat, but he had insisted. "When I got word, I called my father and found out no one had remembered. They were so worried about getting you home."

Maggie grasped his hand, not caring if it was slick with sweat. She could feel blisters forming on his palm. His hands were soft, unused to manual labour. She remembered her father's hands had been calloused by the hours he spent digging in his gardens, trimming his trees, playing at being a farmer.

"Thanks. I hate that he'll come home and Dad won't be here. It's worse somehow. And thank you for coming to get me." She didn't remember much of the train ride back from Montreal. John had handed her tea and food and she had taken what he offered, mechanically. He had talked about his classes if she showed even the slightest interest and kept silent if she turned away. And he had always held her hand. She remembered his eyes, red rimmed and steadily leaking. How she had numbly realized she hadn't cried.

"Will you go back?" John asked.

Maggie shook her head. "No. Mum asked me to stay. She'd be lonely without me. I had my time away. That's all I wanted."

"Won't you miss your friends?"

She bumped his shoulder with her own and tried to smile. "Aren't you my friend?"

"I'm going back tomorrow. I've already missed too much," he said.

"Well, I only had one friend really. And she's trying to get overseas. I'm needed here."

"Maggie—" John swallowed and squeezed Maggie's hand. He cleared his throat and blinked hard a few times, his face contorting. "I hope—when Henry left I promised—" He dropped the shovel and pulled her into a tight embrace. She let herself be crushed into his shoulder. She breathed in the scent of his sweat mixed with dirt from the grave. A few sobs shook out of him. Her eyes stayed dry. Her heart ached as it had since she got the news.

"I know," she said, her voice muffled. "I know."

Twenty-Eight

The cenotaph, intended to memorialize all the lost men and boys, stood mostly as testament to Mrs. Lancaster's grief at losing her only child. True, more names than William's were carved into the base, but the soldier being hoisted to heaven by a strong-armed angel wore William's face. Maggie hated it. No one in town dared to speak publicly against it though, since Lancaster money greased many wheels.

Maggie only looked at it when she had to, mostly at Armistice Day when she laid a wreath for her dead. It had been standing for a few years and had become part of the background scenery in town, standing in a small park beside the town hall.

She almost didn't recognize George, sitting on the bench, his arm stretched along the back of it, contemplating the statue. In her mind, he still looked as he had before enlisting, less wide across the shoulders, darker hair, nicer clothes. Her eyes slid over the hatless man who wore working clothes and whose thick, dark hair was broken up by streaks of silver. Then she recognized him.

When she sat beside him, he tipped a paper bag of candy towards without saying a word or even meeting her eye. She took out a jelly baby, paused to consider its misshapen face and popped it in her mouth. "Still have a sweet tooth, I see," she said.

George smiled and waved the bag at the cenotaph. "So, do you think they'll give it a new face?"

Maggie laughed. "If you'd been at the committee meetings about it, you wouldn't dare suggest such a thing." She could laugh at it now, but at the time, the heated discussions between heartbroken women had left her drained and angry. "Why did they need a public memorial?" she had shouted at John more than once when he asked about the meetings. As if any of them could forget what the war had cost them.

"Maybe they'll just chip his name off," George said. Maggie watched him as he shook the bag of sweets, searching for his favorite color. He smiled, but it didn't reach his eyes. He kept looking up at the angel, his eyes narrowing slightly.

"Mrs. Lancaster hired a European sculptor. She had ideas. And money," Maggie said.

"Yeah. I can see that. Our local hero, ascended straight to heaven, lifted up out of the muck to God himself." George tossed the candy bag into Maggie's lap. "Here. Take the rest. I ate all the red ones."

George lit a cigarette. Maggie ate candy until her mouth felt raw. Neither spoke. As children, they had spent entire afternoons like this. Whenever she heard cicadas, Maggie remembered summer days spent sitting quietly beside George, letting her mind wander.

"Henry's name is on there," he said. "Sometimes—" he sighed, took a drag of his cigarette and blew out smoke rings. Maggie didn't offer something to fill his pause. She watched the rings fade into nothing. Her father would blow smoke rings with his cigars. Had he taught George?

"My name. It would be better if my name were on there too," George said eventually.

She took his hand, but said nothing.

"How did you go on after?" he asked.

She shrugged. "I couldn't stop. The flu came and John needed me. And then Lucy needed me. After that, going on got to be a habit."

"Lest we forget," George read off the cenotaph's base. "Christ. What I wouldn't do to forget for one minute, one second." He crushed the stub of his cigarette under his foot and lit another. Maggie closed her eyes and the smell of the tobacco smoke mingled with the green scent of a humid day. A memory danced on the tip of her mind, conjured up by the smell. She remembered leaning out her bedroom window on summer nights and that smell in the air. George, smoking out of her brother's window on one of the many nights he slept over.

"One of my men killed himself. I reported it as friendly fire, so his family wouldn't know. After, when I got back, I thought about doing it too. But I'd already been dead. It's terrible. There's no angel to yank you up to the sky." George leaned his head back so that his smoke rings floated lazily above them.

Maggie didn't know what to say. She took another candy and looked at the calm face of the angel.

She didn't tell George she knew what he meant. After the telegram about Henry, her mother had turned her face to the wall. Maggie had read that phrase in a book once and had not understood it. It had sounded poetic, not real. But that was exactly what Mrs. Tate had done. When the flu had taken Mrs. Tate, Maggie had thought, "Now I will turn my face to the wall too." But she hadn't because they had been too busy with the sick.

One day, months after her mother's death, Maggie had sat on the dock, watching the current of the river carry leaves to wherever. She had realized that whoever she had been before the war was gone and not coming back. Death was a risk. Who knew what was on the other side? She would stay and be useful.

"I've seen worse memorials, though," George said, pointing at the cenotaph with his cigarette, breaking into Maggie's memories. "At least all that Lancaster money bought some art. Gives William gravitas. He doesn't look so much like a shirt collar ad. Even if it's bit blasphemous to suggest William Lancaster ascended like Jesus himself."

Maggie pinched George's arm, twisting the skin a bit. He grinned and put his arm around her shoulder. "I missed you, Maggie."

"I missed you too."

Twenty-Nine

George walked into the kitchen and into a nightmare. William sat at the table, a smile on his pale face, absorbed in cleaning Henry's hunting rifle. He worked quickly, deftly, the memory of their training still in his fingers. Maggie sat near him, drinking a cup of tea. She watched him work and George saw the rapt attention she sometimes had given William when they were young and falling in love. George wanted to shake her free. He wanted to say, "He's changed, but that doesn't mean he's better." And yet, George could see the beauty in William's dexterity. And he could remember how William had always been good at anything he had turned his hand to.

George saw the gun in William's hand and couldn't move. He rubbed his chest and remembered the feel of the shot. How it felt like a punch between his shoulders. How the pain had exploded and he had dropped to his knees, sure he was going to die. And William had stood over him with that smile.

"George! Good morning!" Maggie smiled at him. She couldn't see him, George realized. She couldn't see his fear. "William's going hunting if you want to join him."

George shook his head. He fought to control himself, to appear normal. William watched, assessing. George swallowed the metallic flood of saliva that filled his mouth. "No thanks. Don't care for guns or killing things," he said.

Maggie got up and placed her empty cup by the sink. "Well, I'm running into town today. Come with me, instead." As she passed through the entrance, she lightly squeezed George's arm. Maybe she did see.

William lifted the rifle and pointed it at George. "Bang," he mouthed and laughed silently. George backed out of the room and collapsed against the wall in the hallway. He put his head between his knees. All around him was the rotten smell of mud and corpses. He was deafened by the gunfire,

124

the shells, the men screaming around him. He was in the middle with William pointing a gun at him. He was always in it.

Thirty

They hid in a deep shell hole, still new enough to not be filled with water. It was so deep, they could stand up and stay concealed. Everything had gone wrong. The shelling was heavier than expected, most of the men were dead. They probably had the wrong directions. Communication had broken down almost completely.

George glanced at William. He would die beside William. He was tempted to climb out and take his chances. Anything to escape. If he was going to die anyway, he didn't want to do it here.

The near constant shelling had done something to William. He didn't smile or wink. He huddled in the muddy bottom of the hole and hugged his knees to his chest. It took George a moment to recognize he pitied William. They had never been friends. But there, in the mud, close to death, William was the only other person who knew what the roses at Apple View smelled like or what it was like to skate down the river on a cold, clear morning.

He sat beside William and put an arm around him. "Once it lets up, we'll get out, find out the hell's going on."

"We're not making it out. We're dying here," William said in a monotone.

William was probably right. They weren't safe, but if they left the hole, they'd be exposed. They could only wait.

"George, remember when I shot that German?" William asked during a brief pause in shelling. George nodded. "I—" William covered his face with his hands. When he pulled them away, he left two dark prints on his face. His eyes stood out, bright blue against the dirt. "What's wrong with me?"

"I don't know what you mean," George said. Fear made him cautious, as if William were a poisonous snake. William never doubted himself, he never showed fear.

"I enjoyed it. Shooting him, like that. Or, I did. And then I didn't feel anything. Nothing. I feel nothing. And then I do something. Something that hurts someone. And then I feel, for a little, then back to nothing. I want to be like you. And I try, but then I—"

George patted William's shoulder. He had no words. He thought of Maggie. He had to make it through this.

"Why are you telling me this?" George asked.

"Because we're going to die. I had to tell someone. You're here. We're friends, right?"

"Sure." George closed his eyes. He was going to die in a mud hole with a crazy man. He tried to picture Apple View in spring, when the blossoms fell from the trees like snow. He pictured lying in the grass, letting blossoms cover him until Henry brushed them off his face and pulled him to his feet laughing. But the stench and the noise kept pushing his imaginings away.

"I wrote that letter. About you. And Henry," William said.

George pulled away from William. "That was you."

"It was wrong."

"Yes. It was," George said.

"No. I mean, what you did was wrong. I couldn't have that in my wife's family. If anyone found out—no. As a friend, I had to take steps."

If I kill him, George thought, no one would know. He had a knife. He could cut William's throat and watch him bleed. But the German boy. The fear in the boy's eyes. William's wink.

"Where are you going?" William asked.

"I'm taking my chances out there," George said.

"Wait!" William called. George turned back. A punch, just off his shoulder blade. His chest felt hot. His hand came away wet, warm. What was that on his hand?

"I've been shot," he said, slow and stupid. William put his gun down and nodded. George fell to his knees.

"I have to save you from yourself. Margaret loves her brother. It has to be you."

George sat back. He pressed his hand to his chest. Stupefied, he watched William climb out of the shell hole. A bang. A flash. William, missing half his head, tumbled down the side. George shook. His breath came harsh and loud. His vision went black while he stared at William's body. "You shot me," he murmured.

Thirty-One

When they were young, William had discovered that a local farmer made and sold strong poteen. William's dangerous ideas for fun were part of why they kept him around. John and Henry were too mild to get into much trouble on their own. George found trouble, but he never brought friends along.

Shaking his empty flask over his morning coffee, George thought of that farm for the first time in years. He wondered if it was still there. Probably. Nothing changed around here. He had been gone ten years and everything was almost exactly the same. Sure, there were more cars and fewer horses. And fine, there were new houses and businesses and unfamiliar faces, but for the most part, everything was just as he had left it.

He borrowed Maggie's bicycle and set off down the road. He got turned around a couple of times, but eventually he found the farm. It had not been prosperous looking when they were younger, but it was even more ramshackle now. The paint on the wood trim had peeled away to expose the silvered wood beneath. The curtains in the windows were askew and very dirty. The grass in the yard was nearly tall enough to be hay. Maybe the farm had been abandoned. But a few chickens scratched on the overgrown drive and a tired dog let out a few huffs to let George know he was being watched.

George knocked on the door.

An old man peered out from behind a dingy curtain and a film of dirt on the sidelight. He frowned, but he opened the door. "I remember you," the old man said. "You're the lawyer's son."

"I was his clerk. You still selling?"

"Not scared of daddy getting angry now, are you? Come in." George followed the old man down a dirty hallway. Everything spoke of neglect. The old man led him into a kitchen. Dirty dishes were stacked high in the sink and the stove was littered with pots and pans. A loaf of bread with chunks torn out of it sat on the table.

"How much do you want?" the old man asked.

"As much as you can give me," George answered. "What I can fit in the bike basket and in here." George held up his rucksack.

The old man nodded. "Price has gone up." The old man took the bag and shuffled to a back room just off the kitchen. George heard the squeal of rusty hinges as the old man opened the basement trap door.

George remembered that there had been sons here ten years ago. He wondered what had happened to them.

The old man came back with the full rucksack and a box of bottles. He set it down on the table with a sigh.

"Tell me," the old man said, peering up at George from under caterpillar eyebrows. "What's going on at Apple View?"

"Nothing you haven't heard. William Lancaster's back from the dead."

"I heard that. Friend of mine was in the woods there, gathering mushrooms. Saw something."

"Your friend was trespassing," George said.

The farmer shook his head. "No. Lawyer gave him permission years ago. And the daughter don't care who's on her land. She don't take care of the place. It's a disgrace to her parents," the old man said. George raised his eyebrows and looked about him. "It's different," the old man spat out. "She's young and rich. I'm an old man. My sons all died in the war. But listen, something strange is going on out there."

"Is there?" George asked. He picked up the rucksack and threw it over his shoulder as a signal that the conversation was over.

"My friend saw that Lancaster boy in the woods. He had a deer carcass and was eating the guts out of it. My friend said that boy was all covered in blood. He just smiled at my friend. My friend got out of there in a hurry, I can tell you."

George fought back a shudder. He thought of William in his bed, smiling at him. "Your friend has a good imagination," he said.

"They say that boy went mad. That's where he's been. The madhouse. You watch him. Folk have put up with a lot up there because they liked the Tates. But a madman's dangerous."

George sighed. Christ, he hated living here. Everyone knew everything and what they didn't know they invented. In a city, he was no one. "Why don't you tell people to mind their own fucking business?"

The old man laughed. "Big words from the likes of you. I used to hunt for rabbits up there. I've seen things too. I know what you used to get up to in that stone house. But I never told. Woulda broke Mrs. Tate's heart to know what I saw."

George threw down some bills, more than he needed to. "I don't know what you're talking about."

He wanted to leave without the poteen, but he couldn't. He needed it. But he wouldn't come back. Someone else had to sell it. George picked up the box, the bottles clinking together. He left to the sound of the old man's creaky laugh. "I know what I saw!" the old man called after him.

George pedaled quickly down the drive. Once he was out of sight of the rundown farm, he stopped and opened one of the bottles. He watched his hands shake as if they belonged to someone else. A thought floated by his mind so quickly, he almost didn't catch it. "This is going to kill you if you don't stop." How did he feel about that? About time something killed him.

He hadn't drunk poteen since his teens. He had forgotten how it burned going down. His lips went numb as the heat spread into his belly. His hands stopped shaking as his body relaxed. George smiled and pushed the cork back in the now half-empty bottle. "Back with your friends," he said to it. A cow in the field opposite lowed at him and he laughed.

As the poteen spread through his blood, George struggled to keep the bicycle straight, catching every rut on the road. The half-empty bottle called to him. So he sipped from it as he rode.

The front wheel balked at a large stone. The grassy edge of the road rose up to meet him. Every part of his body hurt. He pushed the bicycle off and looked up at the sky, closing his eyes against the bright sun. When he opened his eyes next, the sun was further down in the sky. He turned his head.

"Henry?" he asked the shadowy figure sitting beside him. George closed his eyes and opened them. The light had changed.

Henry sat a few feet away from him. In the low light, Henry's eyes seemed even lighter then George remembered. He looks sad, George thought. Oh, but if William could come back, couldn't Henry?

George reached out to him, but Henry was too far away. "Are you really here?" he asked.

Henry shook his head.

"Am I dreaming?"

Henry shrugged and tipped his head towards his shoulder. Maybe. "I'm drunk."

Henry nodded.

"Am I dead?" George asked.

"Not yet," whispered Henry. "But—"

"But I will be if I don't stop," George finished.

Henry came closer and squatted down beside George. George averted his eyes from Henry's disappointed look. "Wake up," Henry whispered and clapped his hands.

George opened his eyes. He was alone. His head hurt and his eyes stung. He wiped his wet forehead. Blood covered his right hand. A piece of glass stuck out of the palm of his left. Wincing, he yanked it out. This poor body, he thought, I can't seem to stop scarring it.

The bicycle and a few bottles had survived the crash. He stood up stiffly. Tomorrow would be painful. He uncorked a bottle and poured it over his wounds to clean them, hissing at the sting of the alcohol. He lifted the bottle to his lips, but, remembering Henry's disappointment, he threw it down. He clumsily wrapped his head and hand in strips torn from his shirt.

George got back on the bicycle and started to pedal home.

*****

"You were drunk," John said before George could even try to lie about what had happened. "If I lit a match, you'd go up like torch. Did you pour it on yourself?"

"A few bottles broke when I went down."

John shook his head. He threaded catgut through a needle and began stitching George's forehead. "I would have given you a ride if you had asked."

George kept still despite the pain of the needle going through his skin. John worked quickly. "I didn't ask because I didn't want you to know," George said.

"I know you're a drunk. But I'm not going to give you a sermon on temperance. You wouldn't listen. You never did. Now, let's see that hand."

The cut followed George's life line almost exactly. Part way through, John looked up and said, "I wouldn't advise you watch this."

"After I fell, I think I was unconscious for a bit," George said. "I thought I saw Henry."

John set down his tools and checked his work. "Try not to sleep for a while. You hit your head pretty hard. I'll let Lucy know to check on you

131

tonight." He sat up straight and rolled his shoulders. "I miss Henry too," John said so quietly, George wasn't sure if he actually heard it or imagined it.

"Aren't you staying here tonight?" George asked.

John shook his head. "No. My parents are having a dinner party tonight; I promised to go." He sighed and pressed his pale lips together.

"Are you feeling well?" George asked. How had he not noticed John's pallor, the shadows around his eyes? Some friend George was.

"I'm fine. Just tired. Ease up on the booze, OK?"

"Are you saying that as a friend or as my doctor?"

"We just got you back. I'd like to keep you around."

George covered his face with his hands. "I'm going to dry out. I promise."

"We'll talk about it tomorrow."

✱✱✱✱✱

He wanted a drink, but then George looked at his stitched hand and remembered his vow. He knew the want would grow on him. At eighteen, he could have crashed that bicycle and felt nothing the next day. Now, when he sat up, every part of his body cried out. Maybe he would lie down for a bit longer.

Someone knocked on the door. "Who is it?" he called. If it were William, no. George couldn't face William, not like this.

"It's me, Lucy. Can I come in?"

"Sure."

She had a tray with a glass of water and buttered toast on it. "How are you feeling?"

"Hell of a headache."

She sat down beside him and pushed his hair back from his warm, sweaty forehead with cool, dry fingers. Her eyes narrowed. She shook her head. "John should have called me. My stitches are nicer."

"It'll add to my mystery," he said with a smile, but she didn't flirt back.

She moved the tray onto his lap, "Try to eat."

His stomach clenched at the smell of the toast. Was he hungry? He took a bite and his tongue recoiled. Swiftly, Lucy moved the tray back to the nightstand and pulled a wastebasket close. "Here," she said and guided him to lean towards it. He spat out the toast. His stomach heaved into his throat and saliva flooded his mouth. He vomited what little was in his stomach. He leaned back.

"Drink some water," Lucy said, putting the glass into his hand. "Slowly, though."

The next few hours passed in a haze of nausea and pain. At one point, he whispered, "I felt so good when I woke up."

Lucy asked. "When did you start drinking? After the war?"

He sighed and clenched his jaw against a rising wave of nausea. When he could speak, George told her no, the war had only helped it along. She lit a cigarette and let him have a drag.

*****

After the shaking, the vomiting and the sweating came hallucinations.

*****

When Lucy left to get him more water, George turned his head to look out the window. When he turned back, Henry was sitting in Lucy's chair. He wore his dress uniform. His light eyes looked empty, almost blank. A poppy tucked behind his ear stood out brightly in the dimly lit room.

"I'm doing it," George whispered. "Just like I said."

"Maybe," Henry said.

"Are you really here?" George asked.

Henry shrugged. "Probably not."

George looked around. He was in Henry's bed. He was in the mud, blood spreading beneath him, mixing with the mud. "Am I dead?"

Henry shrugged. "Isn't everyone?"

Lucy came back in with John. George closed his eyes. When he opened them, Henry was gone. Lucy and John stood above him, speaking in whispers.

"John, how'd you get here? I thought they wouldn't take you, your heart—" He left the sentence hanging. What a nice hospital, though. So much nicer than the other ones.

*****

Then the seizures came.

*****

In between seizures, George had a little time to think, but his mind was so confused. At first, he was afraid he was dying. But he couldn't die because he already had. Did he clutch on to Maggie's arm and tell her that? That he had died in 1918? He thought perhaps he had. Sometimes he saw Henry in the corners, watching him.

"This will help." And John held him up to tip something into his mouth.

George slipped into a dream world, one he'd visited after the second time he'd been shot. It was different, though, emptier. There were no women, no tests, just a bleak landscape and a road leading to a manor in the distance. Inside, the opulent manor looked as if it had been looted. Only tattered furniture and a few slashed paintings remained. He could hear music and followed it down the hall. The grand dining table was piled high with fruit, meat and bread. The smell overwhelmed him. It was the smell of the battlefields, of mud and the sickly sweet smell of decomposing flesh. Flies buzzed around the room.

A laugh from the far end of the table. William. William, strong and healthy and glowing, a smile stretched across his face. His long, white teeth gleamed in the candle light. "George!" He raised a cup. "A toast! To absent friends and long journeys."

George picked up a heavy, metal goblet full of—wine? He wanted to hurl it at William. No, he wanted to beat William with it. He tipped it and dark red liquid stained the table cloth.

"It's not your time yet. I told you, I want you to suffer," William said in a cheerful, conversational tone. "Take a drink. You know you want to."

George wanted to take a bottle and pour it down his throat and make this all go away or at least become bearable. George shook his head.

"I'll have you all. Soon." William licked his red lips. "It's better here."

George put his hands under the table and rocked it a little. In a dream, he could do what he wanted. He flung the heavy table over, sending everything on it crashing to the ground. William snarled like an angry dog. George clapped his hands and yelled, "Wake up!"

He woke to Maggie holding his hand. William lurked in the corner, hidden in shadows.

"Shhh. It was just a dream," Maggie murmured. She wiped his forehead with a cool cloth. He nodded and fell into a dreamless sleep.

Thirty-Two

"Did you see this?" George asked Maggie, handing her the newspaper. "The old bootlegger died. Here." He tapped the obituary. Maggie read the notice and handed the paper back to George.

"I recognize the name, but I don't think I can place him," she said.

William took the paper from George.

"You know who that is?" George asked. "Do you remember him?" William nodded.

"Anyone care to tell me?" Maggie said.

George explained he had bought poteen from the dead man. "He looked healthy enough to me," George said. "I wonder if John knows what happened to the old man." William began to rip the newspaper into long, even strips. The sound was irritating, but George said nothing.

"Maybe. But he won't gossip about patients," Maggie said. She rubbed her hands together. "It's cold in here. I'm going to put the kettle on. I need something to warm my blood. Want any?" She went to the kitchen.

The day was warm. George's shirt stuck to his back. William continued to make a pile of paper strips. The pieces covered his lap and slid to the floor.

"What did you do?" George asked in a low voice. "I know you did something." He leaned down to speak into William's ear. "I know you can speak. I can't wait to hear what you have to say."

Thirty-Three

By the time John came to Apple View to ask for Maggie's help, people were tying cloths over their faces any time they went out. Maggie's mother floated around the house, barely speaking, hardly eating. If Mrs. Tate had closed in at the death of her husband, Henry's disappearance had locked her up.

Maggie felt as if she were a body, going about the business of life while her mind had stopped altogether. She had put away her father's things. Then, a few months later, she had gone to her mother-in-law's and helped to pack up William's life. Then she had packed up her brother's life as much as her mother would allow, but mostly she kept his room as it was and only went in to dust.

The days stretched out long and slow. Maggie ran errands, held brief, meaningless conversations with people she knew and came home to silence. For a time, she tried to be useful and continued knitting socks. But after a few months, Maggie gave up and started to read in the evenings. She found boxes of childhood books in the attic and dragged these down to her room. The simple stories with their minor catastrophes comforted her.

John didn't call ahead the day he came for help. He burst through the kitchen door, startling Maggie. She had been blankly staring out the window while a cup of tea grew cold in her hand. In a rush, he explained that his father's usual nurses were ill, one of them likely to die. They couldn't find anyone else to help. His mother had been pressed into service and he thought, maybe, Maggie could help.

John told her she had enough experience and he had no one else to help him. His eyes were sunk into dark shadows, his lips pale. He had been her brother's closest friend. He was as lonely as she was. She couldn't leave him to fight this alone.

They worked for weeks. People they'd known their whole lives died in front of them. Dr. Mobley, who never got sick, came down with the flu about a week in. Maggie's mother died soon after. Over breakfast, Mrs. Tate complained of a headache. She was gone by midnight. Maggie had been with another patient.

John held Maggie up when she staggered down the church aisle at her mother's funeral service. Mrs. Mobley insisted Maggie stay with them for the week after her mother's death. Maggie dreaded going to her empty house, so she slept in the Mobleys' spare room.

Even John's normal cheer faltered. He worked longer hours and Maggie worked with him. The flu didn't touch them. Maggie felt as if she were losing her mind. She dreamed while awake, talking to her brother and parents as if they were there. John fainted as they walked to his car one day. His lips were blue. He struggled to breathe.

Maggie pounded on his chest, trying to jolt his heart awake. She felt outside of her body, as if she were standing at the side of the road watching a woman raise her fists and strike a pale man again and again. "Don't leave me," she said. His eyes fluttered. Colour began to fill his cheeks and lips as his breath settled. He begged her not to tell his father.

One night, a patient died and John, exhausted, started to cry and couldn't stop. Maggie and someone from the family half-carried him to the car and stuffed him in. Maggie drove out of town, out into the country and pulled over in the drive of a small, wood frame church. John muttered about the plague and the end of the world. They sat in his car and looked up at the sky, the stars so clear against the deep purple-blue of night.

It ended, though. People stopped dying. The sick recovered. Dr. Mobley tended to his patients again.

Dr. Mobley called Maggie and John to his office. He offered Maggie work. She said yes because it ate up the hours that she'd otherwise spend in an empty house. The first day she had been in Apple View after her mother's death, she had felt so small. John had come with her.

Standing in the doorway to Henry's room, Maggie began to cry. At first, she cried quietly, not wanting John to hear. He came to her and held her. She hadn't touched anyone who wasn't a patient in so long. He didn't tell her everything would be fine. He rocked her back and forth and rubbed her back. He cried too.

When the storm subsided, she wiped her face with the handkerchief John gave her.

"I'm sorry," she said.

"Don't be," John said. He wiped his eyes with his sleeve cuff. "We have to feel our hurts. Sorrow comes with joy. It makes us feel the joy more."

"There's no joy," Maggie said. She closed the door on her brother's room.

Thirty-Four

My boy!" a man shouted. He strode into the house uninvited, pushing past Maggie and Lucy in the hall. His clothes were elegant, expensive. Despite his immaculate grooming, he looked sickly. His skin was sallow and bloated. Too many sleepless nights spent eating, drinking and smoking too much were written on his face.

Lucy whispered "Who is that?"

"William's father," Maggie answered.

Mr. Lancaster had not been seen in town for years. His business had prospered during the war, but with a dead son, no one dared to call him a profiteer. And the townspeople pitied Mrs. Lancaster too much to say anything. She would tell everyone he was away on business and was expected back any day. Some had reported seeing him in Europe or in South America, always with a beautiful woman on his arm.

William curled his lip when his father embraced him and brought his arms up stiffly, barely returning the embrace. Mr. Lancaster wiped away tears. "I thought you were lost forever," he said.

He turned to Maggie. "Margaret. You're as lovely as ever. Age has hardly touched you." He bent over her hand and kissed it. She fought to keep her revulsion inside. She had never liked Mr. Lancaster. He was too slick. His stare made her feel as if he were picturing her undressed. His affectionate gestures always lingered too long, were always a little too affectionate. She wanted to wipe her hand on her skirt.

"And who is this vision?" he asked, taking up Lucy's hand. Over Mr. Lancaster's bent head, Lucy grimaced at Maggie. Maggie glanced at William. Had he seen? No, he hadn't. By the time Mr. Lancaster straightened, Lucy wore a wide, thoroughly fake smile.

"This is my friend, Lucy Stoppard. Lucy, this is Mr. Lancaster, William's father. Lucy and I worked together in Montreal. She works for Dr. Mobley now," Maggie said.

"Stoppard? Is your father Fred Stoppard?" Mr. Lancaster asked, still holding Lucy's hand.

"Yes. Do you know him?" Lucy deftly extracted her hand.

"We've done business before. You're a long way from home. Admirable that you continue to serve. I'm surprised your parents let you. You're a beauty. Oh, William, she knows it. I can say it. I bet there's a line of heart-broken men wanting to marry you."

Lucy's false grin widened. "You are so kind to say so. As it happens, I'm engaged to Dr. John Mobley."

Mr. Lancaster barely contained his disapproval. "Ah. Well, may he be happy for as long as he's got. Truthfully, I'm surprised he lasted this long. Last time I saw him, he looked like a walking corpse. Hush, William. She's a nurse. She can see the reality. Look at her. A smart woman like that."

William pulled his father towards the sitting room. When he left, Lucy and Maggie dashed to the front yard. They laughed until tears came to their eyes. "I'm pretty sure he just added you to the possible mistress list," Maggie said, wiping her eyes.

"He's horrible! Poor William. Can you imagine?"

"No. I can't," Maggie said. She couldn't laugh anymore. William had never really spoken of his father. But, when they were young, she could see his discomfort around the man. William would sometimes have bruises he couldn't explain. Maggie remembered teas and dinners where it seemed as if everyone was constantly adjusting to the temperature of the room, to Mr. Lancaster's moods. His bluff good humour could switch to rage with no warning.

Indistinct shouting came from the house. Lucy started to go back, but Maggie pulled her back. "Don't. It's better if we stay here."

The door flew open, banging against the brick wall. Mr. Lancaster stomped across the porch and down the steps. As he walked past the women, he said, "I'll stop in again, Margaret. Talk some sense into him before then." He got into his car and instructed his driver to leave.

William sat at the table with the Ouija board. A crumpled piece of paper on the table before him. Maggie smoothed it out and read it. "He wanted you to go with him? And you said no?" she asked. William nodded. Maggie sighed.

"I'm sorry," she said. She put her hand on his shoulder and he leaned his head against her arm. Then he tapped the board. He wanted to talk. Maggie sat beside him. She picked up a pencil and flipped the crumpled paper over. As he pointed at letters, she wrote.

Never going with him
He said I am dead to him if I do not.

Thirty-Five

In the evening, just as the sun was setting, lighting up the clouds as it sank, William stood on the street, looking up at the hotel his father was staying in. People moved around him as if he were a rock in the river and they were water flowing around him. No one paid attention to him.

He wanted to go in. He never wanted to see his father again. He wanted many things all at the same time and he didn't know what would happen if he went inside.

The revolver was still at his back, tucked into the waist of his trousers, concealed by his jacket, but he checked again, to be sure. It had been with him when he'd arrived at Apple View. Until today, though, he hadn't thought of it, preferring the hunting rifles he was used to from his youth. But he found the revolver in a drawer when he was looking for socks. No one had unloaded it before they put it away. Without thinking, he'd slipped it under his jacket.

When he knocked on the door, his father called out, asking who was there. William knocked again. He heard people talking. His father's voice was an indistinct rumble. There was another, higher voice. A woman's voice. William's fingers curled into fists, his fingernails cutting into his palms. He took a deep breath and knocked again.

His father opened the door. William looked over his father's shoulder into the room. There was no woman, but he did see a brightly colored silk robe draped over a chair and he could smell a too sweet, musky perfume that reminded him of the war.

"William! My boy!" His father crushed him into a tight embrace. William closed his eyes and put his arms around his father. But as soon as he began to relax into his father's arms, his father let him go.

"Come in, come in. Want a drink? Sure you do. Just sit there," his father said, indicating a chair. Mr. Lancaster bustled about the room. William realized he made the man nervous. They were like people who didn't know each other.

He took the glass from his father's hand and sipped at the brown liquid. He couldn't stop his grimace at the taste of it. It was horrible stuff. Had William liked it before? There were still things he didn't know about himself.

"So, my boy. What is it you want? I'll give you anything you want." His father smiled and for a moment, Mr. Lancaster looked as handsome as he had years ago. He reached across and put a firm hand on William's knee.

What did William want?

William thought of a long ago day when he'd walked home from school with Henry after a football game and Mr. Tate had been in the yard, cutting roses. Before Mr. Tate could ask, Henry had shouted out, "Dad! We won!" Mr. Tate had grinned and given each of the boys a quick, firm hug. His light eyes had been shining and for a moment, William had watched the Tates, father and son, look at each other with such open, shining faces. That's love, he'd thought. And he'd known his father had never looked at him like that.

Or another time, when William had passed by Mr. Tate's study and peeked in. George had been puzzling over some schoolwork, his hands clutching his head, pushing his hair up into spikes. And Mr. Tate, pipe clenched firmly in his teeth, had rested a gentle hand on the boy's shoulder. Mr. Tate had said around the pipe, "You'll get it. You're a smart boy." And George's whole body had sagged in relief and he had nodded and smiled. William had seen a man who could love a boy that wasn't his own and he had known no one would ever love him like that.

But he'd wanted that love, for someone to look at him and see him, to tell him he could be better. William had wanted that ease with someone else.

What did he want?

William took another sip of his drink and remembered the night he'd gone to see Henry at school. William had been lonely and he had missed his friends. It had been a late winter night when he'd got off the train and headed towards Henry's house. As William had walked down the street, he'd glanced in the lit-up windows of the houses and apartments. It had seemed everyone in the world had people who smiled at them, who were happy to see them. *No one is happy to see me*, William had thought bitterly, shoving his hands deep into his coat pockets.

But he had thought Henry would at least pretend. And that would have been close enough.

When he had got to the little house Henry and George were sharing, William had hesitated. He and George had never got along and George wouldn't pretend to be happy to see him. But maybe, if William was polite or even, God help him, kind, maybe for one night they could be in the same room together.

He had stepped through the little gate and down the path. Someone had shovelled it clear that day. William had stood on the porch and raised his hand to knock on the door. But he couldn't. Instead, he walked around to the back of the house.

While the curtains were drawn at the front and sides of the house, they weren't at the rear of the house. The little house backed onto the railway tracks. The last time William had been there, a train had passed and it had felt as if the train were going to come through the wall. There was no neatly shovelled path here. No one ever came back here.

Scraggly shrubs reached almost to the windows. The bare branches made William think of claws. The window looked into the small kitchen. From the dark of the back yard, William could see into the brightly lit kitchen. It had been very shabby, with battered cabinets and scuffed walls, but neat.

George had been standing at the old-fashioned stove, stirring something in a pot. William couldn't hear, but he'd thought George was singing. He'd never seen George so happy. Henry had come in and put his arms around George and rested his chin on George's shoulder. In the dark yard, William had stood very still and felt his breath catch in his chest. He shouldn't have seen this. He'd wanted to keep watching. He'd pulled his scarf up over his face and crept closer to the window.

Henry had bit George's earlobe and even from outside, William could hear George's yelp. But then George had started to laugh, turning in Henry's arms so he could wave his wooden spoon in Henry's face. Henry had batted the spoon aside. They'd kissed. Kissed like people who were in love. William had backed away from the window and walked quickly to the front and then out onto the street.

He shouldn't have seen that. They shouldn't have been doing that. He'd realized, his new understanding flowing backwards over his memories, that they'd been in love for years.

A spark of jealousy had bloomed into a fire of rage and he'd tried to smother it. What had he been jealous of? Not them. He had never wanted a man like that. The idea was repulsive. But he'd wanted that easy joy, the way they'd looked at each other as if they were the only two people in the world who mattered. Margaret had never looked at him like that. He'd never loved her like that. It'd always been a different kind of love, possessive and angry, but not easy like what he'd seen.

It'd taken a few months, but eventually, he'd decided what he needed to do to smother his jealousy. He'd written a letter to Mrs. Lancaster, describing things he hadn't seen but he was sure had happened in that little house. For a moment, after sealing the envelope, he'd thought about burning the letter and sparing Henry the pain of what would follow. But then he'd thought of the two men smiling at each other. He had dropped the letter in the mail.

William set down his glass. He went to the desk and found a pencil and a scrap of paper. "Anything?" he scribbled on the paper and passed it to his father. His father nodded.

William took back the paper. "Come home. Come back."

Mr. Lancaster sighed as he read William's rough printing. "I can't, William. I'm sorry. But you can come with me. It'll be just like the old days. Me and you. And Margaret too. We can see the world!"

William tapped the paper. Mr. Lancaster frowned. "I can't live with your mother. I should never have married her."

His entire childhood, he'd been one more thing for his parents to pull between them. Even now, they both wanted him, but only to keep him out of other people's hands. Not because he made them happy.

A woman stumbled into the room. She giggled. "Whoops! I thought you were gone. It's so quiet in here." She came up to William and held out her hand. "I guess I'm your stepmother. But you can call me Lizzie." William stared at her hand. She wore several diamond rings and her nails were lacquered green. He looked at his father. Mr. Lancaster shrugged and offered a weak smile.

When he'd been standing on the sidewalk outside of the hotel, William had thought for a moment of breaking his promise to return to where he'd been. He had thought of rebuilding the life that he had lost, putting it back together differently. He'd thought of growing old with Margaret and restoring the Lancaster family. But he understood now what he needed to do.

"You never loved me!" William shouted at his father. He was angry. It burned in him, white hot and drew the words out of him. He could not be as cool as he'd been with the deer, the bootlegger, the hunter.

"I did. I did," his father cried.

"Prove it, then," William said, shoving his revolver into his father's hands. He forced his father's fingers closed around the handle and stepped back. "Choose me over her." His father's mistress sat, huddled on the ground, crying. "Tell me your son is more to you than a willing cunt."

"I'll leave her! Right now. She can pack her things and go. I'll never see her again. I'll move back home. I promise," Mr. Lancaster spoke fast.

William shook his head. Of course, his father would bargain, even now. Of course, he'd think it was as easy as pretending nothing had happened. "You said that before. You lie. Prove you choose me. Pull the trigger. End it." He pulled his father close. Sweat trickled down his father's face. William licked it. It tasted salty. Saltier than blood. "Do it. You want to."

His father nodded. The sound was loud. It startled his father. William could never be surprised by a gunshot. The woman collapsed. Blood pooled around her. William went to her, while his father keened behind him. The gun fell to the floor with a clatter. William huffed, annoyed. His father was so careless.

She'd been shot through her heart. The shot he'd tried to make on George. He smiled to see it. Then William got on his hands and knees. He lapped up her blood like a dog lapping at a puddle. Each swallow made him stronger.

"What are you doing?" his father wailed. William wiped his mouth with the back of his hand and grinned at Mr. Lancaster. His anger faded as he watched his father turn ashen.

"Your turn," William said.

Thirty-Six

The telephone in the hall rang. Maggie went to it, but didn't hurry. She was tired of prank calls.

"Maggie? Oh thank God," John said after she greeted him. She could hear tension and worry in his voice.

"Is it an emergency? Do you need me?"

"Maggie, can you come to Dad's right now? I need to talk to you. Just you. I can't say more over the phone. Don't bring William."

"Yes. But John—Never mind. I'll be there as soon as I can." Maggie hung up the receiver. She stared at the phone, expecting it to ring again. It stayed silent. She breathed in and out deeply. If she left without telling William, he'd be upset. But he'd want to come with her if she told him she was going into town. In the end, she decided to leave without waking him.

The morning was beautiful. It was still early enough that the dew was on the grass and the air felt fresh and new. Maggie bicycled into town as quickly as she could. John had sounded rattled.

John sat on the curb in front of his parents' house. He was wearing what he'd been wearing the day before. Blood covered his shirt and pants.

Maggie threw her bicycle down on the boulevard. "John, what happened? Are your parents...?" Maggie couldn't finish the question.

"No. It's not my parents. Come inside. Dad's waiting for you." He took her by the arm. Maggie could feel him shaking His breath came in quick little puffs.

Mrs. Mobley handed Maggie a cup of tea as soon as she sat down. Dr. Mobley sat across from her, his hands clasped together.

"What's wrong?" Maggie asked.

"A terrible thing. William's father is dead by his own hand. His mistress too. The maid at the hotel found him in the bath, his throat cut, the razor still in his hand. It was an awful sight. Blood everywhere," Dr. Mobley said. Mrs.

Mobley poked him hard in the upper arm. "Darling, she's a nurse."

Maggie set her tea down carefully. The cup rattled against the saucer. "Was there a note?" she asked.

"Yes. He was a man with a lot on his conscience. It was a sad thing."

"I have to tell William," Maggie said, standing. John held out his arm to stop her.

"Maggie, I believe William is still fragile. The shock of this could undo the progress he's already made," John said, his voice quiet. He sighed heavily.

"Are you suggesting we don't tell him his father's dead?" Maggie asked.

"No. I'm suggesting we don't tell him the cause. We'll say it was a stroke. Did he know that woman was there? No? Good. I'll tell him that it's detrimental for him to view the body. William's mother agreed with us," Dr. Mobley said.

"I don't like lying to him," Maggie said. She felt like a hypocrite. She lied to him all the time and always had. But she didn't want to lie about this.

"I'll tell him. You won't have to lie," John said.

"Then why tell me at all?"

"Because we're concerned about William and we want to put you on your guard," Dr. Mobley said.

Maggie finished her tea. Mrs. Mobley took her cup away to refill it. Maggie automatically accepted the fresh cup and began to drink. "If that's what you advise," Maggie said.

Dr. Mobley patted her knee. "Good girl. I knew you'd be sensible about this."

Thirty-Seven

Maggie woke up to whistling. It wasn't a bird song, it was a song. It was William's favourite song. She remembered he used to whistle all the time. Teachers would punish him for it, but he couldn't stop. He had never seemed to notice when he was doing it.

If he could whistle, could he talk?

Maggie threw a robe over her nightclothes and ran downstairs. The phone rang as she passed by it on her way to the porch. She sighed. Not answering wasn't a choice. She answered. This time, she thought she could hear someone speaking, but it was so faint, she couldn't make out the words. She thought she heard her name, but she wasn't sure. She listened for a few minutes and then hung up without saying anything.

William was on the old swing in the front yard. It hung from the largest branch on the oak tree. He swung back and forth, high in each direction, pumping his legs to go higher. He whistled and laughed.

Maggie watched him swing. She didn't want to break this moment. Since his return, she hadn't seen him look so light and happy. He was almost childlike. She called out to him.

He jumped off the swing mid-flight. She braced for him to crash to the ground, but he landed lightly on his feet, like a cat. "Margaret," he said in a hoarse voice.

"You can talk!" Maggie ran to him and threw her arms around him. He kissed her cheek. She stepped back and took his hands. They swung their arms in excitement.

"I can talk!" he said. And they spun around like children, shouting out.

Thirty-Eight

After she left Montreal, Maggie hadn't expected to see Lucy again. She knew friends drifted in and out of lives. They wrote to each other during the war, but Lucy's letters came less frequently once she returned to her parents. They promised to visit each other, but neither one seemed eager to settle on a date. That was fine. Maggie was learning to live alone. She liked it.

Maggie was surprised when a man turned up at her front door and said he was Lucy's brother, Garnet. Even before he introduced himself, Maggie knew he wasn't from town. His suit was too finely made, the material too expensive for anyone she knew.

He crushed a hat in hands. A red stone set in a heavy ring flashed in the sun. No men she knew wore jewelry like that. "Uh, Mrs. Lancaster?" he asked.

"Yes," Maggie said.

He tried to smile, but it faltered. He held out his hand. His grip was firm, his skin cool and dry. "I'm Garnet Stoppard, Lucy's brother. May I— may I come in?"

"Please. Is Lucy all right?" Maggie felt a spike of something, fear maybe, enter her heart. Lucy had come through the war safe. What could have happened? She should be safe forever.

"Um. Well, that's what I wanted to speak with you about. If I may."

Maggie invited Garnet in. She saw echoes of his sister in his face. He had the same heart-shaped face, but with a heavier jaw. And he had the same wide, dark eyes. But his gaze was not as bold as his sister's and Maggie thought it was not just because he was nervous.

He accepted a cup of tea and proceeded to crumble a biscuit into it, rendering the tea undrinkable. Garnet pushed it away, rattling the cup against the saucer.

"Mrs. Lancaster, my sister considers you her dearest friend," he said.

Maggie waited, not speaking. He needed to warm up to his subject, prepare himself to say whatever it was he came to say.

He cleared his throat. "Did my sister ever tell you about—her beliefs?"

Maggie smiled at the tame description. "Yes. She did."

"After she came back, she was different. I mean, we all were. You never went, did you?"

"No. My father died and I came home to take of my mother. You were there, yes?" Maggie asked.

He nodded. "Yes. My father wanted to protect us, but Lucy and I, we couldn't let others fight while we stayed safe. Our parents used their money to protect us from so much in life." His handsome face twisted for a moment. He caught Maggie's eyes. Yes, he did have the same eyes as his sister. "But they couldn't protect us from this. We wouldn't let them. But they don't understand what it was like. Or they don't want to."

"What happened to Lucy?" Maggie asked. She used the gentle voice she used with patients.

"She didn't hide herself from my parents any more. You know that she's lively. She likes fun. They could overlook that. They hushed up an affair with one of my father's employees. My mother, you understand, wants Lucy to marry well. To align with a family that's advantageous for our business interests. So she needs to guard her reputation."

He sighed. "Lucy wasn't sleeping. She hardly ate. Finally, she collapsed and started to rave about the dead. That they talked to her and wouldn't leave her alone. My parents put her in a hospital."

Garnet reached across the table and too Maggie's hands. He stared into her eyes. "Mrs. Lancaster, it's killing her to be there. If I get her out, can you take her? She's not mad. I know she's not."

Maggie nodded. "Of course. I have an idea."

A week later, Maggie, Dr. Mobley and Garnet escorted Lucy from the hospital. Garnet, with his family's money and influence behind him, convinced the doctors that Lucy would be fine with care provided by a privately hired doctor and nurse.

The first night, while Lucy slept in Maggie's childhood bedroom, Maggie lay awake. She couldn't hear Lucy, but she could sense the presence of another person. Hugging herself, Maggie closed her eyes. She was not alone.

Thirty-Nine

Maggie had told John about Lucy. She'd shown him a picture of two girls in their nun-like VAD uniforms. Lucy was a pretty woman in the photo, so he didn't expect the film star standing with Maggie and his father at the train station. She looked unlike any other woman he had ever seen with her bobbed hair and bright red lips. When Maggie introduced John to Lucy, he knew his life was going to change.

Mrs. Mobley teased John about his sudden care with his clothes. He'd always been neat, but now he added small flourishes. Fancy cuff links, a flower on his lapel. If Lucy noticed the flower, he gave it to her. He felt eighteen again. Or rather, he felt renewed.

Several weeks after she had arrived, John found the courage to ask Lucy to a movie. He saw every film that came to town at least once, often twice. Maggie occasionally came with him, but she didn't share his passion for it. Lucy, though, loved movies too.

John tried not to wonder what she thought of him. He wasn't a handsome man. On his desk, he had a framed photo of himself with Henry after a hockey game. Henry looked like an illustration from a boy's magazine come to life. John was plain, unremarkable. By his teens, he was already balding.

And then there was his bad heart. He was an old man.

He glanced over at Lucy as he drove. I'm a cliché, he thought. He'd read enough of his mother's magazines to know that unimaginative writers paired up doctors and nurses. But she made him laugh. And he made her laugh.

After the movie, they stopped at a cafe to have a snack and talk about the movie. Maggie never wanted to discuss a movie.

"I like you," Lucy said in the middle of John's pondering about the quality of the acting in the film.

"I like you too," he said once he caught up to what she had said.

"Well! That's good. I thought you did, but still. It's hard to say it. Do you know why I came to Apple View?"

"I don't know the details. Since you're technically my father's patient, but I know that you'd been unwell for some time after you came back from the war."

Over cake and coffee, Lucy told him her story. She told him about the war and the things that she saw there. She told him about the dead and her grandmother's séances. And how her brother had rescued her.

He told her how alone he felt when his friends went to war and he was left behind, too ill with rheumatic fever to do anything. He told her that every day he lived, every day his heart kept beating, he was surprised. How he expected to die. He told her about the flu.

The cafe owners stared at them. John looked at his watch. They had sat long past closing time. When they finally left the café, they sat in John's car, not going anywhere. Then she kissed him. His heart fluttered, but for once he didn't worry.

At Apple View, Lucy invited him in. He didn't hesitate. He turned down her offer of a drink and a cigarette.

"How bad is your heart?" she asked.

"Do you have a stethoscope?"

She left the sitting room. He heard her rummaging through something. She came back with a stethoscope. Deftly, she loosened his tie and undid the top buttons of his shirt with one hand. She put the ear pieces in her ears, breathed on the drum to warm it and placed it on his chest. She listened for a few minutes. John tried to breathe calmly, evenly.

"I could hear that murmur without this," she said. She set the stethoscope down and put her ear to his chest. He could smell her hair, feel her breath against his chest. "There it is," Lucy said. "A whoosh. Like a roar."

Lucy sat back beside him. John wondered what Maggie would think if she came in right then. His shirt open, Lucy smoking a cigarette. He felt rakish.

"You must have been very sick," Lucy said.

"At one point, I thought I was going to die. And then I hoped I would because the pain was unbearable. But it passed. My heart, though. It probably saved my life, in a way. I'd have gone off to war with the others."

"Are they all dead? Maggie doesn't talk about them," Lucy said.

"No. I think George is still alive. I got a postcard from him last year. But he never came back. William and Henry are gone." It hurt to talk about them. He still missed them. Especially Henry.

Lucy blew out smoke rings. John watched them float to the ceiling and disappear. He'd never seen a woman do that. "I wish I'd been around when you were sick," she said. "I'm an excellent nurse."

"Well, Maggie spoke pretty highly of you," he said. He wanted to be wittier.

"I would've made you forget about your pain," she said.

"Yes? How's that?"

"Come upstairs with me and I'll show you," Lucy smiled at him, the cigarette dangled from her red lips. She stood in front of him and held out her hands.

He laughed. "Are you flirting with me?"

"No. I'm serious. Come with me," she said.

John looked up at her. "I—my heart. Some things are—"

She yanked him up to standing. "There are a lot of things."

And that had been it for him. They practically lived together after that. At first, she still went with other men, but he didn't mind. She had explained about the voices, what quieted them. He knew the town was scandalized they wouldn't marry. But she didn't want to be a widow. And he didn't want to leave her one.

Forty

After William began to talk, John had contacted someone he remembered from medical school who was using unorthodox methods to help those affected by battle fatigue. He had hesitated to propose a visit to Dr. Blackler. Hypnotism seemed like a parlour trick, but both Maggie and William agreed to do it. John had been surprised when William had asked John and George to go with him, to accompany him into Dr. Blackler's office. It was William who asked if Maggie could hear the recording that Dr. Blackler had made.

John put the roll on the machine. He looked over to Maggie. She clutched a needlepoint cushion so tightly that her hands were white. "Are you sure you want to hear this?" he asked.

Maggie nodded.

"There's nothing—it's odd, but it's not—" John sighed. He didn't have words. "He doesn't explain anything."

"Play it," Maggie said. "I want to hear what he said."

Dr. Blackler: I want you to relax and focus on my watch. Keep your eyes fixed on the watch and your mind focused on the watch. Just relax your body and keep fixed on the watch. Your eyes want to close. Let them close. Stay relaxed. How do you feel?

William: Good. Restful.

Dr. Blackler: Excellent. We'll start with easy questions. Stay as relaxed and easy as you feel now. Let's begin. What's your name?

William: William Lancaster.

Dr. Blackler: Are you married?

William: Yes.

Dr. Blackler: What's your wife's name?

William: Margaret. People call her Maggie. That's a childish name.

Dr. Blackler: When were you married?

William: August 1914, just before I went to Valcartier. Margaret wanted to wait, but you never know with war.

Dr. Blackler: How long have you been married?

William: Two years. No. Wait. Longer. Eleven years. We've been married eleven years.

Dr. Blackler: Do you love your wife?

William: Oh, yes. She is my joy. I have loved her my whole life. I saw her for the first time when I was six years old. I told my mother I was going to marry that red-haired girl. Mother told me I was too young to make promises like that. But I always keep my promises.

Dr. Blackler: Did you promise Margaret you'd come back from the war?

William: Yes. I knew if I promised, I'd come back for sure. It would keep me safe.

Dr. Blackler: William, what happened in 1916? The last time you saw your friend George here.

William: I—I don't remember.

Dr. Blackler: What happened before that? Do you remember?

William: I was afraid. I just wanted to be good, to keep my promise to Margaret. I was in a pit or something with George. He was afraid too. He was shot. He fell into the mud and I got out of the pit. There was a bang. I fell back into the hole. Everything went dark. I was sure I died.

Dr. Blackler: And where did you wake up?

William: It was different, quiet. No artillery. No birds, either. Just silence. I thought my hearing was gone. It happens. The sky was a funny color. It wasn't blue, but wasn't gray. It was hazy, indistinct. At first, I laid there, looking at the sky. And then I realized I was alive and nothing hurt. Which surprised me. I sat up and saw I was alone. George wasn't there. I was out of the pit.

Someone must have moved me. I wasn't on the battlefield. I was in a village. Or what must have been a village. All the trees were broken and burnt. The buildings were shattered.

I got up and walked. I was scared. The silence was strange. I felt exposed.

I came across an old woman crouching under a tree. She was very old. She had a red scarf covering her hair. With bent, knobbed fingers, she was pulling bark from the tree and was eating it. She scooped up dirt and ate that too. Her mouth was ringed with mud and her fingernails were torn and bleeding.

I tried to touch her shoulder, but I couldn't reach her. I can't remember if she spoke French. I know what we said. But I can't remember how. That's strange.

I said, 'Excuse me, can I help you?' She told me she was hungry. I gave her the rations from my pack. She clutched them to her breast and thanked me. I was good. I had done the good thing. I told her I was lost. She pointed towards the church. The steeple was bent. She said someone could give me directions there.

I walked for a long time to the church. There was a woman in front of it. She was not old. But not young. She was on her hands and knees, lapping water out of a puddle. Just like a dog. Her clothes were dirty. I asked if I could help and she said she was thirsty. So I gave her my canteen. She drank until it was empty. I asked her for directions and she pointed me to a large house, a chateau, at the end of the road.

I walked for a long time to the chateau. I reached the gates. The wrought iron was twisted and bent. One gate hung from its hinges. All of the urns along the high walls were split. Dirt and dead plants had spilled out of them. I slipped through the broken gates and passed a fountain with a headless nude pouring nothing from a jug. The steps to the main entrance were broken, but I was able to climb them.

It had been beautiful once. But it looked looted. Everything was damaged. A chandelier had fallen to the floor and shattered glass was scattered across the cracked marble floors.

I looked for my unit in every room. I thought they could be billeting there. But the rooms were empty. In a large dining room, there was food on a table, but it was all rotten.

I felt alone, but as if I were being watched. I felt as if I were the only man left alive.

I went upstairs. All the beds were torn apart and clothes were spilling out of the wardrobes.

At the end of the hall, I saw a closed door. All the other rooms had their doors torn off or kicked in. I knocked on the closed door, but no one answered. I went in. The room was nearly empty. There was only a mattress on the floor. A young woman stood in front of the empty fireplace. She had her back to me. She was very young and her hair covered her to her waist. But she wasn't wearing clothes.

She turned to face me and I could see she was beautiful. The most beautiful woman I had ever seen with white skin and black hair. She smelled like roses. Her lips, hands and feet were blue with cold. She told me she was cold. I gave her my coat and got bedding from other rooms to wrap her in. I also took pieces of furniture to burn. I built a fire for her. I was very good. Very kind.

She asked if she could help me. I told her I was very tired. She unlaced my boots and helped me out of them. She pointed to the mattress I had brought in. I told her I was married. She put her hand over my mouth. It was cold and smooth like marble. She pulled me down to the mattress.

Dr. Blackler: Then what happened?

William: I slept. I woke up in a bathtub. I was up to my shoulders in hot water that smelled of lavender. The girl was gone. The thirsty woman sat beside me. She was clean and wearing a brightly colored dress. She was beautiful too. She washed me like I was her child. I almost cried. I wanted to be clean again.

I asked her where we were. She only said we were here. She told me I'd been tested and found true. Others had laughed at the old woman and kicked her and assaulted the young woman. I asked her what happened to those ones. She shrugged. She said they didn't stay. She said we'd talk over dinner.

The next thing I remember is the dining hall. The table held every kind of food I could imagine. I had been hungry since 1914. I ate and ate while she watched me. I told her about my promise to Margaret. She asked if I wanted to keep it. She said I could go to Margaret as long as I promised to come back. So I did.

Forty-One

William leaned against John. His face, slack with fatigue, almost looked human to George. He wondered if this was what Maggie saw when she looked at her husband. The humid air amplified the stink of the city. George felt gritty. The dirt of the city stuck to his sweaty skin.

"I think I'd better get him back to the hotel," John said. "Dr. Blackler wants to see him again tomorrow and he'll need to rest."

George felt a bit guilty, leaving John alone with William. He wasn't worried for John. For whatever reason, William treated John benignly, mostly ignoring him, almost like a pet of some kind.

"Do you need my help?" George asked. "Because if you don't, I'm tired of sitting around. I need to stretch my legs."

John said he'd be fine. He needed a nap himself, to be honest. The heat really took it out of him. If he didn't see George at dinner, then he'd see him at breakfast in the morning. George helped flag down a cab and stood on the sidewalk, watching it leave. Christ, it was hot. Sweat trickled down his back, pooling at his waist.

Once the cab was out of sight, George pulled a piece of paper out of his pocket. He hailed another cab and read the address on the paper to the driver.

The hallway of the hotel was dark. He could hear muffled voices from behind closed doors. It smelled of tobacco, cabbage and something else he couldn't name.

He checked the piece of paper again. At the end of the hall, he knocked on a door.

"Password?" asked someone from behind the door.

"Jesus Christ. Open the door," George said, laughing.

The door swung open. Alan was on the other side, laughing. "God, I feel like a kid again. Sneaking around in bad hotels."

"Oh my God, stop talking," George said, pushing Alan back into the room, kicking the door shut with his foot.

Later, they traded a cigarette back and forth, lounging on top of the bed, trying to catch a breeze from the open window or the rattling electric fan.

"I had a dream about you," Alan said, breaking the silence. He idly rubbed at George's bullet scar. "I think that's why I came here. Although, I should be pissed at you for trying to leave me for a ghost."

"Do I need to apologize more for that? Your dream. Was it racy?"

Alan laughed. "Is that all you think about? No. It was strange. You weren't there. I was looking for you. In a forest, I think. But there were roses everywhere. It was dark, but the roses were so bright. And I could hear something behind me, breathing heavily. I thought it was a wolf, but I never saw it. I just felt it."

"Did you find me?"

"No. I got lost in the woods. I was calling your name. And I felt really panicked. Then this hunter came out of the trees. He had on a plaid coat, red like the roses and a hat that hid his face. He had a rifle. I tried to see his face, but I couldn't. His eyes were white."

George looked over at Alan. Alan's eyes were unfocused, seeing something that wasn't there. George reached out to smooth away the lines on Alan's pale forehead and brush back his sweaty hair.

"So what happened?" George asked.

"He said that you were in danger. But he would find you. Then he clapped his hands and yelled wake up." George jerked at that. Alan looked up at him. "What? Does that mean something to you?"

With shaking hands, George lit a cigarette. He couldn't get away. "Got any hooch? I need a drink. The day I've had."

"You told me you quit." Alan moved closer to George and rested his chin on George's shoulder. He spoke into George's neck. "I don't know what's happening, but I don't have a good feeling about Apple View. Come home with me."

"I can't. Not yet."

"Then I'll go with you," Alan said.

George sat up, rolling Alan off his shoulder. He turned and took Alan's face in his hands. "No. You can't."

"We could tell them I'm an old war buddy or something. I've got a lot of practice pretending."

"It's not that. I just—you're right. It's not safe. I need you to be safe," George said. He kissed Alan hard.

Alan pulled away. "I'm an old soldier, remember? What the hell is going on there, anyway?"

George shook his head. "Trust me. Please?" And then, because he knew it would work, he kissed Alan again, like he was starving for it. He was. This was home. He knew that now. Apple View was not his home.

When he said he needed Alan to stay safe that meant he loved him, right? If Henry came back like William, what would George do? George quieted his questioning mind and gave himself over to the feel of Alan's hands on his body, the taste of Alan's mouth against his, the sound of their breathing, their hearts beating together.

Forty-Two

"I can't believe your gall," Maggie hissed at Lucy. She hoped Don, seated on the back porch, couldn't hear them speaking in the kitchen. Maggie had never been so angry with Lucy. She wanted to slap her or throw something. Lucy leaned against the heavy oak table, arms crossed. Her hair stuck out in several directions because she kept running her hands through it. Maggie knew that habit. It meant Lucy was angry too.

"I had to," Lucy whispered. "You're miserable. Ever since he came back. You're shrinking into yourself."

"He won't let me go, Lucy. You don't understand," Maggie said. She hadn't admitted that to herself. The words surprised her. She weighed them. Yes, it was true. William wouldn't let her go. He had never meant to.

"I do understand. Get away from him. We'll figure something out. Me and John and George. I promise," Lucy said.

Maggie shook her head. She couldn't ask them to do that. It was dangerous. She didn't know exactly how, but it would be dangerous. William always got what he wanted. He wouldn't let them interfere.

"I can't," Maggie said. "It's not fair. To me. To Don. To William."

"You love him, don't you?" Lucy asked. They were no longer whispering. Surely Don could hear. What did he think? He had come back despite whatever it was that had driven him away. (William. It was William who had scared him off, scared him into exile in the west.) Why did these men want to grasp onto Maggie and hold her? What if Maggie wanted to be alone, to be the one to hold herself? She had been alone before, but she hadn't chosen that. So what if she did that now?

Maggie laughed. She felt wild, trapped. She wanted to throw her head back and scream. "Which one?"

"Either of them," Lucy said.

Maggie shook her head. "I can't see Don. I can't. Lucy. Tell him."

Lucy stamped her foot. Maggie almost laughed. "No. You do it." Lucy grabbed Maggie's shoulders and pushed her towards the back door. Maggie wriggled out of Lucy's grip and went outside.

Don leaned against the porch railing, his back to the door. She had forgotten what he looked like, she realized. Or, rather, she had forgotten what the sight of him did to her. She wanted to touch him, to feel the muscles move under her hand. Heat spread through her as she thought about their last morning together before William's return.

"Don," she said. He turned and words left her. He was tanned and thinner, but he still looked at her as if she was the best thing in his world.

"You won't come, will you?" he said.

"I can't. It's not that I—" she paused. What good would it do to say it? It would hurt them both. "You know how I feel. But I can't. He'd only come find me."

Don nodded. He started to speak, but closed his mouth so hard, she heard the click of his teeth. The muscles in his jaws twitched. He brought his hand up to his eyes and held it there for a moment while he took a shaky breath.

He took Maggie's hand. "Tell me you're safe. I'll leave, but tell me you're safe."

She nodded. His grip tightened, hurting her fingers, but she didn't pull away. She looked into his eyes and thought how hard dark eyes were to read. He pulled her close and wrapped his arms tightly around her shoulders. Maggie rested her forehead on his shoulder and breathed in his smell of outdoors and sweat and coffee. She put her arms around his waist and squeezed as tightly as she could to stave off tears.

"Before I left, he came to me. And he threatened Ruth," Don said, almost in a whisper, his voice calm, flat. "He said if I didn't stay away from you— " he paused. "Well, I had to leave. But I think about you every day. And the dreams. Maggie, I see you in my dreams. You're dead and he's got you forever."

The light breeze became a wind and the warm day turned cold as the sun slipped behind a cloud. Maggie shivered and Don held her closer. She could feel his heartbeat, the heat of his body. He loved her, she knew that. But she couldn't ask him to risk his daughter. He could do without her; he'd already proved that he could. She lied. "I'm safe. I promise."

He let her go and covered his face with both his hands. She heard his breath stutter and he made a sound almost like a sob. When he took his hands away, his eyes were red, his long lashes damp. Oh, she could look at his face forever. She touched his cheek, feeling the roughness of stubble under her fingertips. "I'm sorry," she said. "I would have married you."

His face twisted and she saw lines that she didn't remember. She took his hand and held it palm up. She dropped the engagement ring onto it and then folded his fingers over it.

Don nodded. Maggie stood on her toes to reach up to kiss his cheek, but he used his free hand to cup the back of her head to kiss her lips. She tried to say everything she couldn't with her kiss. To tell him that she loved him, that she burned inside for him.

"Goodbye, Maggie. If— find me if you get free. I'll wait." He left. He walked away, not looking back, and she watched him go until she couldn't see him.

An arm slipped around her waist. "I'm sorry, Maggie. I had to try," Lucy said. Maggie put her arm around Lucy and nodded.

Forty-Three

They didn't sleep much that night. George didn't want to waste a moment before he had to go back.

"I told you my dream. Tell me a story," Alan said. "You're a writer."

"Books for kids, though."

"Still— That weird story your friend told about the castle, you said you recognized it. What did you mean?"

George sighed. Why had he stopped drinking? A drink would help.

"It happened at the end of the war. I came back from patrol and a new man thought I was a Hun. He shot me in the head." George pushed his hair aside and showed Alan the scar. "The bullet went in here and out here." He tapped the back of his head. "The doctors figured it went along the curve of my skull. Never touched my brain. I've got two plates. I didn't pass out right away, though. But I did, eventually.

"I woke up in a hospital far behind the line. I was confused because I thought I'd been awake the whole time. In my mind, I'd opened my eyes and seen sky. My head hurt, but I wasn't bleeding, so I stood up. I was alone.

"I should have known it wasn't real from the sky. It was a hazy yellow. Like before a storm. It had been blue when I closed my eyes. I could see a village in the distance. So I walked to it. Just like William, I saw the old woman and the thirsty woman and I ended up at the castle. Just like William described it.

"I thought maybe the Germans had been in the castle and had ransacked it before retreating. I found the girl in the room and I helped her warm up with a fire and my coat. When she tried to pull me to her, her hand felt like a corpse's hand. You know what I mean? How the skin slips? Her eyes were clouded and her face was bloated, discolored. I pushed her away. She was angry.

"She opened her mouth wide. Much wider than a person should be able to. Her teeth were like a pike's. Ever seen a pike? This noise came roaring out of her mouth, like a storm or a train. She lunged at me. I ran. When I passed through the gates, I woke up in the hospital."

"Jesus," Alan whispered. "What the fuck is going on?"

"I don't know."

Forty-Four

George should have asked Maggie to give him a different room. Henry's old bed was too full of memories. How many nights had he spent here over his life? When they were small, he'd slept in Henry's bed while Henry slept on a cot beside it, exhausted from a day of playing outside. Later, after that first kiss in the snow, he'd scramble into bed with Henry as soon as the door closed behind Mrs. Tate. George sighed and flopped over, trying to find a comfortable position.

He had thought he'd be happy here because he had been happy here. But it just outlined the hole in his life. He felt as if he had not amounted to very much and how that would have disappointed Mr. Tate and, most of all, Henry.

Some nights, when he had spent the night here, all he and Henry had done was talk all night. There had been so much to say. Everything had been more important, more vital than anything he felt now. Other nights, they had silently (or as silently as they could) explored each other's bodies. He could feel Henry's hand clamped over his mouth, stifling George's cries and moans. He'd managed quite a bit with girls from school, more than he thought a lot of other boys had tried, but it was all bold touches under cover of clothes. He had never learned someone else's skin, every inch, all the places to touch, to be touched. Sometimes he wondered if the only thing that had kept their secret safe was everyone's unwillingness to see it.

George got out of bed. Maggie had left the room exactly as Henry had left it. Was it snooping if the person was gone forever? George opened the wardrobe. Old hockey sweaters, arms stretched down by their own weight, hung to one side. George held one to his face and breathed in. It smelled musty, but there was a faint hint of Henry's scent. He tossed the sweater on the bed. George looked up and saw the sketchbooks stacked on a shelf above the clothes rod. He couldn't quite reach. Henry had been taller.

He stood on a chair. The weight of the books in his arms made him waver and nearly tip off the chair, but he regained control. He sat at the small desk to look over the books. He lit a cigarette.

"God, you were pretty," he said to a drawing of himself, reclining like an odalisque. No one had looked at these books, he knew. Or Maggie would know and he didn't think she did. Henry had done this one just before they'd gone home for Christmas the first year they'd lived together. George had teased him. "Afraid you'll forget what I look like?" he had asked. They'd been happy. No one had questioned two friends saving on room and board by living together. It had been heaven. Closing the apartment door behind the world and having Henry to himself.

George clapped the book shut and went back to bed. He stuffed the hockey sweater under his pillow. He fell asleep, clutching the sweater.

Forty-Five

Her wedding ring sat in a drawer in her room. She couldn't wear it on the ward. Her hands had to be clean at all times and her fingers had swelled with work. Maggie had never understood the references in books to working hands before, but now she did.

Lucy teased her that she was trying to fool people into thinking she was single. Maggie would only smile at her friend's joke. But she did forget, from time to time, she was married. Not that she wanted another man. Maggie had quite enough of men.

She'd be working or walking through the city with Lucy or in bed and she'd find herself thinking of her life as if she weren't married. As if she'd never been married. At first, it brought her up short. How could she forget? But soon enough, Maggie began to consider what if she weren't married?

Her pride needed to be wrestled with first. That was hard. She didn't like to admit mistakes. She didn't want to reveal that all William had to do was threaten her. Her parents had meant for her to be stronger. But her father would know what to do.

She considered asking George, but she didn't want him to get the wrong idea. His letters avoided any mention of the night of the party, but it still lurked between every line. She could see the contours of that night in what he didn't say. No. She couldn't ask George. He was in William's unit. And she didn't want William to know. Not yet.

After a few weeks of thinking of little else but her desire to be free, Maggie wrote her father. His reply came within a few days. He would do whatever he could to get her an divorce. She smiled when she read her father's letter. Mr. Tate's handwriting was firm and sure. He could do it. She knew he could. She started to laugh and then cry.

Lucy came into her room, "What is going on?"

Maggie gave her the letter, "I'm going to be free!"

But her father died before he could free his daughter.

Forty-Six

When they were rotated back, George tried to keep his distance from William. He'd go to the Y huts or even church to escape. Yet, William would seek him out.

"Join us for a drink!" William said, clapping George on the back in a very good imitation of being friends. He had a couple of other privates with him, two younger men who followed William around. Thanks to his father, William had more money than anyone else and spent freely, guaranteeing him a crowd of superficial friends. George didn't want to be among William's disciples, but a drink would be nice.

They ended up at a brothel. William had no scruples about throwing money at that sort of place.

Inside, the building had a shabby luxury. The furniture and trims were antique and would not have looked out of place in a fine home, but they were well-worn through constant use. Smoke wreathed through the air like fog, covering everything in a haze. Women of various ages loitered about in flimsy silk dresses.

George ordered a drink. His mother was staunchly temperance, but drink had become one of his chief comforts. George looked forward to his daily rum ration and would do almost anything to be rewarded with more.

William's disciples surveyed the scene. They discussed the merits of different women and egged each other on to choose one to buy a drink for. William mocked them. He gave them money and encouraged them to choose.

"You too, George," he said, throwing some coins towards George. As they rolled past him, George slapped his hand down and slid them back to William. "What? I thought we were old friends."

"I'm here to drink," George said. "You do what you want. I'm sure your wife will understand."

"I'm a married man, risking his life for king and country. She'd damn well better understand. But all the same, for morale, I wouldn't say anything to her. And of course you won't either. Because why would you be writing to an old friend's wife?"

The disciples stopped ogling the prostitutes and turned their attention to William and George. A fight would be a nice addition to the day's entertainment.

"What's the matter?" said one of the disciples. "You got a sweetheart back home, George?"

"Surely it don't matter! We're men after all," another disciple said.

George bolted his drink and signalled for another. His face was hot. William was sharpening some kind of knife.

"Yes, do tell. Got a sweetheart back home?" William asked.

"Wouldn't I tell you, old chum?"

"Well, if you don't, why not pick a girl? My treat. How about that one over there? I seem to remember you liked that blonde McAllister girl. Doesn't she remind you of her?" William pointed to a thin, pale girl in pink, who leaned against the bar. She looked bored.

"No, thanks."

"That's right. You like red-heads. No, I insist. I'll go get that one. Be right back." William stood and as he passed George, he muttered, his false bonhomie gone from his voice, "I hear for a little extra, they'll do whatever you want. Like pretend to be your sweetheart or wife. Do the things you like."

George rolled his eyes and gestured for William to move along. William laughed.

One of the disciples was anxiously discussing if it really would be a bad thing, if one had a girl back home, to partake of the pleasures of the establishment. George sighed. He imagined one of these idiots being the last to see him alive. It depressed him. He signalled for a bottle.

William returned with a red-haired woman. "Here she is, George! Buy her a drink."

And he did. And then he paid Madame and took the red-haired woman upstairs. At least up there, he'd be away from William and his followers.

The girl's room was larger than he had expected, but it was still small. The bed looked clean and comfortable and was the most desirable aspect of the place. Sleeping somewhere clean, dry and comfortable was almost an unthinkable luxury.

The woman introduced herself. "Je m'appelle Hélène," she said. George introduced himself in French and told her he spoke French quite well. She smiled and explained that many of the English did not, making it hard for her. George told he was Canadian and she shrugged. It didn't matter to her.

Why the hell not? It wasn't as if he were married. It was different with a woman, wasn't it? When he got closer to her, he realized that she smelled of violets. She was so clean. She would help him forget everything else for a short time.

After, a maid dropped off a tray of food. Hélène explained all the well-paying clients got this treatment. On it was champagne, omelet for both of them and slices of melon. Eating the melon, George nearly cried. He missed eating ripe peaches straight from the trees at Apple View, the fruit warm and soft, the juices running down his face and arms.

They made small talk over their meal. She asked him if he had a girl waiting for him back home. He told her he did not. She cocked her head to the side and studied his face.

"I think there is someone you're missing very much right now," she said.

Perhaps it was because she was paid to care or because he knew he wouldn't have to see her again unless he chose to, but he told her the truth. He asked her if she had someone she missed. She nodded.

"Love is very difficult," she said. "What I do, what people call love, is very easy. But the heart," she put her hand to her chest, "it would be easier if we didn't have them."

"I don't know about that. I have a friend whose heart is keeping him out of this whole mess," George said, thinking of John. He tried to imagine what John would think of this place and laughed. How had his life brought him here, an ocean away, to a French whore's workspace? He raised his champagne glass, "To hearts!"

Forty-Seven

More people in the house made it feel alive again. Maggie saw with new eyes how tattered and worn Apple View had become. She could see the curtains were faded. The prints on the wall bored her. Even Henry's first, youthful paintings had become dull to her after looking at them for years. While George worked on the outside of Apple View, Maggie began to restore its interior.

While William was out with his mother, Maggie went to the attic to sort through Henry's paintings. The year he had spent living up north had been a productive one for him. There were stacks of landscapes, almost abstracted, showing the changing seasons and aspects of the place of his heart. The colors were vivid. She could feel her brother's love for the scenery. Up close, she could see the brush strokes, the odd fingerprint.

Further back, behind the landscapes, were portraits. Again, the style was not precisely realistic. The colors were a little brighter than natural, the details focused on the most evocative. So George's eyes were bigger than in life, her mother's hair a fiery red it hadn't been since her childhood, their father's wry smile the centre of the piece.

Maggie found a portrait Henry had done of her before he had gone to art school. He had seen color reproductions of pre-Raphaelite works and had tried to imitate them. So Maggie had sat for him in a costume their mother had borrowed from the town players. Her hair had been down, falling over her shoulders. In the painting, she looked up in rapture at something, maybe God. Her hands were full of yellow roses. She smiled and added it to the pile of pictures to hang.

Was it vain to hang that portrait in the sitting room? Maybe. But it reminded her of childhood games, ones where she'd been the princess that George and Henry rescued from a fierce dragon.

"That's beautiful!" Lucy said when she came into the sitting room.

"How old were you Maggie?"

"Fifteen? Sixteen? It took days. I remember that." Maggie sat on the sofa and stared at the painting, seeing her brother in each brush stroke.

"You were beautiful. You still are," William said from behind Maggie. He kissed her cheek and placed a hand on her shoulder. Maggie blushed. He had never told her she was beautiful before. When they were younger, he had fretted over how she dressed, how she did her hair, how she carried herself. He had wanted her to be the perfect match for him. He had never said she was beautiful.

She put her hand over his. He had changed. He was how she had always wanted him to be.

Forty-Eight

No one at Apple View, save John, seemed able to sleep. Maggie could hear George or Lucy prowling around at night and occasionally, she would smell cigarettes. Maggie liked to stay in bed even if she couldn't sleep. Rest was next door to sleep, she told herself. Even so, she didn't like the dark. So she would turn on a lamp and read. Lately, she had returned to the books Henry had loved. Tonight, she read *Idylls of the King* and thought of the time Henry had tried to convince her to pose as the Lady of Shalott and float down the river. He had finally settled for her laid out on the grass, pretending to be on the water.

At first, she thought the steps outside her door were either Lucy or George. Sometimes, Lucy would come lie down with her. They had often shared a bed at the boarding house in Montreal, whispering and giggling until the early hours of the morning. Pretending to be those girls again helped them both sleep. "Come in," Maggie said and startled when the door opened to reveal William.

His light hair stuck out in all directions, making him look like a little boy. "I had a bad dream," he said. None of them were dreaming easy. What was that? Dreams weren't contagious. Maggie waited, not speaking, to see what he wanted.

"Can I sleep in here with you?" he asked. "Only sleeping. I promise. It's just—I don't think I can sleep alone."

She wanted to say no, but he looked so young and scared. "Fine," she said and moved over to make room. Maggie didn't know why he had come to her. They had never really shared a bed. Really, they had only had a few nights together before he had left.

They lay on their backs, stiff and separate, like effigies on a medieval tomb. Maggie pretended to sleep, breathing in small puffs. She couldn't relax. She wondered if he could.

Maggie did sleep eventually. She woke to William's arm around her and his whisper in her ear. The smell that came off him sometimes surrounded her. It was the smell of leaves and dirt freed from snow, a strange, rotting smell. She wanted to pull away, but he held her tightly.

"Take you with me. So impatient here. Come with me," he mumbled.

"Are you awake?" she asked. He didn't answer. He sat up and took Maggie's shoulder, turning her from her side to her back. He straddled her, his knees tight to her ribs. Maggie didn't move. She held her breath. His face was blank, but his eyes were open. He was still asleep. She said his name several times, but he didn't respond.

"Come with me. Now. I'm supposed to be stronger. I think. But I think I know an easier way. Do you want to go?" He mumbled still and he didn't look at her. His eyes rolled up to the ceiling so she could see only the whites. When Maggie shifted under the grip he had on her shoulders, he held her down more tightly.

"Go where?" she asked.

"The other place. Before. Before I came here."

"Where was that?"

"The other place. They said I could have you because I'd promised. Do you want to go?"

John had told Maggie to play along if William seemed confused. It would only agitate him to talk him out of a spell. She tried to stay calm, to be agreeable. "I don't want to go until you're healthier, stronger," she said.

He smiled at her, his eyes still rolled back. She wanted to turn her face away from that weird empty gaze, but she knew he'd know. It wasn't really a smile. These days, he smiled by pulling his lips back to show his teeth. His teeth were very straight and very white. *Didn't he have a canine tooth that stuck out a little?* her memory whispered. He had never showed his teeth when he smiled.

William leaned down and kissed her. When they were young, he only had to kiss her to make her heart flutter and her body burn. He sat up and released her shoulders. He was awake now. "Margaret?" He looked around. "What—? Where—?" He covered his face with his hands. "I'm sorry."

He got up from the bed and left the room before she could say anything.

Later, as she pinned up her hair in the front of the mirror, her robe slipped from her shoulder and she saw a bruise left by his hand. "Where was he?" she asked her reflection.

Forty-Nine

The roses had gone wild in the years since Maggie's mother had died. Every summer, Maggie would intend to trim them back and every summer, she put it off to the next year. She liked how they looked, a red, pink, yellow and white riot of colour. Her mother had kept her gardens neat and ordered. Maggie preferred the chaos of nature. It reminded her of the thorns that concealed Briar Rose.

Since William and George came back, Maggie saw the garden as they must have. Everything around the farm and orchard spoke of her neglect, of her grief. Her parents would have been disappointed that she had let herself, and the farm, become so undone.

She had been hacking at the roses for over an hour when George came out to help her. He took the shears from her hands and gave her a glass of water. Through the green smell of cut branches and the perfume of the roses, Maggie could smell the stale smoke that always hung around George.

Maggie put the cool glass to her sweaty forehead. It felt good. She sat on the grass, not caring if she stained her dress. Sitting became hard, so she lay down on her side, watching George trim the roses. The buzz of bees in the roses and the constant snip of shears charmed her into a doze.

A caterpillar crawled across her hand and startled Maggie awake. The roses looked tamer, more sedate, but not as subdued as they would have been under her mother's care. George had found a balance. Maggie was covered in roses. George was stretched out in the grass, facing her, his shirt bunched under his head as a pillow. Maggie smiled to think how shocked her mother would be to see George in an undershirt and work pants.

"Is that a tattoo?" she asked.

"Hmmm?" George raised himself up on his elbows. "Hello, Sleeping Beauty."

"On your arm, there. Is that a tattoo?"

George twisted to look at his upper arm. "I couldn't stop thinking of the roses here when I was in the trenches. I had it done on leave. This one, it won't die."

"I never really had a chance to be homesick," Maggie said. "I wonder sometimes what it would have been like if I'd left here. For good."

"Why did you stay?" George asked.

"I don't know. I didn't know where to go. Everyone was gone. And then Lucy needed me."

"I should've come home sooner. I know what it's like to be lonely. And I shouldn't have left you to that."

Maggie sat up, scattering her blanket of roses. "Do you? I don't think you've ever really been alone. I know you. You always have some girl willing to let you do whatever you want."

He didn't rise to her bait, making her angry. This was how they had fought when they were younger. One would needle the other who would remain infuriatingly calm. "That's sex. I was still lonely."

"Well, everyone was gone. I was here. Alone. Every day, I woke up and remembered again that Dad was gone, Henry was gone, Mum was gone. Even William was gone. And you didn't want to come home."

George sighed. "I'm here now."

Fifty

His mother talked and talked. Words came out of her in great torrents, but they meant nothing to him. William nodded and smiled. It was as it had been when he was younger, but now he knew she really didn't love him so much as she loved the idea of herself as a good mother. Everything was clear to him now.

He watched her lips move. He thought of the deer. The smell when he sliced it open with Henry's hunting knife, the rich coppery tang of blood, the fetid smell of the guts as they spilled open. He could taste it still. It was like the trenches again.

Or the hunter who had seen him in the woods, feasting on the deer. At first, he had meant to scare the man off. And he had. William had smiled at the hunter and the man had dropped his rifle and run off. But if a deer could bring him so much strength, what could a man do? And it had been so long since he had taken a man.

Then that farmer.

He thought of his father. And how it gave him back his voice.

"I'd like you to come with me, dear." His mother's voice cut through his reverie. William frowned. "Of course," she said, patting his hand, "not if you don't want to. If it's too much for you. It's just that the ladies dedicated so much work to the cenotaph and it would be nice to thank them."

He nodded and his mother smiled. She liked to show off her handsome son. He proved her rightness, her ability. He looked about the room. Everything in his mother's sitting room was expensive, well chosen, a token of her taste. Her china was fine and translucent. He could shatter his tea cup in his fist, grind it into powder.

"I could make a display of her," he thought. How fitting would that be? She claimed to have given him life. Well, now she could.

"What are you thinking of, darling?" she asked.

"I was thinking how glad I am to be here. With you." And he took her hand.

Fifty-One

Summer had gone away. For days, a cold rain fell. Puddles in the fields grew to small ponds. The green leaves on the trees looked wrong. The calendar said summer, but the weather said fall. The roses at Apple View bowed under the weight of water they had collected.

Maggie couldn't get warm. She lit the fire in the sitting room, the earliest it had ever been lit. Her parents had enjoyed a good-natured fight about when to light the fire for the first time once the weather turned cold. Her father had always hesitated until almost winter. Her mother would want to light it at the first chill in the air. The disagreement had extended to the furnace once that had been installed. Maggie didn't want to deal with the furnace yet, so she lit the fire, dragging in logs from the woodpile on the porch.

The house was quiet. Lucy was working, as was John. William was wherever he went when he was not around. Maggie suspected he wandered the woodlot because he often had bits of trees and burrs stuck to him when he came in. He usually took the rifle with him although he never brought back anything that he had shot. George had also become a wanderer. Although, he had told Maggie that he often went to the old stone house.

Maggie tried not to fall asleep before the fire. She was so tired these days. All she seemed to do was sleep or rest. She supposed she should care if she were sick, but she really didn't. Caring was too difficult. Maybe she'd take Dr. Mobley's advice and go somewhere warm for the winter. William's aunt, maybe his aunt, had a house somewhere nice. Florida, she thought. He would go to family, probably. He would go for her. Maybe. He was attached to Apple View, more than he had been when they were younger when all he had wanted to do was get away. Well, he must have missed it while he was away.

Maggie wrapped a blanket around her shoulders. She tried to read, but she couldn't concentrate. She threw her book down as John came into the room. He looked around the room, his face drawn. His jacket collar was turned and he had buttoned his jacket wrong. "Maggie, where's William?" he asked.

"Out for a walk. I don't know where he was going. What's wrong?" She was awake now.

John sat beside her. His coat was wet with rain. He rubbed his forehead and sighed. "It's his mother. She's dead. She—she killed herself last night." Maggie could hear him breathing. "Dad got called in this morning. Her maid found her. It was awful. What should I tell William?"

"You have to tell him his mother's gone," Maggie said.

"No. I mean about how she died. He's still fragile. But to lie about this— I don't know what to do."

"Does he need to know what happened? We already lied to him about his father," Maggie asked.

William came in. He dripped water on the carpet. Drops slipped down his fingers and hit the ground. He stood still, watching them. He knew. Somehow, he knew. And he was waiting for one of them to say something.

John stood up and went to William. He embraced William as he said, "I'm so sorry. Your mother passed last night." William stood for a moment with arms hanging at his sides before lifting them to return John's embrace. Over John's shoulder, William watched Maggie. He blinked or winked. Tears, he blinked back tears. Maggie averted her eyes. She couldn't watch him.

The men parted. "Let me know if I can help in any way," John said. William nodded.

"Thank you," William said in a low voice.

John told William to get out of his wet clothes and into a warm bath. He said he would be back later. Did they need anything from town? No, they didn't, but they appreciated the offer. Maggie caught sight of William's reflection in the mirror over the fireplace. A hint of a smile crossed his face before he turned to go upstairs.

Fifty-Two

Maggie left William sleeping in her bed. She put on her mother's old silk kimono and quietly eased the door closed. Stepping softly and avoiding squeaky floorboards and steps, she went to the dark, quiet kitchen.

When she was little and awake, her mother had always seemed to sense it. Mum would lead Maggie from her room, following the same stealthy path to the kitchen. Then she'd heat up a pan of milk on the stove and toast a slice of bread. Mum would butter the toast and liberally sprinkle it with cinnamon and sugar. Then she and Maggie would either talk about what was keeping Maggie awake or not speak at all. Maggie had been prone to nightmares as a child. She also would lie awake at nights, afraid of dying in her sleep. But her mother could always coax her out of fear.

Stirring the milk so it wouldn't curdle, Maggie sighed. The worst part of being an adult was taking care of herself. There was no one to smooth her hair and tell her not to be afraid. She took down a tin labelled sugar. It concealed a bottle of dark rum. Lucy had taught her to add a bit of rum to her hot milk to help with sleep. She called it hot cow. After adding a splash of rum, Maggie measured out a teaspoon of vanilla. She poured into Henry's enamel camp mug. She knew she should let go of all these mementos and habits that bound her to the past, but she had no idea what to replace them with.

Toast and drink prepared, Maggie sat at the table. She heard a soft knock on the back door. Dr. Mobley smiled and waved at her through the sidelight.

"Do you need Lucy?" she asked when she opened the door.

"No. I saw the light and thought I'd check in on you. You should be sleeping," he said in a quiet voice, not quite a whisper.

Maggie poured out another mug of hot cow and passed it to Dr. Mobley. He took a sip and smiled. "Ah. That warms the heart. What's troubling you, my dear?"

She smiled at Dr. Mobley. If it were anyone else, she would be prickly, offended. Even John couldn't be this solicitous, this kind. But she'd known Dr. Mobley all her life. In her memory, he was old, but now she realized that he had been no older than John when she was a child. And John was the echo of his father's youth. Like his son, Dr. Mobley was not a handsome man, but his kindness made his plain face with its awkward nose and crooked mouth approach something like good looks. His cheeks were rosier than his son's and he still moved with the energy and ease of a much younger man. *This is what John will look like if he ever gets this old,* Maggie thought. *But John won't get this old.*

"Nothing. You know I've never been a good sleeper," Maggie said. Dr. Mobley patted her hand.

"That's true. I remember your mother coming to me when you were about a month old. Her eyes looked like two holes in a sheet, she was that tired. You were keeping her up nights, crying like anything. I finally talked her into hiring a night nurse to sit with you. Well, let's look at you." He took her chin with his fine, long fingers and gently turned her head. He drew a stethoscope from his bag and blew on the drum to heat it. "May I?" Maggie nodded. He listened to her heart and kept count of her pulse in her wrist.

"You young people don't seem to be as strong as we were at your age. But then you've had troubles we did not."

"Oh, we're not so young," she said lightly.

"You're always young to me. Now, as your godfather and your father's friend, I feel as if I am right to offer you some advice. Ignore me, if you like. I'm used to it. That boy of mine does."

Maggie smiled and took one of Dr. Mobley's hands. They really were beautiful hands. Henry had often sketched them surreptitiously. "Please. Advise me. I'm a poor, lonely orphan."

"Leave, Maggie. Go somewhere pleasant with clean air and quiet. I hear Lake Louise is beautiful this time of year. You're fading away. Take John with you."

Maggie shook her head. "I can't. William would never leave."

"Then leave him behind. But you need the rest. You've lost at least ten pounds since I last saw you and you never had the pounds to spare."

"He won't like it if I leave him," she said. She wanted to tell Dr. Mobley that she wanted to go. She saw in his face, the warmth of his dark eyes, that he understood. Maybe he didn't understand everything, but he saw how being here drained her.

"I love you like a daughter, Maggie. I always wished John had married you. Oh, I know he asked you. And I don't blame you for saying no." He took a long drink from his mug. "Good stuff. Your father liked a bit of hot buttered rum. Lucy's a joy, though. Wish he'd marry that girl. Do you know why he won't?"

Maggie laughed. "No. I really don't. I wish they would."

Dr. Mobley set his empty mug on the table. "Well, please consider going on a holiday. Make it a second honeymoon. Tell your husband that."

"I'll think about it."

"Good." He picked up his bag and went to the back door. "And tell that George creature I want to see him at my office sometime this week." He shook his head. "Half my age and you all look as if you're falling apart." He frowned and Maggie saw his age on his face for the first time in the deep lines that bracketed his mouth. John. He was thinking of John, she knew.

After seeing Dr. Mobley off, Maggie dumped the leftover milk down the sink and ripped her uneaten toast into pieces, letting it fall into the bucket of bread scraps for the birds.

She could put on her shoes, open the door and walk away from here. She could get on a train and go west, see the prairies, find Don. She sat down heavily. Would William know she thought of that? Sometimes she suspected he could hear her thoughts. She put her head down on the table.

Fifty-Three

The matron in charge of the VADs came down the hall, holding a telegram. Every woman she passed clutched at her racing heart and waited, braced to have her world shatter. The stern faced woman glided past each one, sparing them. She stopped before Maggie, who was standing at a pot of boiling water, sterilizing bandages.

"Mrs. Lancaster," the matron said.

"Yes?" Maggie said. Her hands shook as she set down her tongs and removed her heavy rubber gloves. She wiped her hands on her apron. For what seemed an hour, she and the matron stared at each other. Telegram. Henry. George. Home. William. That was the wrong order, maybe, but that was the order. Others had already had losses. Not her. Not yet.

"A telegram for you." The matron handed over the envelope. Maggie opened it, her hands steady. She wanted to wipe the sweat and water beading on her forehead. She was not ready for whatever this contained.

"Father dead. John will meet you at boarding house at 5 p.m. To take 7 p.m. train. My sympathy and love. Dr. Mobley."

Maggie turned off the gas and stepped back from the stove. Her legs shook and she didn't want to go down with a pot of boiling water. The matron gripped her arm, holding her up. Maggie gave her the telegram. The older woman nodded and turned to another girl in the kitchen. "Fetch Miss Stoppard. Ask her to come quickly."

Later, Maggie would not remember the walk back to their boarding house. Lucy kept tight hold of her arm. Perhaps they took a cab. Lucy would have been able to bully Maggie into accepting the expense. While Maggie sat, numb and unthinking in a bath, Lucy packed her trunk and laid out her travelling suit. Then Lucy came into the bathroom and washed Maggie as if she were a child. After, she helped Maggie to her feet and dried her off. Then she brushed out and braided Maggie's hair, pinning it tight so it wouldn't come undone during her long train journey. Finally, she helped Maggie dress.

Shaking herself out of her stupor, Maggie turned to her friend. She bit her lip and flapped her hands. No words came and she felt as if all her tears were locked in her heart. It hurt, but she couldn't let them go. "Thank you," she finally whispered. And Lucy flung her arms around Maggie, pulling her tight to her body.

"I'll miss you," Lucy said. "Write to me. Even if you have nothing to say, write that."

"I will. I'll come back." Although, Maggie didn't know if she would. Her mother would be alone. The work here was important. Or at least that's what she told herself when she was emptying pans of vomit and picking up bloody bandages.

Lucy smiled, a small, sad smile. "We'll see. Dad's pulling strings to get me overseas. I am so sorry, Maggie." She hugged Maggie again. When they parted, Lucy dragged the back of her hand across her eyes.

They jumped when they heard a knock on the door. "Mrs. Lancaster, Mr. Mobley is here for you in the parlour," the boarding house's owner called.

"Go," Lucy said. "I'll get your trunk."

John sat stiffly in the parlour, ignoring the curious women who peeked in at him as they passed in the hall. Gentlemen callers were rare and becoming rarer. He stood when Maggie came in and, not paying any attention to the disapproving glare of the proper woman who ran the boarding house, he crushed Maggie to him and kissed her cheek. She felt the rough scrape of stubble against her cheek. He sniffed and swallowed loudly. Her tears were still trapped inside somewhere. She patted his cheek. He looked away from her, his eyes red-rimmed and glossy.

"We should go," she said.

He cleared his throat. "I have a cab waiting outside." He took the trunk from Lucy without looking at her. Maggie quickly said good-bye to the other boarders and left. As she closed the heavy door behind her, she knew she would not see Montreal again. She was going back to Apple View.

Once they were settled on the train, Maggie took off her hat and set it on the seat beside her. John loosened his tie. "John, what happened?"

John looked out the window. It was too dark to see anything but his own face reflected back at him. But he stared out as he spoke. He told her that his father had phoned him at his dormitory. He had just got back from a lecture. Mr. Tate had been found in his orchard. Dr. Mobley thought his friend's heart had given out.

"I'm glad he died in the orchard," Maggie said. John nodded and reached out blindly for her hand.

"I loved him too," John said. "I wrote Henry and George."

Maggie couldn't think of her brother opening that letter weeks from now, when her father would already be in the ground, covered in earth. Or George, for that matter. Even though something had changed between her father and George before the war. So she thought of her father and his orchard. "You know, Dad told me once that he felt like God in the Garden of Eden when he was in the orchard. Walking in the cool of the day, taking pleasure in his creation."

John's mouth twitched into something like a smile. "Dad said Mr. Tate liked to go there to take his mind off the war news. Your mother said he hadn't been feeling well for about a week. Tired and worried. He'd been gone a few hours when they found him. Dad said he looked like he'd fallen asleep in the grass and never woke up. It was peaceful."

It was spring. The orchard would be in bloom. Maggie could see her father, lying on the grass, looking up at the blue sky through the pink and white blossoms of his fruit trees. Maybe he could hear birds singing. Bees from his hives would be feeding on the flowers. And the petals would be falling like snow. She could see him, in his neat vest and trousers, his sleeves rolled up to the elbow, his immaculately trimmed beard, streaked through with gray. He was, had been, a vain man in his way. He'd be covered in petals by the time they found him. Henry could paint it.

Maggie's world had closed in on her that day. When she came home, her mother begged her to not leave her alone.

Fifty-Four

John came across Henry's old canoe when he was searching in the barn for Mr. Tate's hunting rifle. Henry had probably put the canoe away that August when war was declared. John brushed away the cobwebs. It was in fine shape. The paddles rested against the wall beside it. John ran his hand along the canoe. He remembered the day Henry had got it, how excited he had been and how sore they had been the morning after spending hours paddling it down the river.

Every summer, starting when they were sixteen, John and Henry would pack up their camping gear and head north on the train. They would rent a canoe from a local guide and then head out for days of paddling and portaging and making camp wherever they stopped for the night. Henry had wanted to paint landscapes and John had loved to fish. They could be together for days on end, hardly needing to speak to each other.

Once, William had come with them. He had been fine on the trip. Well, except for his habit of making cutting remarks and then saying it had been a joke. But once William had begun to court Maggie, he would never join them.

John picked up a paddle. He could hear the paddles cutting through the water, the loons calling to each other across the water at night. Once, while he had been training in England, Henry had sent John a letter with a drawing of the army camp. "Makes me think of our camping trips!" Henry had scribbled in the margin. "Only, I think I prefer hearing wolves howl at night rather than my neighbor's snoring."

When they were eighteen and George had been sixteen, they had invited George along. John had been sure George wasn't interested in going, but Henry had convinced George to join them. John smiled to think of how much George had hated every minute of that trip. It had rained steadily for the first few days of the trip and then on and off for the rest. Both John and Henry had liked being on the water during a light rain. John had loved swimming in a warm lake on a rainy day. George had hated being wet. He hadn't complained, but he hadn't spoken either. He had sat in the middle of the canoe, glaring at the water, hunched into himself. Every now and then Henry would poke him with a paddle and George would transfer his glare to Henry. At the end of the trip, George had declared, "I like a nice walk in tame woods and sleeping in a dry bed." He had never come with them again.

Those days seemed as if they were a different life. Dr. Mobley had said to John once, "I feel so young inside that it shocks me to see an old man in the mirror." John wished he could understand. He felt old inside.

He set the paddle back against the wall. If anyone had to come back to them, he would have taken Henry.

Fifty-Five

"I remember," George said to William. They were alone. William sat very still, hands clenched into fists on his lap. He had no smile now.

"Remember what?" William asked after a few minutes of silence.

"What happened. Before you died." As he spoke, George could see it as if it were on a screen. He thought William could too. After all, if William could be in his dreams, why not in his head all the time? The lawn disappeared from George's view and he saw only the trench raid, his last one with William.

Alan had once asked "Battle or trench raid?" and George hadn't been able to answer. Battles were chaotic, huge, terrifying. Thousands of men would be consumed in the engine of a battle. But then again, it was a bit like why starlings flocked. If there were a lot of you, it was hard for the hawk to grab you. Trench raids, at night, were another kind of terror. Maybe you'd take the Germans by surprise. Maybe not. But then again, George's only serious wounds had come from Canadian guns, so what the fuck did he know?

That particular trench raid had been a success as far as George was concerned. The Germans had surrendered. No one died. He sent his men back with prisoners and did a final sweep with William who had volunteered to stay behind. For reasons George couldn't understand, William had been popular with the men and they had believed William's story he and George were childhood friends.

They found a young soldier, huddled in a corner, babbling too fast for George to understand. When George had studied German at university, he had meant to read poetry, not use the language to try to calm a scared child. Because the soldier was a child. The boy, so pale, so young, held up his hands and finally George understood that the boy had surrendered. Then a bang and the boy slumped over, red spreading between his pale fingers.

George turned. William still held up his gun. He was laughing. And crying. Almost hysterically whooping.

"What the fuck?" George yelled. William still held his gun at the ready and it shook as he laughed. George eyed it, heart thumping. He stepped forward and grasped it by the barrel and tried to yank it from William, but his grip was too strong. "You need medical leave. You've lost your fucking mind."

William stopped laughing and handed his gun to George. He wiped his eyes. He grabbed George by the upper arm and pulled him close. George could feel William's breath against his face. "No. You won't send me back. Because if you do, I'll report you. And you'll be in prison," William said. "I know all about you."

George set William's gun on the ground. He looked at the German soldier and thought of how the boy may have died listening to William laugh. He walked away. He'd put in for a transfer. He'd get away from William once and for all.

The scene faded from George's mind and he was again looking at Apple View's lawn. William wiped his eyes and smiled at George. "I remember," he said.

"You haven't changed," George said.

"Neither have you. You're still a coward. You'll sit here and talk and talk and talk. But you won't do anything. You're weak. And in the end, I'll still get Maggie and leave you with nothing."

"Why?"

"Same reason I shot that soldier. Because I want to."

"And what if I tell Maggie?"

William smirked. He got up from his chair. George stood too. He couldn't have William standing over him. William pulled George close just as he had in the trench. His hand was cold and George's arm ached with it. "I know where your friend is. He worries about you. But maybe you should worry about him."

William released George's arm. He went back in the house. George rubbed his arm to warm it. There was a white hand print, skin verging on frostbite despite the heat of the day. In a barely controlled fall, George sat on the porch floor. How could he choose? If he left, William would only follow and then, Maggie—

"Help," he whispered and he didn't know to whom. But the word felt almost like a prayer even though he had stopped believing a long time ago. "Help, please."

Fifty-Six

Maggie handed George one of Henry's sketchbooks, opened to a sketch of George sleeping. George flipped through the other pages, a small smile playing over his lips. He glanced up at Maggie. The sadness, or perhaps nostalgia, pierced her. She wanted to let him put his head on her shoulder and cry, but instead she stood and watched him.

"He never did enough self-portraits," George said and handed the book back to Maggie.

"George, did you love him?" she asked.

He raised his eyebrows. "What do you think?"

She nodded. "And he loved you."

George covered his face with his hands. "Christ." He breathed in deeply and she heard the tears around the ragged edges of his breathing. But when he took his hands away, his eyes were dry. "Why? Why are you asking?"

"I didn't know. I was the last to figure it out, I guess."

"It was our secret. Since I was fifteen. And then—someone—found out and told your parents. John always knew. I didn't know that. Henry told him." George sighed.

"You could have told me," Maggie said. But that wasn't true. She wouldn't have understood. At fifteen, she hadn't even known that men could be like that. But it still hurt to know that her best friend, the keeper of all her childish secrets had pulled away from her, had hidden away from her.

She put the book down on the table. George picked up his cigarette case and offered it to her. Habit, she knew. She waved it away and watched as he lit one. His mouth was as beautiful as she remembered from the few years she had been infatuated with her friend. She wanted to reach out and touch his cheek, but she didn't want him to misinterpret the gesture. Her infatuation had passed years ago. She only wanted to touch him to remember.

"Why did you kiss me then? If you were in love with my brother? I'm not angry. I just want to understand. If you don't like women, why were you with Maude that night?" She was fairly certain most of the girls in her class had been kissed by George at one time or another. Maude was the only one she had seen let George take more, but the other girls had likely been more discreet.

George shook his head. "It's not—I can't explain. I loved Henry. But we weren't—that summer." He sighed. "For me, it's not one or the other. I'm not explaining myself very well. Sit down and stop looming over me if you want to have a conversation."

"Did my parents—" Maggie paused. "I don't know what I'm asking. But when they found out, that's when Henry moved up north, isn't it?"

George nodded, biting his lip.

"I'm so sorry. And the party?"

"Fuck, Maggie. What do you want me to say? I'm sorry. I shouldn't have, but you didn't seem to mind at the time. And if I recall, you were engaged to William at the time. I was free to do whatever I wanted with whoever I wanted to."

Maggie took the cigarette from his hand and put it to her mouth. She breathed in deeply. The smoke made her chest feel tight. She coughed and he took the cigarette back.

"I'm sorry," she said. "I knew it was wrong. But I didn't know if I wanted to be engaged. William was suffocating me. And I thought, I don't know. I thought I should see what it was like to kiss someone else." And then she saw it and started to laugh. She laughed to tears and coughing, until George stood up.

She waved her arms. "I'm fine. I just— Oh my God, George. Did you kiss me because you wanted Henry and I was the next best thing?"

His cheeks reddened. He nodded. He looked like a dog that had been caught pulling the roast from the counter.

"So, I helped you make up your mind?" George said.

Maggie shook her head, keeping her face expressionless. This was what William had threatened her with and it didn't matter. It didn't matter at all. She would have still loved Henry.

"You and Henry, did you—?"

"I saw him on leave in England." George flipped through the sketchbook and tapped a colored pencil sketch of Henry's cabin. "He told me about this. He had a plan." He sucked his breath in. Maggie wanted to reach across and take his hand, but she couldn't. His pain hurt her too.

"I miss him," she whispered.

"Yes. Well, we got William back. So I guess we shouldn't count our blessings," George said. He snapped the book shut and took it with him to wherever he was going. Maggie sat alone at the kitchen table.

Fifty-Seven

"This is a place for kids, you know?" George threw his arms open wide, encompassing all of it, the lawn, the barn, the orchards, the river and the fields beyond. "It needs children running around like we used to." He could almost see them, the kids they used to be. John's small smile said he could see them too. But Lucy and Maggie exchanged sharp glances that made him want to claw the words back. William, further away from them, down by the edge of the lawn, hadn't seemed to have heard. So Maggie had been a widow. All right, so why hadn't she remarried before? Filled this place with children? And Lucy and John. George didn't understand what they were doing, why they didn't get married.

"Place like this, should be kids everywhere," he muttered to himself.

"How come you never married?" Lucy asked. George turned to answer her in time to see John clip her ankle with his foot. She kicked back, hard.

"Came close, once," George said.

"What happened? Cold feet?"

"She changed her mind. Everything was set, ready to go. And—" he shrugged. "She was a widow. Her husband came out all right, but before he got back to Canada, the flu got him." George crushed out his cigarette and lit another one. Lucy reached down and plucked it from his lips. She inhaled deeply and handed it back to him. He glared at the lipstick print on the end and gave the cigarette back to her.

"What was she like?" Maggie asked, so quiet, George almost couldn't hear her.

"She liked to dance." He smiled at the memory. It didn't hurt. "She had an answer for everything. She made me laugh. She was tall. Pretty. She could whistle any tune."

"So why did she change her mind?" Lucy asked, jerking her foot away from John's.

George laughed. Fine. It hurt a little. "Because she loved her dead husband more than me. Actually, she didn't love me after all."

And that was almost how it had happened. If it had just been her feelings about her dead husband, he probably could have pressed his case. Well, no. It was pressing his case that had doomed him. She had been sobbing about her dead Robbie's memory and how she couldn't bear the thought of another man touching her, taking his place. He had said, "I know what you mean." She had been hurt he hadn't told her he'd been married before.

When he had asked her if she loved him, she had said yes. It had given him the courage to tell her about Henry. And she hadn't been able to look at him after that. She had said it was rotten of him to lie to her when he was like that, when he had really wanted men the whole time. She had spat that out like it was the most vile thing a person could do. He had tried to explain, but she hadn't understood.

Later, they had each told their families they had changed their minds. And George had left his mother's home.

George didn't tell his friends this story though. "She changed her mind. Probably for the best. I'm too much of a bachelor by now."

William looked over his shoulder and smiled at George. George shivered despite the warm humidity of the evening.

Fifty-Eight

Maggie was so tired, but every time she began to tumble into sleep her body jerked her awake. Maggie felt close to weeping, a feeling familiar from her Montreal hospital days and the long, waking nightmare of the flu. William wasn't there. He hadn't been there for the last few nights. She couldn't sleep without him.

Turning onto her right side, she noticed how her hip dug into the mattress. She had lost weight. Food tasted like ashes. Other than bread and butter or rice pudding, she couldn't finish anything. Her stomach would turn and she'd end up spitting out her food. "What is happening to me?" she whispered to herself.

When she noticed William was not staying with her at night, she said nothing. He would go to bed with her and he would be beside her in the morning, but at night, when she woke up, he was gone. She didn't know where he went. She thought of asking George to follow him.

Her bed felt lumpy. She sat up and flipped and fluffed her pillows. She lay back down. She turned onto her left side. Her knees pressed together and hurt. She flipped onto her back and rested her hands on her stomach. She let her hands explore her body. Her hip bones stuck out. She ran her fingers back and forth over ribs. Was she dying? Oh, but then she could rest.

When she was little, she had liked to sleep on the sofa in the sitting room. With a fire and lots of blankets, it had been very cozy. She had felt safe. She would imagine that she was a little field mouse, warm in its winter nest. Her mother would let her sleep there if she were ill or scared from a nightmare. Well, she thought, I'm ill and scared now.

Maggie gathered her pillows and blankets. The house was dark and silent. Behind each door, someone slept. She hated each one for sleeping so easily.

Downstairs, the steady, heartbeat tick of the grandfather clock broke the silence. Maggie lit a fire in the hearth and created her nest on the sofa. She fell asleep watching the fire.

Maggie dreamed she was in the orchard. Everything had the mellow, golden glow of a fall afternoon. But the grass was a bright, new green and the trees were loaded with blossoms. The scent was heavy, almost overwhelming. Bees hummed, digging deep into the flowers. Birds sang loudly. The entire world was in love with itself.

Petals fell like snow, covering the grass. Maggie realized she was wearing her wedding dress. The hazy film in her vision was her veil. She lifted it back over her head.

Maggie walked through the orchard. She saw her bridal bouquet of white lilies and roses hanging from a branch. She pulled it down.

Ahead of her, she saw something on the ground. As she approached, she saw it was her father. Still carrying her bouquet, she ran to him and dropped to her knees by his side.

He was lying on his back, arms crossed on his chest. His eyes were closed and he was covered in a snowdrift of petals. She brushed petals from his face. His skin was cold. She kissed his pale cheek and put the bouquet in his hands.

He opened his eyes. They were totally white. She was not afraid. She lay down beside him.

"I'm so glad you're here with me," he said.

"I thought you were dead," Maggie said.

"I am. But now you're here with me. I'm glad to have died here, but I was so lonely."

"I'm not dead, though," Maggie said.

"But you will be," he said.

"I've been very sick," Maggie said.

"I thought it was Henry who had come back. He was the missing one. I've been waiting here for him," Mr. Lancaster said.

"Henry's dead. William came back. He wants me to go with him."

Her father turned his head to look at her. She met his weird, cold eyes. "Maggie, are you dead?" he asked.

She shook her head. He uncrossed his arms and her bouquet tumbled to the ground. He took her hands in his cold ones. Her skin burned with cold.

"Don't leave with him. I'm not ready for you yet," he said.

He let go of her hands and turned back to face towards the sky, crossing his hands on his chest again. He closed his eyes. Maggie held up her hands and saw they were blue with cold.

She stood up. The petals fell from the trees and covered her father's body. She started towards the house again. Looking over her shoulder, she saw a man standing at the far end of the row of trees. The man was in shadow. He clapped his hands.

Maggie woke up with the morning sun. The fire had gone out, leaving a pile of ashes. She could only remember pieces of her dream. She thought of her father, lying on the grass. She began to cry. "I'm alone," she sobbed into her pillows.

Someone stroked her hair as if she were still a child. "You're not alone," George whispered. She sat up and held out her arms. Where were her parents? She needed them to hold her. George held her as she cried into his shoulder.

Fifty-Nine

Rain splattered against the windows. Wind whistled at the corners of the house and rushed through the trees. It felt like November even though the calendar swore it was still summer. Lucy pulled her cardigan tighter around herself, as if that would warm her.

Her hands were stiff with cold. She blew on them and rubbed them together. The damp chill dug deep into her bones, making them ache. She wanted to be wrapped in blankets, warm in her bed, preferably with John. She had taught him how to warm a woman. But she had work to do and John was out with his father.

All day thoughts of her notebook kept intruding past whatever she was doing. Someone wanted to speak.

After supper, she feigned a headache and went to her room. She lit two candles and turned off the lights. She placed the candles on her small writing desk and took her notebook from the drawer. She flipped to a blank page. When she glanced out the window, she was momentarily startled by her own reflection in the glass.

Lucy held a pencil loosely in her hand and waited. In her mind, she saw a winding staircase. She pictured herself going down each step. Down and down and her physical surroundings faded from her. The rain and wind became background noise.

"Tell me," she whispered. "Spirit, speak."

Something gripped her hand, guiding the pencil across the page as you would do if you were teaching a child to write. Sometimes the spirits wrote for pages, urgently saying everything they could. This one had little to say. The letters were dark and had been pressed into the page almost to the point of tearing the paper. The loops of the cursive letters were spiky, sharp at their peaks.

"G. Wait for me. I'm on my way. Love, H."

The pencil dropped from Lucy's hand. She ran her fingers over the letters, feeling and reading them.

She went downstairs, stepping carefully through the hallway so that no one would hear her. Feeling like a child playing hide-and-seek, Lucy peeked into the parlour. Maggie and William sat together on the sofa. Maggie held a book open in her lap, but she had dozed off with her head on William's shoulder. William gazed blankly into the fire. Lucy walked slowly down the hall towards the kitchen.

George was there, reading. He had his elbows on the table and rested his chin on his fists. He had a mug of tea beside him and a cigarette dangled from his lips. He looked peaceful. Lucy hesitated. Disturbing him was almost mean. But he had to know. The message was not for her.

"George," she whispered. He looked up. She signalled for him to be quiet and nodded slightly towards the sitting room. "Come with me."

George whispered, "What is it?"

She shook her head. "Quickly."

He shrugged and closed his book. He pushed his chair back without making a sound and stood to follow her. They paused at the door to the sitting room. Again, Lucy looked in. Now William was asleep. Or at least, his eyes were closed.

Lucy pushed the light switch button in her room and invited George to sit at her desk. She put the notebook in front of him.

"I got this message tonight. Does it mean anything to you?" she asked.

George read it. Then, as Lucy had done, he ran his fingers over the deeply scored letters. He left the room. She didn't follow. If he wanted to come back, he would. She waited. He would be back.

A few minutes later, George returned holding a small thin envelope. He took a letter from it and put on the desk beside the message in the notebook. "Look," he said.

Lucy went to the desk. "Who is H?" she asked.

"Who do you think, Lucy?" George asked. "Come on. You know or you wouldn't have asked me."

"Initials aren't much. A lot of names begin with H," she said. "I'd rather not guess. Guessing can make me look—"

"Like a fraud?" He was sarcastic tonight. So maybe he hadn't been as peaceful as she had thought.

"You believed enough the other day. Who is H?"

"Henry. H is Henry."

Lucy read the message again. "With love. But I thought. You and Maggie—"

George stuffed the letter back in the envelope. He tore the note from the book and put both in his pocket. "Don't judge me."

"I'm not. I didn't know."

George flopped onto Lucy's bed. "Remember the hospital? When we met? I used to give you such a hard time about being a flirt."

"I do. I thought you were very handsome. And a terrible flirt. The other girls were wild about you."

"You never flirted with me like you did with the others. I thought you'd found me out somehow. Sensed it."

Lucy shook her head. "No. I had no idea. You teased me so much, I didn't flirt with you to show you up. And you told me different."

At the hospital, she had read books to the wounded men or wrote letters for them. She had asked George if he wanted any letters written. He'd asked her to write to his mother to let her know he was fine.

"And one to your sweetie?" Lucy had asked. When he had blushed, she had laughed and said, "Don't blush like that with the other girls or they'll be even madder for you. So, what do I say to her?"

"Oh. Um, my mother will write," George had said.

"I'm very discreet," Lucy had said.

He had smiled. "Don't look, but the matron has her eye on you. She guards your virtue like a dragon guarding a virgin princess."

Lucy had raised an eyebrow and leaned closer to him. "I don't have a lot of virtue left to guard. How about you?" She had wanted to make him blush again. She had patted his hand. "Don't worry. I don't steal hearts."

George sighed at her story. "My sweetie," he said.

Lucy sat beside him. "I'm sorry."

"Well, I thought William was dead. Saw it with my own eyes. But he's here now. So maybe Henry really can come back," he said.

"I don't get messages from the living," she said.

George blinked hard several times as if he had grit in his eyes.

"What is happening here?" he asked.

"I don't know," Lucy replied.

Sixty

George could almost pretend that they were home again. They sat on a river bank, skipping stones across the water. Birds sang in the trees. Everything smelled green and alive. The birds had different songs and some of the plants were not familiar, but it was close.

He closed his eyes, enjoying the warm orange glow of his own eyelids.

Henry nudged him with his shoulder. "What are you thinking?"

"I'm pretending we're home at Apple View."

"Oh, so it's your home now too?"

"You know what I mean." George flopped onto his back and stared up at the white clouds drifting across the bright blue sky. It felt like a dream to be here after the hospital and before that the trenches. He smiled up at Henry. "My home is where you are."

Henry made a disgusted face, but his cheeks were flushed. "That's sentimental."

"You know what I mean," George repeated and reached out for Henry's hand.

"Did I tell you they wanted me to be a sniper?" Henry asked. His voice was flat. George said nothing, waiting. "Someone found out that I hunted. I was pulled out for training. It wasn't much. I just went with another sniper and he told me where to aim. When to pull the trigger. I was always a good shot. They just came out one after another. Rabbits have more sense. And I picked them off, one-by-one. My first day at it and I got six. Got them all here." He tapped the furrow between his eyes. He hugged his knees to his chest. George sat up. He put a hand on Henry's arm. But Henry didn't look at him.

"When we got back, I said I wouldn't do it again."

"Did you? Do it again?"

"No."

They sat and watched the river, the water moving towards the sea, perhaps. Butterflies fluttered through the tall grass. Dragonflies darted and bobbed around them.

"I might not go back to Apple View," Henry said. "When we were— apart, I bought a little island up north. It has a cabin on it. Nothing much. Practically a shack. Dad gave me the money because—Well, because he felt badly about things. So. Figured I could live up there. Paint. Maybe work as a guide or something."

"Oh." George had pictured what life would be like after the war. He had always planned to return to Apple View. He would get called to the bar and then he would go into practice with Mr. Tate. And he would somehow manage to have Henry too. But he suddenly realized that all of that would be impossible.

Henry nudged him again. "There's a town a boat ride away. They might need a lawyer."

"I'm supposed to live there too? That's what got us in trouble in the first place."

"I know you. Remember? You'd never live in the woods. You're too soft. And I'd get tired of picking up after you. I thought maybe you'd get a place in town. And we'd see each other when we could. Just a couple of old bachelors who like to go fishing together. It's better than nothing."

"It is." George scanned the landscape around them. There was no one there. He leaned over and kissed Henry. As he thought about Henry's plan, he rubbed the spot on his chest where the bullet had gone in. Henry put his hand over George's to still it.

At the train station, George averted his gaze from the tender partings between couples. Envy boiled into rage with each kiss he saw. They couldn't do that. Instead, they had to settle for a handshake, a brisk brotherly hug maybe. The last time he touched Henry could be a handshake, he thought bitterly. And some of these couples may have met just the day before.

Henry started to say something, but the words seemed to catch in his mouth. His face briefly twisted, but he brought himself under control. They got that from their father, George knew. Both Maggie and Henry kept up a chilly outside while their insides seethed. George knew he wore his every thought and feeling on his face. He had to blink hard against tears. It wouldn't do to cry on a train platform.

"Don't worry, George," Henry said, clapping him on the shoulder.

"We'll see each other again. I promise."

"You can't say that. You don't know. I might not be so lucky next time."

"Sure you will. You were born lucky. Do you need a guarantee?"

"It'd be nice."

"Take this, then." Henry undid the chain around his neck. He had had a metal identity disc made while they were on leave. No one trusted the fibre ones would hold up in the damp.

"I can't."

"Take it. I'll come collect it from you when this is done," Henry said.

And then it was a flurry of gathering luggage and boarding trains. And George was alone again. He put the chain around his neck and tucked the disc inside his shirt. He closed his eyes and tried to imagine a cabin on an island.

Two months later, he got a letter from Maggie. Henry had been reported missing in action and was presumed killed. After that, George didn't much care if he ever saw Apple View again.

Sixty-One

George and Lucy sat across from each other on Lucy's bed. Her room was the only one at Apple View that wasn't full of the past for George. She had completely redecorated it with her own things. He put his hands on the coverlet and realized it was silk. She had surrounded herself with luxury. He thought of the hospitals and how they had just the necessities. Nothing more or less. How had she survived it?

Lucy was wearing men's pajamas. If she wasn't John's girl, George knew he would have tried to get her into bed. She'd be fun and wouldn't expect anything more than what he had to give. But she loved his friend and he was glad of it.

She held a notebook. Was this what girls had done when they were young and sleeping at each other's houses? Did they sit around in nightgowns and share secrets? He thought of what he and Henry had done when they were younger and felt his face grow warm. Lucy smiled around her cigarette but didn't say anything.

"I have a practice I keep up when I can. I have to be almost totally relaxed and fully at peace. So, I pretty much do this while John's sleeping," she said.

"After you've tired him out, you mean," George said.

Lucy laughed. "Well, I didn't want to be crass. But I forgot who I was talking to. I'm pretty sure you've got so many notches on your bedpost, there's no post left."

George grinned. He liked this woman. "Why do you have to be John's girl?"

"Oh, please. I hear you on the phone and I see your face when you get your weekly letter."

"You don't miss much, do you?"

"Well, I don't know his name. Back to the subject at hand," she said. She opened the notebook and flipped through the pages. It was full of writing, but the style of writing changed from page to page. Some of it was small and cramped, some of it large and looping.

"What's this?" he asked.

"As I said, when I'm relaxed and fully at peace, I invite the spirits to speak. I let them guide my pen."

George didn't know what to do with this belief of Lucy's. He had tried to sound John out about it, but John had just shook his head and said, "I love her. All of her." Maggie didn't talk about it at all, but she didn't believe. She didn't go to church anymore either. Maggie believed in nothing but the world as it was. George wasn't so sure. And with William's return, he didn't think this world was even as it seemed. Lucy had showed him that message from Henry.

"Did you do this at the hospital?" George asked. "I don't remember."

Lucy shrugged. "I did, but not often. It was hard to relax."

She picked up the book and turned to the most recent pages. "The last few months have been interesting. I've had an increase in messages. Someone is anxious to talk." She held the book out to him. The curlicues on the page looked like a child's imitation of cursive writing, all shape and no meaning.

"I don't see anything," George said.

"That happens when the spirit is not quite able to communicate. The intent is there, but they don't know how or they're not strong enough. It's a bit like talking on a bad telephone line. Only some of the message comes through. But look here, this is from a couple weeks ago." She flipped to another page and held it out to George. His name. Over and over. He looked up at her. Her face was still, serious, all of the lightness gone out of it. If she was crazy, she was fully in it.

"And then here." She flipped to another page. It was a rough drawing of a cabin, surrounded by trees and water. "Home" was written under it. "Do you recognize this?" Lucy asked.

He did. His hands shook as he took the book from her. He closed his eyes.

"George, he's trying to talk to you," Lucy said.

"Do you think he can help us?"

"I don't know."

Sixty-Two

While Maggie and her mother were sewing, Maggie's father came in with the mail. He liked to put William's letters in Maggie's hands with broad hints about love letters. Mr. Tate relished teasing his children and his wife because they all blushed so readily.

"Here's one for you," he said, placing a letter beside his wife.

"Who is it from, dear?" she asked.

"No return address. Probably some sort of chain letter or some nonsense like that. Want me to open it for you?"

"Yes, please. I'm at a tricky spot in this lace," Mrs. Tate said.

Mr. Tate used Maggie's scissors to slit the envelope open. He shook out a thin, typed piece of paper. He read it, then put it back in the envelope and tucked it into his suit pocket.

"Well?" Mrs. Tate asked.

"My dear, when you are finished there, would you join me in my office?" he answered and left the room. Maggie's mother threw down her lace, careless of where she left off. Maggie waited a decent amount of time and then followed them.

There was a small storage closet beside her father's office and a long time ago, Henry had found out that the wall was thin enough he could hear what was being said in the office. The division had been put in after the house had been built. The wall was flimsy and unfinished on the closet side. Maggie and William had taken advantage of the closet for years to eavesdrop on discussions their parents had about them.

Maggie crouched in the closet with her ear against the wall. She regretted discouraging her brother from drilling a peephole in the wall. Her parents weren't speaking. She pictured her father shuffling the papers on his desk and rearranging his pens.

Maggie's mother finally said, "Is someone dead?"

"No. It's—a dirty little bit of gossip and innuendo. I don't know if I should give it to you," Mr. Tate said.

"Don't try to shield me. What is it about?"

"Henry. But I don't want to give too much credence to something that a person didn't have the courage to sign their name to."

"Give it to me," Mrs. Tate said.

"I don't think this has any basis in facts. Someone is trying to smear our family," Mr. Tate said.

"What if it's true? What are you going to do?"

"I'm going to speak with Henry," Mr. Tate said. Maggie could smell his pipe tobacco.

"Are you going to talk to him too?"

"Not until I speak to Henry."

"Who would send something like this?" Mrs. Tate wailed.

Maggie burned to see that letter. She was angry that her mother could believe lies that some stranger told about Henry. But what was it? She shifted carefully, trying not to make a noise.

She had to get out of the closet and back to the parlour. Maggie stepped around the boxes in the closet and carefully closed the door. She shook the dust from her dress and ran her hands over her hair to clear out any dust or cobwebs.

When her parents returned to the parlour, she was busy embroidering a pillowcase. "Not bad news, I hope," she said in as bright a voice as she could manage. Her mother took up her lace and began fretting over losing her place and having to pick out a row. Maggie felt her father studying her. She looked up to meet his light eyes. His stare was unnerving, but she had practice not flinching under it.

"No. Not bad news. It was just a business letter," her father said.

"Oh, that's good," she said and looked back at her work.

Maggie wondered if she would have noticed how stiff her parents were with her brother when he got home, if she had not overheard their conversation about the letter. She could see them both watching him at moments when he wasn't aware of them. Neither of them had listened to his stories about art school life with so much attention. Maggie hoped that when her brother was called to his father's office, her mother would go too so she could eavesdrop again.

After supper, Mrs. Tate suggested to Maggie that she take her coffee in the sitting room. She and Mr. Tate had something to talk to Henry about. Maggie agreed and again waited a decent interval before hurrying down the hall to the closet.

"Read this," Mr. Tate said. "I've told your mother that this is all baseless, filthy gossip. Am I right in saying that?"

No one said anything. Maggie held her breath. She could picture Henry shrugging.

"Henry! Answer your father!" Mrs. Tate spoke sharply. Whatever was in that letter, Maggie knew her mother believed it.

"I assume someone's imagination has run away with him. Is that what you think has happened here? Perhaps you've got an enemy, someone whose feelings you've maybe hurt or who is jealous of you?"

Still Henry said nothing. "Answer him," Maggie whispered.

"Oh my God. It's true!" Maggie's mother cried out. Maggie resolved to find out what was in that letter, even if it meant revealing to her father their secret spy closet.

"Is it?" her father asked.

"You don't need to worry. I'll take care of it," Henry said. Maggie realized that he was neither denying nor confirming anything. It was a trick their father would see through and Henry knew it.

"Henry, you understand this is serious. Your life, your career, could be ruined if this becomes generally known," Mr. Tate said.

"It won't be. You'll never hear about this again. I've made a mistake. I'll fix it," Henry said.

"I knew you were a good boy. You were just misled by that low class—"

"Mother, that's enough. If I may go. I'll see to this right away," Henry spoke flatly with no emotion.

Maggie heard the door of her father's office open. She rushed out of the closet and caught Henry in the hall. "What is going on?" she whispered.

"None of your business. Go back to stitching your trousseau. Wouldn't want to disappoint William, would we?" Henry whispered.

"It's not my fault you're in trouble," she said.

"Shut up. They'll hear. Go back to your sewing. Be mummy's good little golden girl. I've got to go," he said. Maggie made a face at her brother's turned back and immediately felt childish. She heard her brother on the phone, but she couldn't catch who he was calling. "Meet me in thirty minutes," she heard him say. "Yes. The usual spot."

She went to the parlour. She drank her cold coffee and waited for her parents to emerge. What was in that letter?

"She's in the parlour," she heard her brother say to someone.

"Your first night back and you're not staying?" William asked.

"I've got some errands to run that can't wait. I'll see you later," Henry said.

"Oh, well if it's urgent, don't let me keep you." William came into the parlour with a light step. He grinned. Maggie was relieved. A happy William was so much easier to have around.

"What are you working on?" he asked as he sat in her mother's chair and picked up some of her mother's work.

Maggie blushed as she recalled her brother's comment about her trousseau. "Pillowcases. Apparently, my mother is under the impression that our home will have about one hundred pillows that will need fresh cases every day for a month."

"Our home will have whatever you want in it. If you want to have a hundred pillows, you shall have them. Where are your parents?"

"In father's office. Some business matter. I don't know."

"Oh. And Henry's off for the evening? Poor Margaret, if I hadn't come to see you, you'd be all alone." He leaned across the work table and kissed her. She blushed again. That always happened when he touched her.

Maggie's mother came into the sitting room. "William! I had no idea you were here! Did Maggie offer you anything? No? Let me get you something. Did you eat supper? Well, how about some cake and coffee? Let me get that for you. Now, I'm only turning my back on you two lovebirds for a few minutes and Mr. Tate should be out shortly." Maggie heard the forced cheerfulness in her mother's voice and saw her eyes were red around the edges. Did William notice? She didn't think so. He was too entirely happy himself to see.

Mr. Tate did not come out of his office and when Henry came back, he went directly to his room without stopping. Maggie cursed William for being there. Mrs. Tate quite subtly hinted that William's visit should be at an end. William stole another kiss at the gate and assured Maggie he would have a longer visit the next day.

When she came back in, her mother had already gone to bed. Maggie went to her father's office. The door was open and her father sat behind his desk, filling his pipe. Her mother didn't like him to smoke anywhere else in the house. She didn't want the curtains to smell of smoke. Maggie liked the smell of pipe tobacco. When she was little, her father would let her fill his pipe for him.

She knocked on the door. "May I?" she asked. He gestured for her to join him. She sat across from him and debated whether she should ask what was going on.

"Do you know what a father wants for his children more than anything in the world, Maggie?" he asked.

"What do you want for us, Dad?" she asked.

"A father wants his children to be happy above all else. He worries that the world will hurt them and he knows he can't protect them from everything. Sometimes, he has to cause them present pain to ensure future happiness. Or at least, he hopes that what he's doing. It's hard to know." He lit his pipe and took a few puffs.

"I'm happy," she said, although she wasn't sure if she was telling the truth.

"Good," he said. "I know you're curious. You were born curious. When Dr. Mobley first gave you to me, you looked around with those big eyes and I could see you wouldn't miss anything. It's not your concern, though."

"Isn't it? If it's something that affects our family, isn't it my concern?"

"No. It doesn't really affect the whole family." He sighed. He rummaged in a deep drawer in his desk and came up with two glasses and a bottle. "Don't tell your mother. But I need a drink and only a sad man drinks alone when his mind is troubled."

"What's troubling you?" Maggie sipped the whiskey her father gave her. It burned her lips and tongue and throat. But the warmth of it felt good in her belly.

"I wonder if I made the right decision about something," he said.

"Now you're just teasing me."

"I know, but it's not my place to say more than that. Maggie, you'll understand when you have children of your own. Sometimes, you tell them no for their own good and it hurts. Because you know if you said yes, they'd be happy for a time."

She reached across the desk and patted her father's hand. "I think you and Mum have done well for us. You can't protect us from everything."

"Maggie, be gentle with your brother for a little while, promise me? And don't cross-examine him, either."

"I promise."

"Now, have you set a date for the wedding?"

Maggie knew her father was changing the subject. But she saw that he was hurt about something and so she humoured him with chatter about her wedding plans. She suggested wild, expensive schemes just to see him make comically pained faces and clutch at his heart. They even laughed.

Henry came into the office. He glanced at Maggie. She got up, but he gestured for her to sit again.

"It's done," he said. He threw the letter on his father's desk. "Burn that." He walked out without looking at his sister.

"I'm leaving on a fishing trip tomorrow," Henry called out as he went down the hall. "Alone. Don't know when I'll be back." Maggie's father nodded. He picked up the envelope. He placed it in his ashtray and then lit it with a match. He and Maggie watched it burn in silence.

"It's done," her father said. "I'm going to bed. So should you, young lady."

After her father was safely in bed and Maggie saw the light go out from under his bedroom door, she went down the hall to her brother's room. His light was still on. She put her ear to the door. She could hear him moving around the room, packing, probably. She knocked on the door. "It's me," she whispered.

"Go away," he said.

"But you just got home and you're leaving again."

He opened the door. "I'm sorry. I can't stay."

"Henry, what is going on?" Maggie asked. She stepped inside his room. Henry's suitcase was on the bed. A pile of clothes sat next to it.

"There was some trouble. I took care of it. And now I'm going away," he said.

"Yes and you usually take John with you. So what is going on?"

"John's sick. He can't come."

"He's sick?" Maggie hadn't heard that. News went through town like a grass fire, quickly before burning out.

"I stopped in to see if he could come with me. His father said they'd picked up from school a week ago. Rheumatic fever."

"Oh my God. Is he all right?"

"I guess so. His father said not to worry or to put off my trip since he won't be strong enough even when he's better. So I'm leaving tomorrow. You should visit John, though. Take Mum. She loves a mission of mercy."

"Does George know?" Maggie asked.

Henry shrugged. "I have to pack and be on the early train tomorrow. Go to bed, Maggie." He kissed her forehead. "I'm sorry if I was sharp with you earlier."

She hugged him. "Be safe. Come home soon."

The first half of summer was long and boring for Maggie. John was sick and confined to bed, Henry was gone to the woods and William had left on his trip with his father. George didn't come around Apple View that summer. William wrote Maggie every day.

She tried to write him every day, but often had very little to say. Her days were the same: reading, sewing, wandering through the orchard, alone.

Sixty-Three

Every time they came back for the summer, for the first few weeks, George would feel as if their meetings were tawdry. It was strange to hide and lie and misdirect after months of living together over the school year. On the surface, they shared an apartment to save costs. But it was home to George. He hated coming back to their old routine of speaking carefully, acting carefully. He knew Henry hated it too.

They met in the old house as they had for years. Mr. Tate always talked about tearing down the old stone house. But he never did.

When George arrived, Henry was already there. He paced back and forth across the old dining room.

"Couldn't make it one night?" George asked. He pulled Henry towards him for a kiss. At first, Henry kissed him eagerly. Then he broke it off and pushed George away.

"Don't. This is hard enough," Henry said. He stepped back. He looked over George's shoulder, not meeting George's eyes. George started to shake. His heart thrummed hard in his chest. Something bad was about to happen. Or, no, something bad was happening.

"My parents got this letter," Henry said. George took the piece of paper Henry held out to him at arm's length. He read it and gave it back to Henry.

"And? What did you say?" George asked.

"What could I say? They asked if it was true. I can't lie to them," Henry said. He covered his eyes with a shaking hand.

"Why? You've been lying for years," George said.

"They've never asked. I never lied. And don't get high and mighty with me. You've never told anyone either." Henry started to pace again. George stepped in front of him, blocking his path.

"And now what?" George asked.

Henry looked down at his feet. He swallowed hard. George closed his eyes. He wanted to freeze this moment, to stop it before everything broke.

"I can't do this anymore," Henry said. "They're right. The price is too high. If this gets out—You can't be a lawyer. I can't do this to them."

"So that's it?" George asked. His nails dug into his palms. Anger rose in him. Henry's misery made him bitterly happy.

"I'm sorry," Henry whispered.

"Me too. I'm sorry I met you and your fucking family."

"Don't blame me," Henry said. He was angry too. George hated the pleasure he felt at Henry's red face and flashing eyes. He wanted Henry to push him again so he could swing out.

"Why not? If you'd left me alone, none of this would've happened."

"Maybe not with me. But with someone. This is who we are."

"No. It's who you are. I would have been happy if you'd let me be. I'd never even thought about—until you," George said.

"You keep telling yourself that. I know it's not true."

"God damn it, Henry. I'm not arguing with you about this again. We can just—I don't know, lay low for a while. Why blow up everything over a letter?"

Henry said nothing. His jaw tightened, but he didn't speak.

"So that's it? We'll never see each other again?" George thought back to earlier that morning when he had woken up beside Henry, when their lives had been entwined.

Henry shrugged. George clenched his fists and held his arms stiff to his sides. He wanted to break Henry's calmness, his dutifulness. "It's a small town. I'm sure we'll see each other around," Henry said.

"That's not what I meant. I mean—," George broke off. He couldn't speak without crying.

"It's done. We're done. I—" Henry sighed. His lower lip trembled. He bit it. "I love you. But I can't give up everything for that." He turned and walked out the door. George stood in the empty room. He leaned against the wall. He slid to the floor and let himself cry.

Sixty-Four

Money could overcome anything. Despite the rush, Maggie and William had a proper church wedding followed by a garden party at the Tates'.

George hadn't expected to be invited. Henry refused to speak to him and all his letters came back. He still clerked for Mr. Tate, but he never came to Apple View. Maggie wrote to him, but they weren't close as they'd been as children. Sometimes, he thought he should break away.

But he went to Maggie's wedding. He came alone and sat apart in the church, taking a seat among Tate relatives from out-of-town, towards the back. Henry was an usher. He showed George where to sit, but said nothing. He was in khaki too.

During the party, George slipped away to the river. He'd missed Apple View nearly as much as he had missed Henry. Last year, he had thought he'd never see the orchard again, stand by the river and look across to the woods and the stone house beyond. His head was fuzzy with champagne. "Welcome home," he whispered.

"You look like hell." Henry's voice. It had been a year since George had heard it.

"You look a proper soldier," George said.

"Thanks. But I'm serious. You look terrible," Henry said.

"I had a hard year." George shook his head. His mind was slow. He wished he hadn't had so much champagne. "I can't do this. I can't pretend we're old friends, catching up. Leave me alone."

Henry stood beside him. "I don't want to be your friend."

"Then fuck off."

Henry sighed. "What I mean is—I—Oh hell." He grabbed George, almost pulling George off his feet, and kissed him. George pushed him away.

"What are you doing?"

218

"A bad job of asking you to take me back," Henry said.

"I leave for training in a week."

"I thought about you every day. I wanted to keep your letters. To talk to you," Henry blushed.

"Why didn't you just talk to me?" George asked.

"Because I'm a coward."

"I don't think I can forgive you," George said. He sat down on the grass, not caring about his uniform. Henry sat beside him.

"I won't do it again. I promise. Us—it's worth the risk," Henry said. He smiled at George, but he was waiting for George's answer. His smile flickered.

"What if I'm with someone else now?" George asked.

"Are you?" Henry turned pale. His smile died. George didn't enjoy it.

"One of my classmates, his sister. I take her dancing. We go to shows. She's nice."

"Oh," Henry said. He started to stand. George grabbed his hand and pulled him down, hard.

"It's nothing. She's not you. Come on. Let's get out of here."

Henry smiled. "Really?" George nodded. He stood up and helped pull Henry to his feet.

As they crossed the footbridge, George asked, "If it wasn't for the war, would you have asked?"

"It might have taken me longer. But I had to say something."

George glanced around. No party guests had wandered down to the river. The music and laughter and conversation was faint and indistinct. George kissed Henry.

Sixty-Five

Maggie realized she had not seen her brother for a few hours. The party was busy, though. People milled around and kept stopping her to offer congratulations. She tried to escape without talking to any one person for too long, but some were persistent.

George walked by with a glass of champagne. He grinned at her, but didn't stop to talk. She made an excuse to her father's aunt and chased George. "Have you seen Henry?" she asked.

"He's down by the river," George said. "Thanks for inviting me to this bash, kiddo."

"You're drunk!"

George laughed and gulped his glass of champagne. "Course I am. Want your dad to get his money's worth." He kissed Maggie's cheek. It was sloppy and he reeked of cigarettes and champagne.

Maggie found her brother on the footbridge. "You used to tell me everything," Maggie said to Henry. "Won't you tell me what's on your mind?"

Henry shook his head.

"They say it will be over by Christmas," Maggie said.

He shrugged. "I don't know. I hope so."

"What if you don't come home? What if you're killed? I don't think I could bear it."

"You could." He sighed. "I never wanted to leave here. How about you?"

"I've never had the chance to go anywhere else," Maggie said.

Henry kicked a pebble into the water. A duck rushed to it and then turned back, disappointed.

"Is there a girl? Did you get some girl in trouble?" Maggie asked.

Henry let out a bark of laughter, "Why would you ask that?"

"I don't know. I'm trying to think of what you could do that would make Mum so angry. She wouldn't even say your name until you enlisted."

"It's not a girl and that's all I'm telling you," Henry said.

"Fine. Have secrets then."

"Why not? You do."

"Why are you so exasperating?" Maggie asked.

"Admit it, you love when I'm in trouble."

"I don't love it. It's serious this time, isn't it? She's really angry."

"She's forgiven me now there's a chance I could die. Anyway, your wedding distracted her quite a bit, so thank you for that." Henry shoved Maggie a little.

"There you go. Get married. She'll love you forever then. But who to marry? I'm pretty sure you wouldn't find a girl in town that would go canoeing with you or be happy to let you disappear in the woods for weeks. And you'll probably starve in a hovel with your paintings. Not a great prospect."

"It's the bachelor life for me, then. I'd never give up my paintings or the woods."

"Henry?"

"Yes?"

"Come back. Promise?"

"Promise," he said.

They held hands as they had when they were small and looked out over their family's land. Maggie felt they were already separated.

Sixty-Six

William sat beside her. As he moved the air, his scent pushed towards Maggie. He didn't smell of sweat, but instead a dank, vegetable smell. Mushrooms, she thought. He smelled like the morels and puffballs Henry would collect in the woods every spring and fall. William smelled of the forest floor, of shadowy places, of decay.

He grasped her hand and she had to stop herself from pulling out of his cold, waxen grip. His touch, though, became warmer after a few minutes. Even his pallor diminished and his cheeks became almost rosy, as she'd remembered them. His eyes brightened.

William bent to kiss her hand, the inside of her wrist, as he used to do when they were younger. They'd sit in the bottom of the old rowboat while it was tethered to the dock and chastely kiss for hours. His other arm wrapped around her shoulders, tentatively, hardly touching. She breathed in and his familiar, almost spicy smell brought her back to sixteen.

"Couldn't you feel me trying to get to you?" he whispered. "I'm sorry it took so long. Time is so odd there."

"Where?" she asked.

He shook his head. "I—," he frowned. "I can't remember. Before I was here."

He leaned towards her. She turned her head, forcing him to kiss her cheek. His lips were cold and dry.

Sixty-Seven

"I can hear your mother's needles clicking when I sit here. She was very beautiful, wasn't she? Tall. She had long fingers. Henry used to draw her hands. And you used to draw her too. She had a big emerald ring and she loved roses. Where is she?" William asked.

Maggie thought for a moment. She assumed William knew that her parents were dead. He had never before asked where they were. She hadn't thought to tell him.

Her mother's roses nodded in the breeze.

"She died. We lost her when the flu came," Maggie said.

"Flu?" William asked, frowning. No one talked about the flu. It was as if it hadn't happened. Or it was too much to think about. One more wave of death that swept people away.

"Just after the war, Spanish flu came. It was everywhere. A lot of people died. It's when John asked me to work with him. Don't you remember the flu?"

William shook his head. "I don't think it came where I was."

Maggie wanted to ask where he was, but she didn't. He insisted he didn't know. It always made him angry and sullen for the rest of the day. So she said nothing and let silence fill the space between them.

A red admiral butterfly with bright orange-red and black wings landed on the porch railing. William smiled to see it and reached towards it. The butterfly fluttered onto his hand and William laughed. Maggie held her breath.

Another butterfly landed on him. And then another. Butterflies came until his arm was covered and seemed to pulse with colour as they gently flapped their wings. William smiled at them. A tear spilled down his cheek, surprising Maggie. He stood and slowly walked down the porch steps, keeping his butterfly arm extended before him. He swung his arm up. The butterflies swirled up into the sky and flew away.

Sixty-Eight

"Everyone's having strange dreams. John wakes up in the night, crying because he can't save them all. He won't talk about it. I've been dreaming about the field hospital. Blood and pain and misery without end. They grab at me with skeleton hands and beg me to kill them. Or I'm holding their guts in my hands while they beg for me to spare them. What about you, Maggie?"

Maggie shrugged. Lucy knew the lie was coming before Maggie spoke. "I never remember my dreams."

"I had a dream about you the other night. You were looking out over the river. The sky towards the lake was full of dark, greenish clouds. The wind picked up and you wavered in it. But you stood firm at the river's edge, even when the lightning started. You stood firm even as a tornado came down from the sky and ripped apart the orchard. Blossoms swirled all around you and you stood there," Lucy said.

Maggie raised her eyebrows, but Lucy caught her small shiver. "Are you going to tell me the meaning?" Maggie asked, laughing.

Lucy shook her head. "I don't know. Summer storms?" Trouble, she thought, but didn't say. Trouble and how Maggie kept still, not moving, even in the midst of trouble.

Lucy put her arms around Maggie. She pulled her friend close enough to feel Maggie's heartbeat. "It's all terrible. It's all been terrible. It will all be terrible until we're all gone and no one remembers us."

Sixty-Nine

William kissed Maggie's hand as he used to do. Then he licked her hand and arm. He sucked and bit at her fingers. It didn't hurt at all, it felt wonderful. She shook with the pleasure of it. She watched as he chewed on fingers, blood ringing his lips. He drew back and she looked at the stumps of her fingers. She laughed and wiggled her bleeding fingers. William licked his lips. He leaned down and kissed her with his bloody mouth. It tasted sweet. And then, with his sharp teeth, he tore out her tongue.

Maggie woke up with a grunt. She held her hands in front of her face and was relieved to see her fingers, whole and untouched. Her nightgown clung to her sweaty skin, but she shivered. William muttered in his sleep and draped a heavy arm across her. He licked his lips.

Seventy

"I had my fortune told once. At a fair. And it was all wrong. She said I'd have an easy life and I'd marry a light-haired woman," George said.

Lucy laughed. "Fortunes change. Our choices cut off some roads and open others. Other people's choices do that to us too. Give me your hand."

His large hands dwarfed hers. She touched his palm with her fingertips. Working on the house over the summer had created calluses on his hands. "You're a hard worker. Weren't you studying law before the war? So there's a road that forked."

"You don't need to be a seer to know I can do a hard day's work," George said.

Lucy ignored him. She ran her fingers over his palm. She let her vision relax and go unfocused. She wasn't really reading lines as much as she was opening herself up to whatever messages came across. "You walk through fire, but it doesn't burn you on the outside. It burns out your heart. Your life line. See how long it is?"

"That's where I sliced it," George said.

"Still, it's your life line. You have a long life ahead of you," she said. She caught his grimace. "But it's a lonely one. Look at your love line. It's doubled, but broken up. You can't keep lovers. You charm them with your beautiful face and your golden tongue, but you don't keep them."

"I told you that," George said. "And you know what it's like. You're like that too."

She shook her head. "No. You don't want to be alone, but you push them away. I'm a hedonist. Until John, I never wanted to keep any of them. You don't want your heart to break again."

Seventy-One

As Maggie became weaker, Lucy insisted that she go outside more. Maggie laughed because her mother had also believed the sun could heal. On a late September afternoon that mimicked summer, Lucy proposed they have a picnic by the river to enjoy the weather before winter came.

As they passed by the orchard, Maggie could smell the sour tang of the windfall apples. Mr. Tate would have harvested those and made them into cider. For years, Maggie had left the apples where they fell. In the winter, deer would come and paw through the snow for the frozen, wizened apples.

Sitting by the river, throwing cracked corn to the ducks, Maggie felt as if fifteen years had been erased. Well, somewhat. Lucy replaced Henry. But the number of people was right. Lucy took a cigarette from George with a grin. Henry hadn't smoked, but George had started when they were ten or eleven. William sat apart, silent.

The illusion couldn't last. Even the mellow light of fall couldn't soften the changes age brought to all of them. John was frailer than he had been as a boy. He had gone bald young and wore a hat to shield his head from the sun. Dark circles surrounded his eyes. George had lost his softness. His face was leaner, carved with lines. His dark hair and week-old beard were streaked through with white. Maggie looked down at her hands and saw how thin they'd become. Her red hair had faded. Lucy's dark bob had a stripe of silver near the front and wrinkles fanned out around her eyes when she laughed.

John chuckled. Lucy asked him what was funny. "I was thinking of the time Maggie fell in the river. We'd been skating. All of us. She'd been waltzing with George. You remember, Maggie? You'd lost your temper. You'd always been red-headed. You'd taken off your skates and came stomping back to tell us off about something. And you stomped right through a weak spot. That cooled you off quick."

"I remember," Maggie said. John didn't need to know her memory didn't line up with his. He saw their past as golden. "And then you and William got into a fight over who should give me their coat. When Mum saw you carrying me up the hill, she went running out in the snow with only her slippers on. She made you run for your father, even though you had no coat."

"And George, where were you?" Lucy asked. George blew smoke out of his nose and shrugged.

"I was around," he said. "I don't remember it being all that funny. We were all hot-headed then."

"You and Henry skated off as fast you could," John said. "They were always like that, Lucy. First sign of trouble, they were gone. Henry sneaked back in while my dad was wrapping up Maggie's sprained ankle. Their mother tore a strip off Henry for leaving his sister to freeze. And he just shrugged at her. Remember how he used to do that? No words, just a shrug. Your mum was almost purple, she was so angry. And your dad stepped in and said he thought we'd all had enough excitement."

Maggie shivered. Lucy put a shawl around her shoulders and Maggie pulled it tight around herself. She caught George's eye. He remembered too. Did William? He could hear them from where he sat. She looked over. William was pulling grass up by fistfuls and scattering it on the water.

The golden summer river faded. Maggie could see the river as it had been on that day. It was sunny, but very cold. Everything was blue and white and gold. The river had frozen after days of bitter cold and, bored of being inside, they decided to go skating. Henry and John had been mad for hockey; they took their sticks and a ball down to the river to practice. William had never been able to get the knack of skating. He hated being left behind.

Henry warned Maggie about the thin ice at the edge. Reeds poked out of the ice and Henry shattered the ice around them with his skate blade. It sounded like glass. It was still and quiet, almost as if they were the only people in the whole world. It was so cold, her eyelashes frosted with her breath.

Maggie was a good skater and she easily outpaced the boys. She raced down the river, knowing that it would anger William and not caring. He was openly courting her, but she wasn't sure if she wanted that.

George caught up to her and grabbed her hand. He asked her to dance. He hummed a song and they spun in circles. The landscape blurred as they whirled and Maggie felt somewhere between sick and hysterical. She felt like a little girl. They spun towards William who watched John and Henry pass the ball back and forth. They were so graceful and precise.

William reached out and pulled Maggie towards him, but she stumbled and twisted her ankle. The pain sparked anger. After George helped her up, she shoved William, knocking him to the ice. When William got back to his feet, George skated between the two of them, holding them apart at arms' length. They glared at each other across George. Finally, Maggie left.

After Maggie took her skates off, she glanced back. William and George were talking and she could see by their gestures they were arguing. They both kept pointing towards her. She was something to squabble over like a toy. She threw her skates down and hurried back to the ice, forgetting about the weak edges. The cold water was even more painful than her twisted ankle and deeper than she had expected. Her heavy wool skirt and petticoat held her back as she tried to hoist herself back onto the ice.

John and Henry flew down the ice, skating faster than she'd ever seen. They lay on their stomachs and held out their hockey sticks. "Grab hold, Maggie!" her brother shouted. She gripped the sticks with numb hands and pain flared through her stiff fingers. Together, John and Henry pulled her out. Henry lifted her to standing and she buried her face in his shoulder and cried from fear and rage. John offered her his coat. William argued that he had more right to give her his coat. John dropped his coat on the ice. Maggie thought it looked like a dead animal's skin lying on the ice.

Henry wrapped her in William's coat, kissed her cheek and said, "I can't stand this." He lifted her and passed her to John. As John ran back to the house with her, she looked over his shoulder to see Henry grab George by the arm and skate away down the river. She watched them until they disappeared around the bend.

William, not burdened with Maggie, ran ahead. By the time John had struggled up the hill with her, Mrs. Tate was in the yard, wearing only her house dress and slippers.

For days, Maggie was confined to her bed. Her mother had an abiding fear of pneumonia. Finally, she was allowed to lie on the sofa in the sitting room. William was waiting for her. Her mother left to chaperone discreetly from the next room.

Maggie felt the heat of anger rising up in her, flushing her skin. William took her hands in his. "Please forgive me, Margaret," he said. "I'm so sorry. When I saw you fall—you're everything to me."

Maggie yanked her hands free. "Maybe we should stay friends. I've known George since I was three years old and now, because you're walking me home, I'm not supposed to be his friend? No. I won't do it."

William nodded. "You're right. I made a mistake," he said. She looked into his eyes. His grey eyes? His green eyes? She looked into his eyes and believed him. Then, after he glanced towards the door separating them from Mrs. Tate, he kissed her. It was just a quick press of lips, but it was their first kiss.

Seventy-Two

The room was dark. Candles were the only light, throwing shadows on their faces. They held hands, even William. Lucy had mesmerized him and called out for the spirits to speak through him. She didn't know if he would speak or something would speak for him. John and Maggie didn't believe, but they were humouring her and that was enough.

"Who am I speaking to?" Lucy asked.

"No one. You don't know me," William said.

"Where are you?"

"In the castle. We are in the castle," William said. His voice was quiet. He spoke as if he were asleep.

"All of you?" Lucy meant the dead.

"No. Only the chosen. There are many places for the dead." William's eyes were open, but they had rolled back in his head.

"Is there a king?"

"No. There is only a queen. She chooses her consorts."

"Who does she rule?"

"The dead. Not all. She slept for centuries. She had been forgotten. Her kingdom slipped away."

"What woke her?"

"The war. All those souls."

"Where is her castle?"

"There. Everywhere. Nowhere."

"Do you know William?"

"Yes. He has been to the castle. He sits with you."

"Is he dead?"

"He's not here. The dead are here."

"Yes, but is he dead?"

"She says I can't tell you our secrets."

"Who is she?" Lucy asked.

"She has no name."

"Who are you? Were you a soldier?"

"I think so. I'm no one. I'm from the castle. She allows me to speak."

"May I speak with her?"

"No. You don't reverence her as you should. She is like a mother. She is very kind." William smiled.

"Is Henry there?" Lucy felt Maggie and George squeeze her hands.

"No. He did not choose to stay."

"So he's dead?"

"Yes."

"What about William?"

"He has a body and breath in that body."

"Can I please speak to your queen?"

"No. You are like ants to her. You don't see the world beside this one."

"What world is that?" Lucy asked.

No answer came. A mirror slid from the wall and shattered on the floor. A shock of electricity went through them all, forcing them to release each other's hands. William left and went out into the night.

Maggie shook her head. "This is absurd." She pushed back from the table and left the room. Lucy heard her steps across the floor, up the stairs, down the hall and to her room. A door upstairs slammed shut.

Lucy sighed and rubbed her eyes. Her head ached. John stood behind her and handed her a glass of water. She leaned her head against his hip. He pressed his hand against her head.

Seventy-Three

He'd learned to be careful. After his mother's death, he saw George watching him. George knew, had always known. It would be, William supposed, easier to get rid of George, but he took too much pleasure in drawing out George's pain. Why? He didn't know. It had always been. Something about George made William want to cause him pain.

He'd always been a hunter. William and Henry, sometimes John, had spent days in the woods on the Tates' property, hunting rabbits, deer, game birds. Those had been days when William could have said he was happy. Days when his tongue wasn't full of mean words. He had always felt calm in the woods, with his friends beside him and a gun in his hands.

John had hated dressing the animals. For someone who would grow to cut into people, he had been oddly squeamish. Henry and William had been the one to field dress anything they caught. William had enjoyed it. Had enjoyed how skilled he had been with the knife. Henry, well, he had been softer. Not as soft as John, but still soft. Because Henry had always knelt to the animal's ear and whispered something. And he had always kindly stroked its fur or feathers as if soothing it.

Had Henry done that in the war? Killed because he had to, but easing the path of the dead?

William wanted to hunt. Every human soul he took made him stronger and he needed to be strong if he wanted to take Maggie with him. But he also wanted the pleasure of the hunt. Life should be pleasant. One should feel good as much as possible. Isn't that why George drank and Lucy fucked? They made their lives about chasing their desires, so why couldn't he?

William found a girl. He had learned something from George when they were young. George had shown them how to read a girl, to select the one you could take out back or to another town or wherever he had taken his women. William reflected that George had probably been able to do this with men too. But no, he wouldn't think of that.

William went to another town, to a dance and he found himself a girl. She had smiled at him with a question in her eyes. Her lips were painted red and her dress was as flimsy as lingerie. "Do you want to see shooting stars?" he asked her and she laughed.

"I'd like to see whatever you want to show me." She had put her arms around his neck and bit his earlobe.

"Well, I know the perfect place."

When Mr. Tate had bought the neighboring farm, had he known what uses that old house would be put to? Likely not. William smiled at how shocked Mr. Tate would be. He almost wished the man were alive so he could show the proper lawyer what went on his paradise.

To calm her, keep her docile, William let the girl climb all over him, pawing at him, leaving her lipstick marks all over, like bloody mouths. Then he pushed her aside, drawn out the hunting knife, showed her his long white teeth. And she knew, the way the deer knew when the predator came. "Run," he told her.

Her flimsy high-heeled shoes made her clumsy and slow on the uneven ground. She crushed a patch of mint and the smell filled his nose. He could smell her fear, the metallic tang of her sweat. He crept along behind her, not really running, not really needing too.

Mice and other night creatures scuffled through the undergrowth, disturbed by her crashing steps. A few times she fell and stood again. Her breath came in hoots and choked sobs.

Finally, bored of the chase, he leapt and pulled her to the ground. As he slit her throat, he thought of Henry whispering to the deer. So he tried it. He whispered his thanks and stroked the leaves out of her bobbed hair. He felt nothing. Why had Henry done it? It seemed useless. He put his mouth to hers and drew out her strength.

Seventy-Four

"What if I won't go with you?" Maggie asked. William's jaw tightened, the muscles flexing in his face. But he smiled at her.

"Then I would follow you. We'll never be apart again. And you will come with me. When the snow comes, you'll be with me," William said.

"I don't want to leave. My life is here," Maggie said. She tore her hand out of his and stood up. Anger made her restless. She paced back and forth across the sitting room. It wasn't true. She did want to leave. Her life here was nothing. But he offered her nothing different.

"Your life was here. What have you done with it? Nothing. You've been waiting all this time. I know you have. Even if you won't admit it. Why do you always go against me?"

"Against you? I did nothing but what you wanted for years. The only time I did what I wanted was when I went to Montreal and then asked you for a divorce. And you refused."

"I still love you. And I forgive you," William said. He got up and stood in front of her, stopping her from pacing. He grabbed her arms and pinned them to her sides. Maggie wanted to struggle against his hold, but she felt weak, tired.

When he let her go, Maggie pushed him. He laughed at her. Her push had been nothing. He hadn't even moved. "I never loved you. But I hate you now," she said. A hot spike of angry joy went through her as his face turned pale. She wasn't afraid of him. Or that's what the anger told her. But another, smaller voice whispered that she was afraid and always had been afraid. He'd never let her go. This would be the rest of her life.

He raised his hand and she readied herself to be slapped. He had never struck her before. She flexed her fingers, ready to pick something up, to strike out. But he put his hand down. "I won't let you goad me. Why are you so hateful? What happened to you?"

"I've always been like this," she said. "You never saw me."

"No. You've changed. You're being influenced by bad people. They need to leave."

Maggie stamped her foot. It was childish, but she felt childish. She was angry, but too weak to do anything. Her life was beyond her control. It was like being a child again. So she stamped her foot. "No. This is my house. They won't leave."

"No. It is my house," William said. "What is yours is mine. They're leaving."

She couldn't be alone with him. Her friends stood between her and him even if they didn't know it. If she left, if she ran, he would always look for her. Her only way out was his death or hers. She put a hand to her chest. Her breath and heart stopped at that. Death was the only way out.

"I'm done talking to you," she said. She walked away, expecting to feel his hands on her, pulling her back. But for once, he let her go.

Part Three

One

George lay back in the cool bath water. After a long day repairing the house's roof, he was too sore and tired to swim, but he wanted to feel cold water. So a bath instead of the river. In the bath, he could write a letter on a board he'd laid across the tub. He heard Lucy and Maggie laughing outside and he smiled. This was contentment. In the middle of all that was strange and unsettling, he'd found this moment. So maybe that's why he was considering inviting Alan. Despite William. Despite his own doubts. Despite his fear for Alan.

They'd been writing to each other all summer. Words on a page came readily to George. He could write things that he couldn't say. Alan was a thin thread connecting George to a world that made sense, that wasn't full of the dead.

George lit a cigarette and put the letter aside. He'd finish it later. His eyes kept closing and his writing had turned into looping scrawls. He tucked a towel under his head and tried not to fall asleep until his smoke was finished. Working on the roof had felt good. He still couldn't quite think of himself as part owner of Apple View, but he liked restoring it to as it had been in his childhood.

He dozed. His cigarette dropped into the water. Lucy and Maggie's laughter and indistinct words drifted through his mind like a dream. Just as he started to sink into a deeper sleep, he jerked awake. The water had grown cold.

William knelt at the edge of the tub, resting his chin on his folded arms. He grinned at George. "Shhh. Just relax. I'm going to help you." He picked up George's half-finished letter. In his other hand, he held a match. The match lit itself and William held it to the letter. "I'm saving you from yourself."

George was caught in William's dark stare. He couldn't move. It was the night William had come to his bedroom all over again. His pulse quickened and he started to breathe shallow, fast. William blew the ashes of the letter into the tub. "You just can't help yourself, can you? I wanted to be patient. Margaret is fond of you, but I think it's time."

George watched as William turned and rummaged through the medicine cabinet above the sink. He turned back with a blade from a safety razor in his hand.

George flinched. He moved, just a little, but still. "You can't kill me. You already tried," he whispered.

William reached out his free hand and touched the scar on George's chest. George hissed. William's touch burned with ice. "I've been killing you by inches for years." William held the blade out to George. "Take it."

And George reached up and took the blade. Even though he fought it, he couldn't stop his fingers from closing around it. "No," he said.

William shook his head. "Yes. I'm going to tell you a little secret. I haven't killed most of them. Some do it themselves." He dropped his voice to a whisper and leaned close to George's ear. "Don't tell me you haven't thought of it before."

"No," George whispered, but he couldn't look away from William's flat eyes, his wolfish grin. His arms shook as he fought against whatever was pulling them. He held out his left forearm, wrist up. And quickly, his right arm brought the razor across the delicate skin of his inner wrist, slicing through, opening the arteries. Blood spurted out, splashing across William's face. He licked his lips.

William lifted George's arm to his mouth and licked along the cut. All George could do was watch, trapped inside his body, shrieking in his mind. He tried to say something, but he could only say "no." William smiled at George with lips as red as if he were wearing Lucy's lipstick.

"Oh my God," George said. He looked down at his wrist, blood running between William's fingers. He pulled his arm from William's grasp and pushed William away. George stood. He had broken free. "You want me to suffer because you can't stand it."

William's smile faltered. His eyes shifted away from George, breaking the remnants of whatever hold he had on George.

George grinned. He had power for once even though he was bleeding out. It didn't matter. Not if he could knock William back, cast his own spell. George stood up and spread his arms out, throwing blood like paint across

William, across the room. It splattered across the mirror above the sink.

"You want to fuck me. That's what all of this has been about. Isn't it? Well, have me. Do it. I don't care. Just stop whatever this is. Do what you've wanted to since—when?"

William bared his teeth at George. He was like a cornered animal. George looked down at the water in the tub. The water was red. His knees buckled and his vision began to go black at the edges, closing in until he could only focus on William with difficulty.

"You can't kill me. You keep trying, but it never takes." George felt himself starting to faint. He collapsed to his knees and rested his head back against the wall. He thought of Henry, clapping his hands and telling George to wake up. Where was Henry? He had promised Henry he'd take care of Maggie, but he was too weak. He closed his eyes. Maybe he'd find Henry.

A clap. He was clapping. George clapped his own hands and yelled "Wake up!" He sat up. Someone was knocking on the door.

"George?" Lucy called from the other side.

William was gone. George was alone. And bleeding.

"Help," he said. "Lucy, help me."

Lucy came in and bit back a scream, clamping it in her mouth, snapping her teeth shut. Her face went from shocked to calm in seconds as her training took over. She gently closed the door behind her. "What did you do?" she asked even as she fashioned a tourniquet from a towel.

"William," George whispered. He couldn't stay awake. It was cold. Maybe Lucy would add more water to the bath and warm him up. His teeth chattered and his arm hurt. "He made me. Fuck. I'm cold. It hurts."

Lucy closed her eyes and pulled down the scarf around her neck to show a small cut held together with one stitch. "William. But he couldn't hold me."

"How do we stop him?" George asked.

She shook her head. "I don't know. I'm trying to find out. George, I have to stitch you up. You've lost a lot of blood."

He nodded. "Don't tell Maggie, or John. Please."

She nodded and went out of the room to get supplies. George slumped over the edge of the tub. Everything had slowed. He felt peaceful. Ready for something, but patient. His eyes closed. Lucy was with him. Henry was waiting for him.

TWO

"We need to ask for help," Lucy said. George nodded.

Maggie pulled her shawl tighter around her shoulders. All night, she had been lifting it to her face and breathing in the smell of her mother's lavender sachets. She wanted to wail for her mother.

"Ready?" Lucy asked. Maggie took George's hand and John's hand. Lucy held George's hand and John's hand. Lucy asked them to concentrate on their need for help. She murmured under her breath.

Wind blew down the chimney. The fire and the candles guttered out. The room went dark. Maggie began to lift herself from her chair, meaning to turn on the lights, but Lucy held up her hand. "Wait," she said. Maggie sighed. She didn't believe in this. It wouldn't help. She was tired of it all. She wanted to sleep and never wake up.

The wind blew hard again, rattling tree branches against the windows. The front door opened with a bang. Maggie looked down the hall, towards the door. William stood at the threshold, his eyes glowing like a cat's.

John cried out and put his hands to his head. Maggie rushed to the light switch. Nothing happened when she pushed it. She looked into the hall again. William was gone. The door was closed.

"John!" Lucy shouted. "John!"

John tried to speak. His words were muddled and indistinct.

"Look at his arm," George said. John's left arm curled against his body. His face sagged. He held his forehead with his right hand. He tried to get to his feet and fell against the table. Lucy screamed as he clattered to the ground. George ran around to the other side of the table, throwing John's chair aside. He scooped his friend up in his arms.

Lucy ran past to the telephone stand in the hallway. Maggie tried the switch again and the lights came on. "Yes, yes. Get me Dr. Mobley. I'm at Apple View. Tell him it's an emergency. John's sick," Lucy said into the phone.

Maggie followed George up the stairs, into Lucy's room. George set John down on the bed. John was unconscious.

"What's wrong with him?" George asked.

"I think he's had a stroke," Maggie answered. "Help me get his jacket and shirt off. Lucy's called his father."

"Will he die?" George asked.

Maggie shook her head. "I don't know." She put a hand to John's face. He hadn't been well for a long time, she knew. He had looked tired, worn out. But she'd been too caught up in herself to tell John to rest, to take care of himself.

Three

John realized he did know this place, in a way. It was the dream William had described at the doctor's office. The one George claimed to have had too. John's head hurt and his left side felt strange. He held out his hands. They seemed all right and identical. He remembered the candles going out and seeing William at the window. A bolt of pain in his head. "I've had a stroke," he said, hearing the words disappear into the still air.

He started for the castle. It was just as William and George said. He first came to an old woman, on her hands and knees, eating fistfuls of dirt. He started to say he had nothing to give her, but he realized he had a rucksack. He gave her the loaf of bread he found inside. She snatched it away greedily and started biting huge chunks out of the loaf. His stomach turned at the sight of her muddy mouth print on the clean, white loaf.

He continued on and met with the middle-aged woman. Or, really, he supposed, a woman his own age. She was lapping water out of a stagnant puddle. Again, he found what he needed in his rucksack. She opened her mouth wide, tilted her head back and poured the water from the canteen down her throat. When finished, she pointed him to the ruined chateau.

It was a formerly opulent home, now ruined. Its treasures had been ransacked and left to rot. He went up the grand staircase, covering his nose and mouth with his shirt collar. The place smelled strongly of decay.

The girl waited for him in the bedroom. He gasped at her beauty. His poor, ruined heart struggled to keep a steady beat. He did as the others had and covered her and led her to the fire. She whispered in his ear, her voice soft and hissing. She told him a guest waited for him in the banquet hall.

That detail made him pause. It had not been in either George's or William's descriptions. Or, if it had, he couldn't remember. His head hurt more than ever. He struggled to see through it. His left eye wept. Still, he went down the grand staircase again and searched for the banquet hall.

The smell of rotting food made him gag when he opened the giant double doors. Flies buzzed around great piles of meat that bled onto the floor. Piles of fruit oozed their fermenting juices onto the fine white tablecloth. William sat at the head of the table.

William raised his glass to John. "John! My friend! So good of you to come. Pull up a chair. Eat."

John shook his head. He couldn't see out of his left eye now. And his leg, he couldn't make his leg move. He dragged it behind him as he walked towards William.

"Just what the doctor ordered for your head." William drank something, maybe wine, out of his cup as greedily as the woman had drank her water. Red liquid ran down his chin. He wiped it away with the back of his hand and smiled at John. His teeth were stained red.

John tried to speak, but the words came out garbled.

"I will have her. Even if I have to bring you all with me. You, your whore, the filthy sodomite. All of you. I'll feast on you here," William said in a friendly conversational way as if they were discussing the weather.

John grasped the back of a chair. William held him by the arm. His grip tight and cold. His icy fingers burned John's skin.

"John!"

John recognized that voice. William, in surprise, released him. Suddenly, he felt stronger, his tongue freed. "No!" he cried out and pushed William back. William spilled his cup. The strong metallic smell of blood filled the air.

"John!" the voice called out again. And then a whistle. It was the whistle he and Henry had used on their hikes if they got separated. He ran towards the sound. He saw Henry's silhouette in the doorway.

Four

Henry's hunting knife felt good in George's hand. The bone handle was smooth, comfortable. It was heavy, but not so heavy as to be unwieldy. Its heft gave it reality, something George sorely needed.

William had left the house. George, armed with Henry's hunting knife, searched for William. He left the barn and crossed the yard towards the house. Lights shone through the windows of the house, comforting him. He relaxed a little. Maybe William had run away to wherever he had come from.

The wind picked up and leaves scattered on the walk, sounding like the scuttle of little claws. Like rats. Like the rats in the trenches. The ones that ate the dead and sometimes the living. Don't think of the rats. Stay here. George gripped the knife more tightly, willing himself to stay in the present. He looked over his shoulder, back towards the barn. There was nothing behind him. He turned back and came face-to-face with William.

William grabbed for the knife, trying to grasp the blade. Blood dripped from his closed fist and down his wrist. The knife slipped from William's hand. George pushed the knife into William's gut, putting one arm around William's waist to bring him firmly onto the blade. George pulled the knife out and stepped back. In the dim light, he could see blood spreading out from the hole in William's shirt.

William smiled and lifted his shirt to reveal a bloodied but unwounded stomach. He laughed at George's amazed stare. No. That couldn't be. George had felt the flesh and muscle give way to the blade. He had heard it.

"I'm a dead man," William said. "I am like a god. I feel nothing." He gripped George's arm with both his hands. George tightened his grasp of the knife, although William's blood ran down the blade, making his hand slick. William's fingers pressed into George's arm. George dropped the knife. He tried to pry William's fingers off his arm, but they felt like iron.

The trench smell of William made George gag.

William grinned at George and broke his arm like a stick. The snap of the bones giving way made George's stomach tighten. The pain flared bright, emptying his mind. He stared at William, into William's blank eyes, at William's wolfish grin and wondered who was screaming. George realized he was screaming. William released his grip. George looked down to see white jagged edges of bones (radius, ulna, his mind supplied through the haze of pain) emerging from a deep bloody gash. Yellow fat oozed out with the blood. George collapsed to his knees and vomited.

"Death made me stronger. What did living get you?" William asked. He lifted his foot and placed it flat against George's chest. He pushed George to the ground.

George couldn't stop screaming. How was he still awake?

"George!" Maggie called. "George!" Her hand was on his cheek. Was he still screaming?

"Lucy, call Dr. Mobley! Get John's kit. His arm's broken." Maggie sat on the ground beside him. He wanted to tell her she'd get muddy, but he couldn't speak. She cradled his head in her lap and leaned down to kiss his forehead. He began to shake. "Shhh. We'll help you." She wiped his face with her skirt hem. "I'm so sorry," she whispered.

"He's going to kill you," George thought he said, but he couldn't be sure.

Dr. Mobley offered George chloroform so he wouldn't feel his arm being set. He refused. He didn't want to be unconscious with William still out there. Instead, he let Dr. Mobley give him morphine.

"I should be driving you to the hospital. This needs traction," Dr. Mobley said. George shook his head.

Maggie and Lucy kept their faces still when Dr. Mobley set George's arm, not reacting to George's screams. Maggie wiped George's face with a cool cloth while Lucy helped Dr. Mobley with the cast.

"What is happening here?" Dr. Mobley asked. George wanted to tell him, but he couldn't talk. The world was getting soft and indistinct.

"George thought he heard a prowler," Lucy said. "He was attacked."

"Don't lie to me, Lucy. Not with my son dying."

George fainted from the pain before he could hear Lucy's answer.

Five

The snow fell so thick that all Maggie could see out of the window was white. The world had disappeared. William was somewhere out in the whiteness. John was with parents, still not awake.

Someone knocked on the door three times. They all jumped, startled. Maggie's throat closed. Her heart beat fast and her hands were numb. She had never been this afraid.

"Answer it," said Lucy. "We've summoned it. It can't come in unless we ask it." The candles flickered. A wind came down the chimney causing the fire to flare up and die down again.

Another three knocks. George opened the door. "Oh my God," he said. "Oh my God."

"Hello, George. Aren't you going to invite me in?" said a man at the door.

Maggie stood up, knocking her chair to the floor. It was Henry. Her brother had returned. She didn't hear George's answer. She ran to the door. George and Henry stood just inside the doorway, kissing. Henry held onto George as if he were holding him up.

"Henry!" Maggie cried. George broke away and stepped back. Maggie ran to her brother. He was thin and pale. He was dressed for the trenches, including his helmet. And she knew he was dead, that this wasn't really him. But it was him. She threw her arms around his neck. He had the same wet, earthy smell that William had, but she didn't care. He put his arms around her and rested his head on her shoulder.

"You're just some revenant, some piece of Henry," George muttered.

Henry lifted his head from Maggie's shoulder. "I can't explain it, but it's me. I'm here."

"You're still dead. And when this is over, you're gone again, aren't you?" George's voice was rough and caught at some of the words.

"Yes," Henry said.

"Can you help us?" Maggie asked.

"I think so. I hope so. Where is he?"

Maggie shook her head. She let go of her brother and led him to the sitting room. "I don't know. He said when the snow comes, we'll be leaving here. And it snowed last night." She shivered. She couldn't stop shivering. Her teeth started to chatter. Henry knelt beside where she sat and put his arms round her.

"I won't let him take you," Henry said. "Do you have my hunting knife?"

"That won't work," George said. He leaned in the doorway, holding his broken arm against his body with his good arm. His eyes were red. "I stabbed him with it. He laughed at me. It didn't even leave a mark. Then he broke my arm like a stick. You can't kill the dead."

"Where's the knife?" Henry asked.

"Still out there. But it won't work. I already tried."

"Trust me, George. Show me where."

Lucy helped George into a coat and boots. "I'll stay here with Maggie. If he comes back, I'll call for you." George nodded.

Maggie watched them go out the door. She felt alone. She felt like she had when her mother died. "I just want this to be over," she said. Lucy grasped her hand.

Six

The snow was still falling. It was heavy and wet and came straight down. The flakes were fat and on any other night, George would have been happy to be out. This night, he felt as if they were being buried. His arm throbbed.

"Show me where," Henry said. George led him to the path between the house and the barn. He thought of the bone sticking out of his arm and his stomach tightened. He held it closer to his body.

"Here. It was right here." George pointed down. They were both up to their knees in snow. Henry kneeled and began to dig in the snow with his bare hands. "You'll get cold," George said.

"I'm not cold," Henry said. He scooped handfuls of snow up and sifted it through his fingers. George watched him. Snow filled George's hair and gathered on his shoulders. His feet hurt with cold. But he couldn't go back inside. He watched Henry dig. He looked at the face he knew so well and saw he hadn't remembered it quite right. In his memory, Henry's face had begun to combine with Alan's in his mind. He had forgotten about Henry's cheekbones, high, but also round, his deep-set eyes. He wanted to touch Henry, but he couldn't make himself move. George thought of their kiss at the door and a shiver went through him. It was like being young again save for the dark thread of mourning running through his desire.

"Henry," George said.

Henry looked up. It was strange to see him in a field uniform. George had never seen him in it. He always thought of him as he had looked their last day in England in a white shirt with the sleeves rolled up. His eyes were lighter than George had remembered.

"Yes?" Henry said.

"Can you stop him?"

Henry frowned and looked back at his hands, red with cold. "I don't know."

"If he hadn't come back, would you have returned?"

"No." Henry went back to digging.

"You broke my heart twice."

"I know."

"Don't do it again. I don't think I can stand it."

"I will and you can," Henry said. "Wait. Here it is." He held up the knife and grinned at George. George had expected the blade to be stained with William's blood. It gleamed by the light of the flashlight. Henry stood up and brushed snow from his legs. He tucked the knife into his belt. He faced George. George willed his arm to act and put a hand to Henry's cheek. Henry leaned into George's hand and closed his eyes. "You called for me, but I have to go back when this is done," he said.

"I know," George said. He sniffed. His problems were small and stupid compared to Maggie's. And even John's. They were fighting for their lives. He was selfish.

Henry stepped closer and pulled George to him. "I'm sorry."

"You're here for Maggie, not me. She needs you."

But they stayed outside a few minutes more.

Seven

Wood squealed against wood. Maggie woke. She was alone. Lucy had wanted to stay with her but Maggie had convinced her to go to John.

William slipped through the open window. He moved fluidly like a cat. She wanted to move or scream, but she couldn't. William stood beside the bed and grinned. His teeth were so long. The air around him was cold and smelled of snow.

"Are you ready, Margaret?" he asked.

She couldn't speak. Her tongue sat heavy in her mouth. Sound died in her throat.

He lifted her up. William kissed her and she felt as if she were suffocating. He smelled of decay. His lips tasted of dirt. "Did you think your brother was going to save you?" He shook his head. "No. He's been distracted by his lust. Don't you see? I'm saving you."

"No," she whispered. "They're my friends."

"Don't worry. You will have so many friends where we're going. You'll be a queen. You'll never age. You'll always be beautiful," he said, holding her close to him.

"I'll be dead," she said, her voice hoarse.

"Yes. In this world. But you'll live in another, better one."

"I never loved you," she said. He flushed and his grip tightened on her. She could make him angry. She still had some power over him.

"You're lying. They told you to say that. They don't want you to go with me. But I'll win. I always win," he said.

"No. You won't."

He grunted. She watched the muscles of his jaw tighten. If she could keep him angry, maybe he would be distracted. Maybe she could gain time. She felt like Bluebeard's wife, hoping her brother would come save her.

William carried her outside. It had stopped snowing and the night was clear. The drifts glittered under the full moon.

He waded through the deep snow, down the hill, towards the river. The water was inky against the white fields. She tried to scream, but could only make hoarse sounds. She wanted to call to Henry. Henry was dead. She didn't need to speak. She closed her eyes and tried to calm her mind, to reach out to him. She thought of Lucy, sitting in front of a candle, calling out to Henry. In her mind, Lucy said, "Henry, he's taking her to the stone house."

Despite the snow, it had not been cold enough to freeze the water. Still, rather than take the bridge, William forded the river, holding Maggie above the water. Maggie gasped as her feet skimmed the surface. Her nightdress trailed in the water.

He carried her through the woods. She wanted to reach out and grab at the trees, but her arms stayed limp. When they reached the small cemetery, William kissed her. "Do you remember when I proposed to you here?" Maggie didn't answer. "I wanted to be part of your family. You were happy. My family wasn't happy. I was so jealous. But I was wrong to be. Your parents loved you and Henry, but that didn't save you."

"We're human," she whispered. Anger sparked hot in her, bringing back her voice. "We were happy. I should never have married you."

"I can save you. I'm taking you home." William carried her across the threshold of the stone house.

"I don't want to go," she said. And then she screamed, a wild, piercing noise that she couldn't believe was her own voice. She thrashed in his arms like a fish on a line, but William held firm. She heard shouting.

George and Henry were shouting her name over and over. Their voices grew louder. The door flew open. Henry had kicked it. William dropped Maggie to the ground. "Henry!" Maggie yelled, reaching out towards her brother.

George ran to Maggie, but Henry and William ran towards each other. At the last moment, though, William changed direction and stepped abruptly towards George. He picked George up by his jacket and flung him against a wall. It was as if he were throwing a doll, George seemed so weightless in his grasp. William threw his head back and laughed.

Maggie screamed. She felt like she was drowning. "Stand up," a voice said. It was her mother. "Stand up," she said again. Maggie looked around, but Mrs. Tate wasn't there. She stood.

George threw something to Henry. It landed on the floor by Maggie. She snatched up Henry's knife. Henry had wrapped his hands around William's throat.

"You can't kill me," William gasped out. "I'm already dead."

"So am I," Henry said. He bared his teeth and squeezed harder. William pulled at his hands, but couldn't move them.

"If you don't give me Maggie, I'll tear your boy up before your eyes. I'll eat the heart right out of him. I'm stronger than you. And I've been so hungry."

Henry glanced at Maggie and nodded. "I'm hungry too. All of us are on the other side." He let go of William's throat and pinned William's arms to his side. He put his mouth over William's. It wasn't a kiss; it was more like he was devouring William's mouth. He seemed to be breathing in, pulling something out of William.

William struggled out of Henry's grasp. When he pulled away, Maggie could see blood on his mouth. He was smiling. His teeth were red. Henry turned away and vomited blood. Maggie heard George groan.

She realized this wouldn't end. William would hurt everyone until he had what he wanted. She thought of Lucy sitting by John's bed and George's broken arm. And the others. William's parents, the farmer, the hunter, the girl in the woods. Maybe others. She thought of George's bullet scar. It was so simple.

"I'll go!" she said.

"No!" Henry yelled. He tried to grab at her, but she avoided him.

"He won't stop until I say yes," Maggie said. "I have to. He's my husband."

William went to her. "My love!" He wiped the blood from his mouth with his hand. Maggie gripped the knife in her hand.

She smiled up at him. He held his arms out to her. She raised her hand and plunged the knife into his chest, burying it to the hilt. She sawed the blade down and pulled it out. Blood poured from the wound. William stared down at his chest. His face grew pale. His cheeks began to sink.

Maggie threw the knife down.

She reached in with both hands and spread his ribs apart. He didn't fight her. She felt stronger than she ever had before. He came apart in her hands as if he were made of paper. Her anger ran through her, hot like a fever. All her life, William had tried to keep and hold her.

When his ribs were apart, he looked down, his expression blank, his mouth hanging open. She wanted to laugh. She reached into the cavity. She thought of Lucy, straddling a man, holding his guts in, trying to stuff the life back in. Maggie felt around until she found his beating heart. She yanked and twisted, pulling it free.

"Maggie!" William cried out.

His heart stopped beating and began to shrivel in her hand. Blood poured out of his open chest and onto the floor. His lips were red, his cheeks sunken.

She stared into his eyes. She lifted his shrunken heart to her lips. "I'm so hungry," she said and bit into the heart. Her stomach clenched at the metallic taste, but she forced herself to bite and chew and swallow. William fell to his knees. She reached down and grabbed him under the arms to lift him back to his feet. He was light in her hands. His head was half gone. She heard George moan from behind her. This was his last view of William. She could see what he had seen.

William fell apart in her hands, his flesh and bones coming to pieces. Maggie felt arms around her and she fought against them. "Shhhh. It's me." Her brother spoke in her ear. She began to shake. She dropped the remnants of William from her hands. Henry lifted her like a child. He carried her back to Apple View, back to home. Henry set her down on the sofa by the fire.

Maggie kept wiping at her mouth with her hands. She could taste William's heart still. George held a bottle to her lips. "Drink this," he said. It burned. Fire would clean it out. She swished the whiskey in her mouth and spat it onto the rug. She took the bottle from George. Tipping her head back, she took a long swallow.

"Fire," she said. "Fire." George and Henry looked at each other. Henry nodded.

She laid her head back on a cushion and closed her eyes. It was done.

Eight

George knelt beside Maggie and kissed her cheek. Her breathing was soft and easy.

"Stay with her," he said to Henry. "I'll be back." Henry helped him stand. For a moment, George leaned against Henry. He was so tired. But there was still work to do. It wasn't quite over.

"Where are you going?" Henry asked.

"She said fire," George answered. He brushed his fingers against the bottle of whiskey on the table. It would be so good. Instead, he clumsily took out a cigarette and lit it one-handed. Fire, she had said. There was kerosene in the barn and he always had matches.

William's body, or rather, the collection of bones and flesh and rags that had been William was where they had left it. George poured kerosene over it. He splashed more around the floor of the house.

Before he lit a match, George rested his forehead against the wall. He had been in love here. His heart had been broken here. More than any part of Apple View, he had carried this place with him. "Goodbye," he whispered.

At the threshold, he lit a match and threw it down into a puddle of kerosene. His broken arm ached. He clutched it with his good arm as he sat on an old gravestone and waited for the fire to really take.

When he came back to the house, Henry was sitting on the floor. Maggie was asleep on the sofa. Henry stroked her hair. He wiped at his eyes. "Is it done?" he asked. George nodded. Henry handed George a piece of paper.

"What's this?"

"He can't keep ruining your lives after he's dead. It's his confession." Henry said. "I've always been a good forger."

George read the letter. In it, William claimed all the deaths. He was haunted by the battlefield and he sought the solace of death. "It's over," George said, setting the letter down.

George held out his hand to Henry and pulled him to his feet. "She'll be fine for a little bit. Come with me," George said. He led Henry to his room. They sat beside each other on the bed. Outside, the wind tapped branches against the window. Snow swirled in all directions. George wanted to talk. He wanted to touch Henry. He didn't want to. Henry was dead. He wasn't really here. This body was a construction and not really the body he had known.

"I was happy you got out," Henry said.

"I didn't get out," George said. "I'm still there. I can't get out. Unless—unless you take me with you."

Henry sighed. "I don't know if I can. I don't want to." He looked at his hands. George wanted to reach out and touch Henry's face, run his thumb against his jaw.

"Actually, I do want to take you. But I want you to live. Be happy. I know you found someone to love. Do that. Get old. Otherwise—what did we do it all for?" Henry asked.

"Nothing. It was for old men and politicians."

"No, I mean, this. Me coming back. Saving Maggie from William. George, she needs you. I love you. But I can't take you with me."

"I'll kill myself," George muttered. Henry put his arms around George. George fought against him, wanted to break away, but his broken arm hurt and he was tired. So he gave up and leaned against Henry.

"I don't know if that would work. I don't know how any of this works." Henry held George tighter. He rested his chin on George's head. "But I think John's dying and I want to try to bring him back with me. Can I do that?"

George laughed. All those years he had been jealous of John. Henry and John were leaving him behind. But, Henry could be there, wherever that was, and not be alone.

"Yes," George said against Henry's chest. He took a deep breath, but it caught in his chest. He began to weep, huge sobs that shook his body. Henry stroked his back, but he didn't tell George that it would be all right. Finally, George pushed Henry away.

"Go. Please. I can't," George said. His voice shook. He covered his face with his good hand.

Henry nodded. "I wanted everything to be different." He got up and walked out of the room. When the door closed behind Henry, George began to cry again.

Nine

"I have to go," Henry said. He wanted to cry, but nothing would come. Maybe this body couldn't cry. Maggie sat up and patted the cushion beside her. He sat down. She leaned against him.

"I don't want to go," Henry said.

"I know you have to, though," Maggie said. She sniffed and then laughed and then cried.

"Maggie, promise me you'll do what you want with your life," Henry said. Maggie nodded. "And, if you can help George? Please?"

"I will," Maggie said. She burrowed into him. "Thank you. For coming back. You saved me."

"You beat him. You did that."

Maggie shook her head. "I couldn't have if you hadn't broken his hold on me. If you hadn't made him weak."

He kissed her head. "I love you."

"I love you too."

Henry eased her back to lying down. She started to drift off almost right away. He brushed a hand along her cheek and swallowed hard. No tears came. This body. He was so tired of it. He didn't understand it. It wasn't his. He was almost himself, but he wasn't.

Ten

"He's not waking up," Lucy said. "You're here to take him, aren't you?"

Henry nodded. Her face crumpled and her breath caught in a hiccup, but she smoothed her emotion away. She'd learned that, he knew, during the war. Henry had a clear vision of a younger Lucy in her blue and white uniform, hands thrust into a man's guts. She had more inner steel than anyone he'd ever known. She'd survive this.

Lucy wiped under her eyes with her fingers. "I'm not ready. I always knew, but I'm not ready."

"He's not either. Very few are. I wasn't."

"He'll be with you?" she asked. She was trying so hard to be brave. Her wobbly smile made him doubt this. Could Henry do anything to save John? He didn't think so. There should be no magic. Whatever William had done to come back had disrupted things too much already.

"Yes. I think so. It's—" He struggled to describe it. It was beyond understanding. "It's different there." Henry put his hand over John's chest. He could feel the sluggish beating of John's heart. "He loves you." Lucy nodded and this time, she allowed a few tears to track down her face. She sniffled and then laughed.

"Can I say goodbye?" she asked.

Henry nodded and left the room. When the door closed, he sat down in the hallway. He wanted to be done with this world. He hadn't wanted to come back. It was hard, too hard. He had to see their hurt, witness their sorrow. It wasn't right. Even gone, William kept hurting them.

He covered his ears to block the sound of Lucy's grief. After a few minutes, he knocked on the door. She opened it and pushed past him. When he started to speak to her, she held up her hand and shook her head. He let her go.

Henry went into the room and closed the door, "Ready, John?"

"Yes."

Eleven

Maggie knocked on George's door, but George didn't answer. She opened the door. George was on the bed, his back to the door. Maggie stood in the doorway. Was he asleep? He sniffled. Tears came to her eyes. She lay down beside George and put her arm around him. "He's gone," she said.

George nodded. He held onto her hand. She kissed the back of his head. She felt so old. She felt so young. "Thank you," she said.

He sighed. "I'm so tired."

Maggie pulled her hand from his and sat up. She took a quilt from the end of the bed and pulled it over them. "John's gone too," she said.

"What do we do now?" George asked. Maggie didn't answer. She didn't know.

They fell asleep, curled up together in Henry's bed under a quilt made by Mrs. Tate. Outside, it began to rain.

Twelve

After John's funeral, they came back to Apple View. No one spoke.

Lucy and George smoked, filling the kitchen with a haze. Lucy paused between cigarettes, but George lit the next with the dying embers of the last. His hands shook and his eyes kept sliding towards Lucy's glass.

Alan put the teapot on the table. He fixed everyone a cup and then sat down beside George. Maggie took up her cup and held it to warm her hands. The wind had been cold at the graveside.

She liked Alan. What a time to meet him. She watched him and George together and found she didn't mind. It didn't disgust her as people said it should. She liked Alan, but she still wished that it was Henry sitting at the table with them. If he had told her, they could have had this. Maggie put her arm around Lucy's waist, drawing her friend closer.

"I knew, you know, that I wasn't going to keep him. But that doesn't make it easier," Lucy said.

"I know," Maggie said. She pressed a kiss to Lucy's cheek. After John died, Lucy clung to Maggie. They went everywhere together and slept in the same bed. Or tried to sleep.

"What are you doing now?" Lucy asked. "Are you going west? To Don?"

Maggie sipped her tea. It was strong, hot. "I don't know. Maybe. He wrote and said he'd wait."

"What do you want to do?"

Maggie set her tea cup down and stirred in some more sugar. "I think I want to go somewhere warm. I want to see the ocean."

"Well, then go," Lucy said.

"What about you?" Maggie asked. "Why don't you come with me?"

"I sent Garnet a telegram. He's coming to get me in a couple days. I'm moving in with him."

"Oh." It was after the war again. Everyone was leaving Apple View and she'd be alone.

"I have to be close to the university. I'm going to be a doctor." Lucy laughed. Maggie wondered if she looked as surprised as George.

"Really?"

Lucy nodded. "I was always going to do it, but it seems like the right time now. I didn't want to leave John. He's gone, so—" Her lips shook. She tried to take a drag on her cigarette, but coughed. Tears welled in her eyes, but didn't fall. "It's time."

"I want to paint," Maggie said. "And tell everyone about Henry's work. Like Van Gogh's sister-in-law."

George nodded. "Yes. Do that."

"But first, I want to rest," Maggie said. "George, come with me. Let's find somewhere warm." George glanced at Alan. "Alan too. Let's rent a house. You can write and I can paint. And Alan, you can—what do you do?"

"I keep accounts," Alan answered, laughing. "I can manage a household budget. And I can be very good at sitting in the sun reading and telling people they're geniuses."

Lucy stood up from the table. She went to the basement and came back with several bottles of champagne. "George, I know you won't drink a glass, but please take one for the toast and I'll drink it for you." She opened a bottle while Maggie got out glasses.

They lifted their glasses and looked to Lucy, waiting for her words. She tried to smile, but couldn't quite make her mouth turn up. "To John!" she said. They repeated her toast and clinked glasses. "To Henry!" she said next. Finally, she said, "To breaking free!"